# CAMELOT'S DEATHLESS LEGACY . . .

"Get out," I said to Miss Lytton, the guards.

"Sir, I—"

I shot her a look, and she backed away. Then the old man spoke, and once again I heard that wonderful voice of his, like a subway train rumbling underfoot, "Yes, Amy, allow us to talk in privacy, please."

When we were alone, the old man and I looked at each other for a long time, unblinking. Finally, I rocked back on my heels. "Well," I said. After all these centuries, I was at a loss for words. "Well, well, well."

He said nothing.

"Merlin," I said, putting a name on it.

"Mordred," he replied, and the silence closed around us again.

—From Michael Swanwick's
*The Dragon Line*

*Books in This Series from Ace*

# Isaac Asimov's Camelot

Edited by
## Gardner Dozois
and
## Sheila Williams

ACE BOOKS, NEW YORK

This book is an Ace original edition,
and has never been previously published.

ISAAC ASIMOV'S CAMELOT

An Ace Book/published by arrangement with
Dell Magazines

PRINTING HISTORY
Ace edition/May 1998

The Penguin Putnam Inc. World Wide Web site address is
http://www.penguinputnam.com

Check out the Ace Science Fiction/Fantasy newsletter, and much more,
at Club PPI!

ISBN: 0-441-00527-6

ACE ®
Ace Books are published by The Berkley Publishing Group,
a member of Penguin Putnam Inc.,
200 Madison Avenue, New York, NY 10016,
ACE and the "A" design are trademarks
belonging to Charter Communications, Inc.

PRINTED IN THE UNITED STATES OF AMERICA

10  9  8  7  6  5  4  3  2  1

# CONTENTS

# Acknowledgments

The editors would like to thank the following people for their help and support: Susan Casper, Shawna McCarthy, and George Scithers for having the good taste to buy some of this material in the first place; Scott L. Towner, Sharah Thomas, and Torsten Scheihagen; Cynthia Manson, who set up this deal; and thanks especially to our own editor on this project, Susan Allison.

# Isaac Asimov's
# Camelot

# THE LAST DEFENDER OF CAMELOT

## Roger Zelazny

*"The Last Defender of Camelot" was purchased by George Scithers, and appeared in the Summer 1979 issue of* Asimov's SF Adventure *with an illustration by Frank Borth. The late Roger Zelazny only ever published a few stories in* Asimov's, *but each was memorable, and important to the magazine, his novelette "Unicorn Variations" winning a Hugo Award in 1982, and his novella "24 Views of Mt. Fuji, by Hokusai" winning another Hugo in 1986. The story that follows, Zelazny's only other* Asimov's *story, was also well-received and critically acclaimed. Most stories dealing with Arthurian themes and the Matter of Britain take place somewhere around the glory days of Camelot itself, but here Zelazny shows us that the consequences of our actions can stretch thousands of years into the*

*future beyond our own times, and that, in the words of that wise sage, Yogi Berra, it's not over until it's over . . . no matter how long it takes.*

*Roger Zelazny began publishing in 1962, and his subsequent career would be one of the most meteoric in the history of SF. By the end of that decade, he had won two Nebula Awards and two Hugo Awards and was widely regarded as one of the most important American SF writers of the sixties. In subsequent decades, until his untimely death in 1995, he would win many more major awards, and his series of novels about the enchanted land of Amber would make him one of the best-selling SF and fantasy writers of our time. His other books include, in addition to the multi-volume Amber series, the novels* This Immortal, Lord of Light, The Dream Master, Isle of the Dead, Jack of Shadows, Eye of Cat, Doorways in the Sand, Today We Choose Faces, Bridge of Ashes, To Die in Italbar, *and* Roadmarks, *and the collections* Four For Tomorrow, The Doors of His Face, the Lamps of His Mouth and Other Stories, The Last Defender of Camelot, *and* Frost and Fire. *Among his last books are two collaborative novels,* A Farce to Be Reckoned With, *with Robert Sheckley, and* Wilderness, *with Gerald Hausman, and, as editor, two anthologies,* Wheel of Fortune *and* Warriors of Blood and Dream.

The three muggers who stopped him that October night in San Francisco did not anticipate much resistance from the old man, despite his size. He was well-dressed, and that was sufficient.

The first approached him with his hand extended. The other two hung back a few paces.

"Just give me your wallet and your watch," the mugger said. "You'll save yourself a lot of trouble."

The old man's grip shifted on his walking stick. His shoulders straightened. His shock of white hair tossed as he turned his head to regard the other.

"Why don't you come and take them?"

The mugger began another step but he never completed it.

The stick was almost invisible in the speed of its swinging. It struck him on the left temple and he fell.

Without pausing, the old man caught the stick by its middle with his left hand, advanced and drove it into the belly of the next nearest man. Then, with an upward hook as the man doubled, he caught him in the softness beneath the jaw, behind the chin, with its point. As the man fell, he clubbed him with its butt on the back of the neck.

The third man had reached out and caught the old man's upper arm by then. Dropping the stick, the old man seized the mugger's shirtfront with his left hand, his belt with his right, raised him from the ground until he held him at arm's length above his head and slammed him against the side of the building to his right, releasing him as he did so.

He adjusted his apparel, ran a hand through his hair and retrieved his walking stick. For a moment he regarded the three fallen forms, then shrugged and continued on his way.

There were sounds of traffic from somewhere off to his left. He turned right at the next corner. The moon appeared above tall buildings as he walked. The smell of the ocean was on the air. It had rained earlier, and the pavement still shone beneath streetlamps. He moved slowly, pausing occasionally to examine the contents of darkened shop windows.

After perhaps ten minutes, he came upon a side street showing more activity than any of the others he had passed. There was a drugstore, still open, on the corner, a diner farther up the block, and several well-lighted storefronts. A number of people were walking along the far side of the street. A boy coasted by on a bicycle. He turned there, his pale eyes regarding everything he passed.

Halfway up the block, he came to a dirty window on which was painted the word READINGS. Beneath it were displayed the outline of a hand and a scattering of playing cards. As he passed the open door, he glanced inside. A brightly garbed woman, her hair bound back in a green kerchief, sat smoking at the rear of the room. She smiled as their eyes met and crooked an index finger toward herself. He smiled back and turned away, but . . .

He looked at her again. What was it? He glanced at his watch.

Turning, he entered the shop and moved to stand before her. She rose. She was small, barely over five feet in height.

"Your eyes," he remarked, "are green. Most gypsies I know have dark eyes."

She shrugged.

"You take what you get in life. Have you a problem?"

"Give me a moment and I'll think of one," he said. "I just came in here because you remind me of someone and it bothers me—I can't think who."

"Come into the back," she said, "and sit down. We'll talk."

He nodded and followed her into a small room to the rear. A threadbare oriental rug covered the floor near the small table at which they seated themselves. Zodiacal prints and faded psychedelic posters of a semi-religious nature covered the walls. A crystal ball stood on a small stand in the far corner beside a vase of cut flowers. A dark, long-haired cat slept on a sofa to the right of it. A door to another room stood slightly ajar beyond the sofa. The only illumination came from a cheap lamp on the table before him and from a small candle in a plaster base atop the shawl-covered coffee table.

He leaned forward and studied her face, then shook his head and leaned back.

She flicked an ash onto the floor.

"Your problem?" she suggested.

He sighed.

"Oh, I don't really have a problem anyone can help me with. Look, I think I made a mistake coming in here. I'll pay you for your trouble, though, just as if you'd given me a reading. How much is it?"

He began to reach for his wallet, but she raised her hand.

"Is it that you do not believe in such things?" she asked, her eyes scrutinizing his face.

"No, quite the contrary," he replied. "I am willing to believe in magic, divination, and all manner of spells and sendings, angelic and demonic. But—"

"But not from someone in a dump like this?"

He smiled.

"No offense," he said.

A whistling sound filled the air. It seemed to come from the next room back.

"That's all right," she said, "but my water is boiling. I'd forgotten it was on. Have some tea with me? I do wash the cups. No charge. Things are slow."

"All right."

She rose and departed.

He glanced at the door to the front but eased himself back into his chair, resting his large, blue-veined hands on its padded arms. He sniffed then, nostrils flaring, and cocked his head as at some half-familiar aroma.

After a time, she returned with a tray, set it on the coffee table. The cat stirred, raised her head, blinked at it, stretched, closed her eyes again.

"Cream and sugar?"

"Please. One lump."

She placed two cups on the table before him.

"Take either one," she said.

He smiled and drew the one on his left toward him. She placed an ashtray in the middle of the table and returned to her own seat, moving the other cup to her place.

"That wasn't necessary," he said, placing his hands on the table.

She shrugged.

"You don't know me. Why should you trust me? Probably got a lot of money on you."

He looked at her face again. She had apparently removed some of the heavier makeup while in the back room. The jawline, the brow . . . He looked away. He took a sip of tea.

"Good tea. Not instant," he said. "Thanks."

"So you believe in all sorts of magic?" she asked, sipping her own.

"Some," he said.

"Any special reason why?"

"Some of it works."

"For example?"

He gestured aimlessly with his left hand.

"I've traveled a lot. I've seen some strange things."

"And you have no problems?"

He chuckled.

"Still determined to give me a reading? All right. I'll tell you a little about myself and what I want right now, and you can tell me whether I'll get it. Okay?"

"I'm listening."

"I am a buyer for a large gallery in the East. I am something of an authority on ancient work in precious metals. I am in town to attend an auction of such items from the estate of a private collector. I will go to inspect the pieces tomorrow. Naturally, I hope to find something good. What do you think my chances are?"

"Give me your hands."

He extended them, palms upward. She leaned forward and regarded them. She looked back up at him immediately.

"Your wrists have more rascettes than I can count!"

"Yours seem to have quite a few, also."

She met his eyes for only a moment and returned her attention to his hands. He noted that she had paled beneath what remained of her makeup, and her breathing was now irregular.

"No," she finally said, drawing back, "you are not going to find here what you are looking for."

Her hand trembled slightly as she raised her teacup. He frowned.

"I asked only in jest," he said. "Nothing to get upset about. I doubted I would find what I am really looking for, anyway."

She shook her head.

"Tell me your name."

"I've lost my accent," he said, "but I'm French. The name is DuLac."

She stared into his eyes and began to blink rapidly.

"No . . ." she said. "No."

"I'm afraid so. What's yours?"

"Madam LeFay," she said. "I just repainted that sign. It's still drying."

He began to laugh, but it froze in his throat.

"Now—I know—who—you remind me of. . . ."

"You reminded me of someone, also. Now I, too, know."
Her eyes brimmed, her mascara ran.

"It couldn't be," he said. "Not here. . . . Not in a place like this. . . ."

"You dear man," she said softly, and she raised his right hand to her lips. She seemed to choke for a moment, then said, "I had thought that I was the last, and yourself buried at Joyous Gard. I never dreamed . . ." Then, "This?" gesturing about the room. "Only because it amuses me, helps to pass the time. The waiting—"

She stopped. She lowered his hand.

"Tell me about it," she said.

"The waiting?" he said. "For what do you wait?"

"Peace," she said. "I am here by the power of my arts, through all the long years. But you—How did you manage it?"

"I—" He took another drink of tea. He looked about the room. "I do not know how to begin," he said. "I survived the final battles, saw the kingdom sundered, could do nothing—and at last departed England. I wandered, taking service at many courts, and after a time under many names, as I saw that I was not aging—or aging very, very slowly. I was in India, China—I fought in the Crusades. I've been everywhere. I've spoken with magicians and mystics—most of them charlatans, a few with the power, none so great as Merlin—and what had come to be my own belief was confirmed by one of them, a man more than half charlatan, yet . . ." He paused and finished his tea. "Are you certain you want to hear all this?" he asked.

"I want to hear it. Let me bring more tea first, though."

She returned with the tea. She lit a cigarette and leaned back.

"Go on."

"I decided that it was—my sin," he said, "with . . . the Queen."

"I don't understand."

"I betrayed my Liege, who was also my friend, in the one thing which must have hurt him most. The love I felt was stronger than loyalty or friendship—and even today, to this

day, it still is. I cannot repent, and so I cannot be forgiven.
Those were strange and magical times. We lived in a land
destined to become myth. Powers walked the realm in those
days, forces which are now gone from the earth. How or why,
I cannot say. But you know that it is true. I am somehow of
a piece with those gone things, and the laws that rule my
existence are not normal laws of the natural world. I believe
that I cannot die; that it has fallen my lot, as punishment, to
wander the world till I have completed the Quest. I believe I
will only know rest the day I find the Holy Grail. Giuseppe
Balsamo, before he became known as Cagliostro, somehow
saw this and said it to me just as I had thought it, though I
never said a word of it to him. And so I have traveled the
world, searching. I go no more as knight, or soldier, but as
an appraiser. I have been in nearly every museum on Earth,
viewed all the great private collections. So far, it has eluded
me.''

"You *are* getting a little old for battle.''

He snorted.

"I have never lost,'' he stated flatly. "Down ten centuries,
I have never lost a personal contest. It is true that I have aged,
yet whenever I am threatened all of my former strength re-
turns to me. But, look where I may, fight where I may, it has
never served me to discover that which I must find. I feel I
am unforgiven and must wander like the Eternal Jew until the
end of the world.''

She lowered her head.

". . . And you say I will not find it tomorrow?''

"You will never find it,'' she said softly.

"You saw that in my hand?''

She shook her head.

"Your story is fascinating and your theory novel,'' she
began, "but Cagliostro was a total charlatan. Something must
have betrayed your thoughts, and he made a shrewd guess.
But he was wrong. I say that you will never find it, not because you are unworthy or unforgiven. No, never that. A more
loyal subject than yourself never drew breath. Don't you
know that Arthur forgave you? It was an arranged marriage.
The same thing happened constantly elsewhere, as you must

know. You gave her something he could not. There was only tenderness there. He understood. The only forgiveness you require is that which has been withheld all these long years—your own. No, it is not a doom that has been laid upon you. It is your own feelings which led you to assume an impossible quest, something tantamount to total unforgiveness. But you have suffered all these centuries upon the wrong trail."

When she raised her eyes, she saw that his were hard, like ice or gemstones. But she met his gaze and continued: "There is not now, was not then, and probably never was, a Holy Grail."

"I saw it," he said, "that day it passed through the Hall of the Table. We all saw it."

"You thought you saw it," she corrected him. "I hate to shatter an illusion that has withstood all the other tests of time, but I fear I must. The kingdom, as you recall, was at that time in turmoil. The knights were growing restless and falling away from the fellowship. A year—six months, even—and all would have collapsed, all Arthur had striven so hard to put together. He knew that the longer Camelot stood, the longer its name would endure, the stronger its ideals would become. So he made a decision, a purely political one. Something was needed to hold things together. He called upon Merlin, already half-mad, yet still shrewd enough to see what was needed and able to provide it. The Quest was born. Merlin's powers created the illusion you saw that day. It was a lie, yes. A glorious lie, though. And it served for years after to bind you all in brotherhood, in the name of justice and love. It entered literature, it promoted nobility and the higher ends of culture. It served its purpose. But it was—never—really—there. You have been chasing a ghost. I am sorry Launcelot, but I have absolutely no reason to lie to you. I know magic when I see it. I saw it then. That is how it happened."

For a long while he was silent. Then he laughed.

"You have an answer for everything," he said. "I could almost believe you, if you could but answer me one thing more—Why am I here? For what reason? By what power? How is it I have been preserved for half the Christian era while other men grow old and die in a handful of years? Can you tell me now what Cagliostro could not?''

''Yes,'' she said, ''I believe that I can.''

He rose to his feet and began to pace. The cat, alarmed, sprang from the sofa and ran into the back room. He stooped and snatched up his walking stick. He started for the door.

''I suppose it was worth waiting a thousand years to see you afraid,'' she said.

He halted.

''That is unfair,'' he replied.

''I know. But now you will come back and sit down,'' she said.

He was smiling once more as he turned and returned.

''Tell me,'' he said. ''How do you see it?''

''Yours was the last enchantment of Merlin, that is how I see it.''

''Merlin? Me? Why?''

''Gossip had it the old goat took Nimue into the woods and she had to use one of his own spells on him in self-defense—a spell which caused him to sleep forever in some lost place. If it was the spell that I believe it was, then at least part of the rumor was incorrect. There was no known counterspell, but the effects of the enchantment would have caused him to sleep not forever but for a millennium, and then to awaken. My guess now is that his last conscious act before he dropped off was to lay this enchantment upon you, so that you would be on hand when he returned.''

''I suppose it might be possible, but why would he want me or need me?''

''If I were journeying into a strange time, I would want an ally once I reached it. And if I had a choice, I would want it to be the greatest champion of the day.''

''Merlin . . .'' he mused. ''I suppose that it could be as you say. Excuse me, but a long life has just been shaken up, from beginning to end. If this is true . . .''

''I am sure that it is.''

''If this is true . . . A millennium, you say?''

''Just so.''

''Well, it is almost exactly a thousand years now.''

"I know. I do not believe that our meeting tonight was a matter of chance. You are destined to meet him upon his awakening, which should be soon. Something has ordained that you meet me first, however, to be warned."

"Warned? Warned of what?"

"He is mad, Launcelot. Many of us felt a great relief at his passing. If the realm had not been sundered finally by strife it would probably have been broken by his hand, anyway."

"That I find difficult to believe. He was always a strange man—for who can fully understand a sorceror?—and in his later years he did seem at least partly daft. But he never struck me as evil."

"Nor was he. His was the most dangerous morality of all. He was a misguided idealist. In a more primitive time and place and with a willing tool like Arthur, he was able to create a legend. Today, in an age of monstrous weapons, with the right leader as his catspaw, he could unleash something totally devastating. He would see a wrong and force his man to try righting it. He would do it in the name of the same high ideals he always served, but he would not appreciate the results until it was too late. How could he—even if he were sane? He has no conception of modern international relations."

"What is to be done? What is my part in all of this?"

"I believe you should go back, to England, to be present at his awakening, to find out exactly what he wants, to try to reason with him."

"I don't know. . . . How would I find him?"

"You found me. When the time is right, you will be in the proper place. I am certain of that. It was meant to be, probably even a part of his spell. Seek him. But do not trust him."

"I don't know, Morgana." He looked at the wall, unseeing. "I don't know."

"You have waited this long and you draw back now from finally finding out?"

"You are right—in that much, at least." He folded his hands, raised them and rested his chin upon them. "What I would do if he really returned. I do not know. Try to reason with him, yes—Have you any other advice?"

"Just that you be there."

"You've looked at my hand. You have the power. What did you see?"

She turned away.

"It is uncertain," she said.

That night he dreamed, as he sometimes did, of times long gone. They sat about the great Table, as they had on that day. Gawaine was there, and Percival. Galahad . . . He winced. This day was different from other days. There was a certain tension in the air, a before-the-storm feeling, an electrical thing. . . . Merlin stood at the far end of the room, hands in the sleeves of his long robe, hair and beard snowy and unkempt, pale eyes staring—at what, none could be certain. . . .

After some timeless time, a reddish glow appeared near the door. All eyes moved toward it. It grew brighter and advanced slowly into the room—a formless apparition of light. There were sweet odors and some few soft strains of music. Gradually, a form began to take shape at its center, resolving itself into the likeness of a chalice. . . .

He felt himself rising, moving slowly, following it in its course through the great chamber, advancing upon it, soundlessly and deliberately, as if moving underwater . . .

. . . Reaching for it.

His hand entered the circle of light, moved toward its center, neared the now blazing cup and passed through. . . .

Immediately, the light faded. The outline of the chalice wavered, and it collapsed in upon itself, fading, fading, gone. . . .

There came a sound, rolling, echoing about the hall. Laughter.

He turned and regarded the others. They sat about the table, watching him, laughing. Even Merlin managed a dry chuckle.

Suddenly, his great blade was in his hand, and he raised it as he strode toward the Table. The knights nearest him drew back as he brought the weapon crashing down.

The Table split in half and fell. The room shook.

The quaking continued. Stones were dislodged from the walls. A roof beam fell. He raised his arm.

The entire castle began to come apart, falling about him, and still the laughter continued.

He awoke damp with perspiration and lay still for a long while. In the morning, he bought a ticket for London.

Two of the three elemental sounds of the world were suddenly with him as he walked that evening, stick in hand. For a dozen days, he had hiked about Cornwall, finding no clues to that which he sought. He had allowed himself two more before giving up and departing.

Now the wind and the rain were upon him, and he increased his pace. The fresh-lit stars were smothered by a mass of cloud and wisps of fog grew like ghostly fungi on either hand. He moved among trees, paused, continued on.

"Shouldn't have stayed out this late," he muttered, and after several more pauses, *"Nel mezzo del cammin di nostra vita mi ritrovai per una selva oscura, che la diritta via era smarrita,"* then he chuckled, halting beneath a tree.

The rain was not heavy. It was more a fine mist now. A bright patch in the lower heavens showed where the moon hung veiled.

He wiped his face, turned up his collar. He studied the position of the moon. After a time, he struck off to his right. There was a faint rumble of thunder in the distance.

The fog continued to grow about him as he went. Soggy leaves made squishing noises beneath his boots. An animal of indeterminate size bolted from a clump of shrubbery beside a cluster of rocks and tore off through the darkness.

Five minutes . . . ten . . . He cursed softly. The rainfall had increased in intensity. Was that the same rock?

He turned in a complete circle. All directions were equally uninviting. Selecting one at random, he commenced walking once again.

Then, in the distance, he discerned a spark, a glow, a wavering light. It vanished and reappeared periodically, as though partly blocked, the line of sight a function of his movements. He headed toward it. After perhaps half a minute, it was gone again from sight, but he continued on in what he thought to be its direction. There came another roll of thunder, louder this time.

When it seemed that it might have been illusion or some short-lived natural phenomenon, something else occurred in that same direction. There was a movement, a shadow-within-shadow shuffling at the foot of a great tree. He slowed his pace, approaching the spot cautiously.

There!

A figure detached itself from a pool of darkness ahead and to the left. Manlike, it moved with a slow and heavy tread, creaking sounds emerging from the forest floor beneath it. A vagrant moonbeam touched it for a moment, and it appeared yellow and metallically slick beneath moisture.

He halted. It seemed that he had just regarded a knight in full armor in his path. How long since he had beheld such a sight? He shook his head and stared.

The figure had also halted. It raised its right arm in a beckoning gesture, then turned and began to walk away. He hesitated for only a moment, then followed.

It turned off to the left and pursued a treacherous path, rocky, slippery, heading slightly downward. He actually used his stick now, to assure his footing, as he tracked its deliberate progress. He gained on it, to the point where he could clearly hear the metallic scraping sounds of its passage.

Then it was gone, swallowed by a greater darkness.

He advanced to the place where he had last beheld it. He stood in the lee of a great mass of stone. He reached out and probed it with his stick.

He tapped steadily along its nearest surface, and then the stick moved past it. He followed.

There was an opening, a crevice. He had to turn sidewise to pass within it, but as he did the full glow of the light he had seen came into sight for several seconds.

The passage curved and widened, leading him back and down. Several times, he paused and listened, but there were no sounds other than his own breathing.

He withdrew his handkerchief and dried his face and hands carefully. He brushed moisture from his coat, turned down his collar. He scuffed the mud and leaves from his boots. He adjusted his apparel. Then he strode forward, rounding a final corner, into a chamber lit by a small oil lamp suspended by three delicate chains from some point in the darkness overhead. The yellow knight stood unmoving beside the far wall. On a fiber mat atop a stony pedestal directly beneath the lamp lay an old man in tattered garments. His bearded face was half-masked by shadows.

He moved to the old man's side. He saw then that those ancient dark eyes were open.

"Merlin . . . ?" he whispered.

There came a faint hissing sound, a soft croak. Realizing the source, he leaned nearer.

"Elixir . . . in earthen crock . . . on ledge . . . in back," came the gravelly whisper.

He turned and sought the ledge, the container.

"Do you know where it is?" he asked the yellow figure.

It neither stirred nor replied, but stood like a display piece. He turned away from it then and sought further. After a time, he located it. It was more a niche than a ledge, blending in with the wall, cloaked with shadow. He ran his fingertips over the container's contours, raised it gently. Something liquid stirred within it. He wiped its lip on his sleeve after he had returned to the lighted area. The wind whistled past the entranceway and he thought he felt the faint vibration of thunder.

Sliding one hand beneath his shoulders, he raised the ancient form. Merlin's eyes still seemed unfocussed. He moistened Merlin's lips with the liquid. The old man licked them, and after several moments opened his mouth. He administered a sip, then another, and another . . .

Merlin signalled for him to lower him, and he did. He glanced again at the yellow armor, but it had remained motionless the entire while. He looked back at the sorceror and saw that a new light had come into his eyes and he was studying him, smiling faintly.

"Feel better?"

Merlin nodded. A minute passed, and a touch of color appeared upon his cheeks. He elbowed himself into a sitting position and took the container into his hands. He raised it and drank deeply.

He sat still for several minutes after that. His thin hands, which had appeared waxy in the flamelight, grew darker, fuller. His shoulders straightened. He placed the crock on the bed beside him and stretched his arms. His joints creaked the first time he did it, but not the second. He swung his legs over the edge of the bed and rose slowly to his feet. He was a full head shorter than Launcelot.

"It is done," he said, staring back into the shadows. "Much has happened, of course . . . ?"

"Much has happened," Launcelot replied.

"You have lived through it all. Tell me, is the world a better place or is it worse than it was in those days?"

"Better in some ways, worse in others. It is different."

"How is it better?"

"There are many ways of making life easier, and the sum total of human knowledge has increased vastly."

"How has it worsened?"

"There are many more people in the world. Consequently, there are many more people suffering from poverty, disease, ignorance. The world itself has suffered great depredation, in the way of pollution and other assaults on the integrity of nature."

"Wars?"

"There is always someone fighting, somewhere."

"They need help."

"Maybe. Maybe not."

Merlin turned and looked into his eyes.

"What do you mean?"

"People haven't changed. They are as rational—and irrational—as they were in the old days. They are as moral and law-abiding—and not—as ever. Many new things have been learned, many new situations evolved, but I do not believe that the nature of man has altered significantly in the time you've slept. Nothing you do is going to change that. You may be able to alter a few features of the times, but would it really be proper to meddle? Everything is so interdependent today that even you would not be able to predict all the consequences of any actions you take. You might do more harm than good; and whatever you do, man's nature will remain the same.''

"This isn't like you, Lance. You were never much given to philosophizing in the old days.''

"I've had a long time to think about it.''

"And I've had a long time to dream about it. War is your craft, Lance. Stay with that.''

"I gave it up a long time ago.''

"Then what are you now?''

"An appraiser.''

Merlin turned away, took another drink. He seemed to radiate a fierce energy when he turned again.

"And your oath? To right wrongs, to punish the wicked . . . ?''

"The longer I lived the more difficult it became to determine what was a wrong and who was wicked. Make it clear to me again and I may go back into business.''

"Galahad would never have addressed me so.''

"Galahad was young, naïve, trusting. Speak not to me of my son.''

"Launcelot! Launcelot!'' He placed a hand on his arm. "Why all this bitterness for an old friend who has done nothing for a thousand years?''

"I wished to make my position clear immediately. I feared you might contemplate some irreversible action which could alter the world balance of power fatally. I want you to know that I will not be party to it.''

"Admit that you do not know what I might do, what I can do.''

"Freely. That is why I fear you. What *do* you intend to do?''

"Nothing, at first. I wish merely to look about me, to see for myself some of these changes of which you have spoken. Then I will consider which wrongs need righting, who needs punishment, and who to choose as my champions. I will show you these things, and then you can go back into business, as you say.''

Launcelot sighed.

"The burden of proof is on the moralist. Your judgment is no longer sufficient for me."

"Dear me," the other replied, "it is sad to have waited this long for an encounter of this sort, to find you have lost your faith in me. My powers are beginning to return already, Lance. Do you not feel magic in the air?"

"I feel something I have not felt in a long while."

"The sleep of ages was a restorative—an aid, actually. In a while, Lance, I am going to be stronger than I ever was before. And you doubt that I will be able to turn back the clock?"

"I doubt you can do it in a fashion to benefit anybody. Look, Merlin, I'm sorry. I do not like it that things have come to this either. But I have lived too long, seen too much, know too much of how the world works now to trust any one man's opinion concerning its salvation. Let it go. You are a mysterious, revered legend. I do not know what you really are. But forgo exercising your powers in any sort of crusade. Do something else this time around. Become a physician and fight pain. Take up painting. Be a professor of history, an antiquarian. Hell, be a social critic and point out what evils you see for people to correct themselves."

"Do you really believe I could be satisfied with any of those things?"

"Men find satisfaction in many things. It depends on the man, not on the things. I'm just saying that you should avoid using your powers in any attempt to effect social changes as we once did, by violence."

"Whatever changes have been wrought, time's greatest irony lies in its having transformed you into a pacifist."

"You are wrong."

"Admit it! You have finally come to fear the clash of arms! An appraiser! What kind of knight are you?"

"One who finds himself in the wrong time and the wrong place, Merlin."

The sorceror shrugged and turned away.

"Let it be, then. It is good that you have chosen to tell me all these things immediately. Thank you for that, anyway. A moment."

Merlin walked to the rear of the cave, returned in moments attired in fresh garments. The effect was startling. His entire appearance was more kempt and cleanly. His hair and beard now appeared gray rather than white. His step was sure and steady. He held a staff in his right hand but did not lean upon it.

"Come walk with me," he said.

"It is a bad night."

"It is not the same night you left without. It is not even the same place."

As he passed the suit of yellow armor, he snapped his fingers near its visor. With a single creak, the figure moved and turned to follow him.

"Who is that?"

Merlin smiled.

"No one," he replied, and he reached back and raised the visor. The helmet was empty. "It is enchanted, animated by a spirit," he said. "A trifle clumsy, though, which is why I did not trust it to administer my draught. A perfect servant, however, unlike some. Incredibly strong and swift. Even in your prime you could not have beaten it. I fear nothing when it walks with me. Come, there is something I would have you see."

"Very well."

Launcelot followed Merlin and the hollow knight from the cave. The rain had stopped, and it was very still. They stood on an incredibly moonlit plain where mists drifted and grasses sparkled. Shadowy shapes stood in the distance.

"Excuse me," Launcelot said. "I left my walking stick inside."

He turned and re-entered the cave.

"Yes, fetch it, old man," Merlin replied. "Your strength is already on the wane."

When Launcelot returned, he leaned upon the stick and squinted across the plain.

"This way," Merlin said, "to where your questions will be answered. I will try not to move too quickly and tire you."

"Tire me?"

The sorceror chuckled and began walking across the plain.
Launcelot followed.

"Do you not feel a trifle weary?" he asked.

"Yes, as a matter of fact, I do. Do you know what is the
matter with me?"

"Of course. I have withdrawn the enchantment which has
protected you all these years. What you feel now are the first
tentative touches of your true age. It will take some time to
catch up with you, against your body's natural resistance, but
it is beginning its advance."

"Why are you doing this to me?"

"Because I believed you when you said you were not a
pacifist. And you spoke with sufficient vehemence for me to
realize that you might even oppose me. I could not permit
that, for I knew that your old strength was still there for you
to call upon. Even a sorceror might fear that, so I did what
had to be done. By my power was it maintained; without it,
it now drains away. It would have been good for us to work
together once again, but I saw that that could not be."

Launcelot stumbled, caught himself, limped on. The hollow
knight walked at Merlin's right hand.

"You say that your ends are noble," Launcelot said, "but
I do not believe you. Perhaps in the old days they were. But
more than the times have changed. You are different. Do you
not feel it yourself?"

Merlin drew a deep breath and exhaled vapor.

"Perhaps it is my heritage," he said. Then, "I jest. Of
course, I have changed. Everyone does. You yourself are a
perfect example. What you consider a turn for the worse in
me is but the tip of an irreducible conflict which has grown
up between us in the course of our changes. I still hold with
the true ideals of Camelot."

Launcelot's shoulders were bent forward now and his
breathing had deepened. The shapes loomed larger before
them.

"Why, I know this place," he gasped. "Yet, I do not know
it. Stonehenge does not stand so today. Even in Arthur's time
it lacked this perfection. How did we get here? What has
happened?"

He paused to rest, and Merlin halted to accommodate him.

"This night we have walked between the worlds," the sorceror said. "This is a piece of the land of Faërie and that is the true Stonehenge, a holy place. I have stretched the bounds of the worlds to bring it here. Were I unkind I could send you back with it and strand you there forever. But it is better that you know a sort of peace. Come!"

Launcelot staggered along behind him, heading for the great circle of stones. The faintest of breezes came out of the west, stirring the mists.

"What do you mean—know a sort of peace?"

"The complete restoration of my powers and their increase will require a sacrifice in this place."

"Then you planned this for me all along!"

"No. It was not to have been you, Lance. Anyone would have served, though you will serve superbly well. It need not have been so, had you elected to assist me. You could still change your mind."

"Would you want someone who did that at your side?"

"You have a point there."

"Then why ask—save as a petty cruelty?"

"It is just that, for you have annoyed me."

Launcelot halted again when they came to the circle's periphery. He regarded the massive stands of stone.

"If you will not enter willingly," Merlin stated, "my servant will be happy to assist you."

Launcelot spat, straightened a little and glared.

"Think you I fear an empty suit of armor, juggled by some Hell-born wight? Even now, Merlin, without the benefit of wizardly succor, I could take that thing apart."

The sorceror laughed.

"It is good that you at least recall the boasts of knighthood when all else has left you. I've half a mind to give you the opportunity, for the manner of your passing here is not important. Only the preliminaries are essential."

"But you're afraid to risk your servant?"

"Think you so, old man? I doubt you could even bear the weight of a suit of armor, let alone lift a lance. But if you are willing to try, so be it!"

He rapped the butt of his staff three times upon the ground.

"Enter," he said then. "You will find all that you need within. And I am glad you have made this choice. You were insufferable, you know. Just once, I longed to see you beaten, knocked down to the level of lesser mortals. I only wish the Queen could be here, to witness her champion's final engagement."

"So do I," said Launcelot, and he walked past the monolith and entered the circle.

A black stallion waited, its reins held down beneath a rock. Pieces of armor, a lance, a blade and a shield leaned against the side of the dolmen. Across the circle's diameter, a white stallion awaited the advance of the hollow knight.

"I am sorry I could not arrange for a page or a squire to assist you," Merlin said, coming around the other side of the monolith. "I'll be glad to help you myself, though."

"I can manage," Launcelot replied.

"My champion is accoutered in exactly the same fashion," Merlin said, "and I have not given him any edge over you in weapons."

"I never liked your puns either."

Launcelot made friends with the horse, then removed a small strand of red from his wallet and tied it about the butt of the lance. He leaned his stick against the dolmen stone and began to don the armor. Merlin, whose hair and beard were now almost black, moved off several paces and began drawing a diagram in the dirt with the end of his staff.

"You used to favor a white charger," he commented, "but I thought it appropriate to equip you with one of another color, since you have abandoned the ideals of the Table Round, betraying the memory of Camelot."

"On the contrary," Launcelot replied, glancing overhead at the passage of a sudden roll of thunder. "Any horse in a storm, and I am Camelot's last defender."

Merlin continued to elaborate upon the pattern he was drawing as Launcelot slowly equipped himself. The small wind continued to blow, stirring the mists. There came a flash of lightning, startling the horse. Launcelot calmed it.

Merlin stared at him for a moment and rubbed his eyes. Launcelot donned his helmet.

"For a moment," Merlin said, "you looked somehow different. . . ."

"Really? Magical withdrawal, do you think?" he asked, and he kicked the stone from the reins and mounted the stallion.

Merlin stepped back from the now completed diagram, shaking his head, as the mounted man leaned over and grasped the lance.

"You still seem to move with some strength," he said.

"Really?"

Launcelot raised the lance and couched it. Before taking up the shield he had hung at the saddle's side, he opened his visor and turned and regarded Merlin.

"Your champion appears to be ready," he said. "So am I."

Seen in another flash of light, it was an unlined face that looked down at Merlin, clear-eyed, wisps of pale gold hair fringing the forehead.

"What magic have the years taught you?" Merlin asked.

"Not magic," Launcelot replied. "Caution. I anticipated you. So, when I returned to the cave for my stick, I drank the rest of your elixir."

He lowered the visor and turned away.

"You walked like an old man . . ."

"I'd a lot of practice. Signal your champion!"

Merlin laughed.

"Good! It is better this way," he decided, "to see you go down in full strength! You still cannot hope to win against a spirit!"

Launcelot raised the shield and leaned forward.

"Then what are you waiting for?"

"Nothing!" Merlin said. Then he shouted, "Kill him, Raxas!"

A light rain began as they pounded across the field; and, staring ahead, Launcelot realized that flames were flickering behind his opponent's visor. At the last possible moment, he shifted the point of his lance into line with the hollow knight's blazing helm. There came more lightning and thunder.

His shield deflected the other's lance while his went on to strike the approaching head. It flew from the hollow knight's shoulders and bounced, smouldering, on the ground.

He continued on to the other end of the field and turned. When he had, he saw that the hollow knight, now headless, was doing the same. And beyond him, he saw two standing figures, where moments before there had been but one.

Morgana le Fay, clad in a white robe, red hair unbound and blowing in the wind, faced Merlin from across his pattern. It seemed they were speaking, but he could not hear the words. Then she began to raise her hands, and they glowed like cold fire. Merlin's staff was also gleaming, and he shifted it before him. Then he saw no more, for the hollow knight was ready for the second charge.

He couched his lance, raised the shield, leaned forward and gave his mount the signal. His arm felt like a bar of iron, his strength like an endless current of electricity as he raced down the field. The rain was falling more heavily now and the lightning began a constant flickering. A steady rolling of thunder smothered the sound of the hoofbeats, and the wind whistled past his helm as he approached the other warrior, his lance centered on his shield.

They came together with an enormous crash. Both knights reeled and the hollow one fell, his shield and breastplate pierced by a broken lance. His left arm came away as he struck the earth; the lancepoint snapped and the shield fell beside him. But he began to rise almost immediately, his right hand drawing his long sword.

Launcelot dismounted, discarding his shield, drawing his own great blade. He moved to meet his headless foe. The other struck first and he parried it, a mighty shock running down his arms. He swung a blow of his own. It was parried.

They swaggered swords across the field, till finally Launcelot saw his opening and landed his heaviest blow. The hollow knight toppled into the mud, his breastplate cloven almost to the point where the spear's shaft protruded. At that moment, Morgana le Fay screamed.

Launcelot turned and saw that she had fallen across the

pattern Merlin had drawn. The sorcerer, now bathed in a bluish light, raised his staff and moved forward. Launcelot took a step toward them and felt a great pain in his left side.

Even as he turned toward the half-risen hollow knight who was drawing his blade back for another blow, Launcelot reversed his double-handed grip upon his own weapon and raised it high, point downward.

He hurled himself upon the other, and his blade pierced the cuirass entirely as he bore him back down, nailing him to the earth. A shriek arose from beneath him, echoing within the armor, and a gout of fire emerged from the neck hole, sped upward and away, dwindled in the rain, flickered out moments later.

Launcelot pushed himself into a kneeling position. Slowly then, he rose to his feet and turned toward the two figures who again faced one another. Both were now standing within the muddied geometries of power, both were now bathed in the bluish light. Launcelot took a step toward them, then another.

"Merlin!" he called out, continuing to advance upon them. "I've done what I said I would! Now I'm coming to kill you!"

Morgana le Fay turned toward him, eyes wide.

"No!" she cried. "Depart the circle! Hurry! I am holding him here! His power wanes! In moments, this place will be no more! Go!"

Launcelot hesitated but a moment, then turned and walked as rapidly as he was able toward the circle's perimeter. The sky seemed to boil as he passed among the monoliths.

He advanced another dozen paces, then had to pause to rest. He looked back to the place of battle, to the place where the two figures still stood locked in sorcerous embrace. Then the scene was imprinted upon his brain as the skies opened and a sheet of fire fell upon the far end of the circle.

Dazzled, he raised his hand to shield his eyes. When he lowered it, he saw the stones falling, soundless, many of them fading from sight. The rain began to slow immediately. Sorceror and sorceress had vanished along with much of the structure of the still-fading place. The horses were nowhere to be seen. He looked about him and saw a good-sized stone. He headed for it and seated himself. He unfastened his breastplate and removed it, dropping it to the ground. His side throbbed and he held it tightly. He doubled forward and rested his face on his left hand.

The rains continued to slow and finally ceased. The wind died. The mists returned.

He breathed deeply and thought back upon the conflict. This, this was the thing for which he had remained after all the others, the thing for which he had waited, for so long. It was over now, and he could rest.

There was a gap in his consciousness. He was brought to awareness again by a light. A steady glow passed between his fingers, pierced his eyelids. He dropped his hand and raised his head, opening his eyes.

It passed slowly before him in a halo of white light. He removed his sticky fingers from his side and rose to his feet to follow it. Solid, glowing, glorious and pure, not at all like the image in the chamber, it led him on out across the moonlit plain, from dimness to brightness to dimness, until the mists enfolded him as he reached at last to embrace it.

HERE ENDETH THE BOOK OF LAUNCELOT,
LAST OF THE NOBLE KNIGHTS OF THE
ROUND TABLE, AND HIS ADVENTURES
WITH RAXAS, THE HOLLOW KNIGHT,
AND MERLIN AND MORGAN LE FAY,
LAST OF THE WISE FOLK OF CAMELOT,
IN HIS QUEST FOR THE SANGREAL.

*QUO FAS ET GLORIA DUCUNT.*

# THE THREE QUEENS

## Esther M. Friesner

*"The Three Queens" was purchased by Gardner Dozois, and appeared in the January 1993 issue of Asimov's, with an illustration by Carol Heyer. Friesner's first sale was to Asimov's, under George Scithers in 1982, and she's made several sales here subsequently under Gardner Dozois. In the years since 1982, she's become one of the most prolific of modern fantasists, with more than twenty novels in print, and has established herself as one of the funniest writers to enter the field in some while. Her many novels include* Mustapha and His Wise Dog, Elf Defense, Druid's Blood, Sphinxes Wild, Here Be Demons, Demon Blues, Hooray For Hellywood, Broadway Banshee, Ragnarok and Roll, Majyk By Accident, Majyk By Hook or Crook, Majyk By Design, Wishing Season, *and* The Water King's Daughter. *Her most recent books include* The Sherwood Game, Child of the Eagle, *and* The Psalms

of Herod. *Her* Asimov's *story "Death and the Librarian" won a Nebula Award in 1996. She lives with her family in Madison, Connecticut. In the moving story that follows, a distinct change of pace from her usual Funny Stuff, she treats us to a haunting and powerful look at the reality behind the mask of Legend . . .*

Long after Guinhwyfar has gone, I gaze at the old man in the chair. The damp wind off the marshes blows in through the unglazed windows, lifting his elflocked white hair until some strand or other is whipped across dripping nose or rheum-encrusted eyes, and there it sticks. It always happens so. He never even tries to brush the pale, limp threads away. I do not move. To move would be to break the slender spell that is all that keeps me from lurching to my feet, grabbing him by the scrawny, wattled neck, shaking him until his toothless gums clapper together and demanding, *"What have you done with my father?"*

So slim a spell, at once impossibly strong and frail as adamantine spiderweb. Yet for all that, I know its power would be useless, kept or broken. No cave so deep nor elfland so faraway could hold the man *this* excuse for breath has stolen from me. From us all.

My father was a hero. Many times in my travels I saw how the mere mention of his name would cleave the chatter from a gathering of common men. The sound of it alone would fall upon them like Rome's old might, Byzantium's awesome splendor. I saw how it filled their meager souls with fire, made their heavy lips twist into smiles that lingered over wondrous dreams.

His name, and for a time they shook the dung from their cracked leather shoes, put aside the wooden plow, and rode with him in search of holy glory. I saw raw hands that had never so much as touched a dagger curl themselves around the gemmed hilts of invisible swords while the phantom bodies of the proud black knights their fancies slew stacked themselves three deep around the smoky daub walls of the drinking house. My father's name hung in the air, a glamour more golden than any homely casting of my dam's, and lent these earthworms wings. Had Guinhwyfar been there as witness, she'd cross herself and move bloodless lips around her tame catchword: *miracle*.

Yes, hero and miracle both, my father and his name. But now . . .

I pace the small, cheerless chamber. It lies in the southern-most quarter of my keep, far from the prying eyes of those servingfolk I may not entirely trust. The slaves I permit to come and go at their pleasure. They know, by the warning bite of their iron collars, that a word spoken incautiously will buy them a fiercer bite of iron at the neck. I do not like to play the cruel man's part, but he has given me no choice. I glower at my captive, my captor, and demand, "What have you done with him?" awaiting some reply.

There is none. There can be none. And who am I to expect a miracle? No, I set my sights lower. I would be satisfied to have some contrary spark of hellfire itself light those empty eyes with their old, keen flame. I would dice with the Christians' own devil for the hope of having this clatter of old bones rise once more and say to me, "Still the fool, boy? What an hour I wasted in your begetting! Not even the memory of pleasure can make up for having fathered a weak-spined thing like you, Modred."

Why do I continue to shelter him from the world, and the world from what he has become? Surely not for love. I wonder if perhaps I ought to summon my men to me, to escort me from this place. The cold marsh wind is not good for my aching bones. *He* bears it well, of course. Cold is nothing to him, who rode so late, so long, over so many lives to hammer out a realm. And now the owlish, elfin voice behind my ear creeps in like the soft soughing of the wind to ask, *And for what?*

That is not for me to say.

I will not summon my men just yet. Instead I will drink a leisurely memory of my—of our—late visitor.

Guinhwyfar was charming, of course. To that sole end these petty kings breed their daughters, to win in bed what they may not in battle. She came for Christian charity, she said, and stayed long enough to spoon a pan of gruel into the gaping red hole of his mouth. More than the half of it dribbled down into his lap where she left it for lesser souls to wipe away.

She said, "His lips look a little blue, Modred. Is that all right?" and hurried back to the warmth and serenity of her convent walls without listening to my reply.

She will not much like what I plan to do this day, I think, but what in her god's name will the white woman ever be able to do about it? Milk-skinned, milk-souled, she is too sickly-sweet to raise any quarrel she cannot win by pouting or wheedling or running off to hide. Yet she shall play her part.

One comes. "My lord?" My men-at-arms flank him with cold steel against the unlikely event of his attempted departure without leave. I weigh him by eye: Not much meat, birdie bones, dirt, the smell of stale beer. So this is a poet.

"Leave him," I command. "Let the slaves bring us food and wine. The Falernian." My men have heard me—their eyes, at least, still kindle when another human being speaks to them. But I am more and less than human, if what the poets sing of my dark mother can ring true. Black Morgan's get from her own brother's loins, I must have stolen some of that cunningwoman's skill for sifting souls. How else explain that even now my men-at-arms carry a Modred-imp inside their skulls? And the imp scampers among their thoughts to spy the fear each feels whenever he looks upon my father's face. The fear clothes itself in words that shiver like beggars in the rain: *And in this, too, the end that waits for me?*

I think these men-at-arms who aid me now, in this hidden chamber, in this desolate place, will become my boldest steel. This instant I could command them to go forth and conquer me the world, and they would do it. One last look on my father's face and they would gallop to their deaths without demur. So Arthur still retains a scrap of power to work miracles even now. He casts a new spell that, singing, weaves its strength around strong men: *Better to throw your life against the lances of your enemy than purchase safety, cradle your bones, go home to dandle babes that grow and fly away to leave you lone, awaiting the erosions of time and the death that cruelly will not come.*

Only I am immune to his witcheries. Keen death, quick death, death with a whetted edge—such won't be mine. My father said it best himself, long since: "Can such a coward be my son?"

But I am brave. Just coming here each day takes bravery. Where is Lancelot, who once was held up before my eyes as goading whip and bright *exemplum* every chance my father got? Lancelot, the grail of gallantry! He too has fled. He huddles among monks and whimpers psalms piteously at the gates of heaven like a starving dog scratching for admittance at a kitchen door. Against the iron face of age, Lancelot is the coward, not I.

"My—my lord?" It is the poet, piping like a cricket from his perch on that blackwood stool beneath the window. My men-at-arms have left us two alone, as ordered.

I am being a sorry host. My guest has taken the only other seat in this room, apart from the siege where my father sits. I lean upon my staff and turn to him. "What is your name?"

His mouth opens and closes many times. My imp leaps in at his ear and reads that he is balancing the wisdom of truth against several clever lies. Whichever choice will lengthen his days, allow him to escape my keep alive, that will be the one he'll make. Not what is right, but what will serve him best to save his skin. Oh, good. I like this man better by the moment.

"Never mind," I say. "I need a man who can keep a secret."

The poet shifts uneasily in his place. My father's head nods, slumps down. Long gurgling snores fill the stone chamber. The poet's eyes shift left and right. To gaze upon my father's face once filled men with dread, yet lifted up their hearts. Now there is only the dread, and that is chiller than the marsh winds. Monks claim they love to meditate upon the body's frailty, the better to adore the imperishable soul, yet I have yet to hear of one monastery where they take special pains to gather in and contemplate the old.

A slave comes with food and wine. I serve my guest my-

self, although my ache-gnarled legs make such service difficult. When I look at him, will his eyes presume to hold a
measure of pity? They had better not. Not for me.

There are three slabs of bread to hold our cold meat and
cheese, three cups also. Some fool kitchen knave will need a
talking-to, I see. It's not as if we are three full men here. My
father has lacked the means—teeth and inclination both—to
deal with food like this since Mother's elfin henchmen
brought him to my keep all those months past. Still, for old
times' sake, when he stirs I kneel beside him and tilt his cup
against his lips. I smile to see the silver-stubbled cords of his
neck move greedily as he gulps the wine.

"Falernian," I tell the poet. "Imported from the southron
lands, when the sea-wolves permit the ships to cross unhin-
dered. It was his favorite—*is*. There are times I find it hard
not to speak of him as dead. A shame there is not more of
this fine vintage in store—I was lucky to get this much.
Sometimes I like to think it only wants enough of a draught
of the wine he loved—loves—to bring him back to the land
of the living."

The poet sips his own wine charily. To his eyes, I babble,
and so am an even greater danger than rumor tints me. What
have I in store for him? No one of my people has let slip a
word, for I have given them no words to let slip. Being who
I am, I must be up to no good. He is a poet: He believes the
tales, even to those he weaves on his own account. He should
know better, but logic sleeps apart from poetry. His imagination flutters wildly from one baseless surmise to another.
Now I see it fold its wings and drop to roost upon the matter
of this wine.

How prudently he savors every mouthful of the liquid silk!
Perhaps he dreams my black sorcery knows limits, that my
poisons are trifles that a man's tongue can detect, so long as
he tastes each mouthful cautiously enough. Foolish notion:
My venoms surpass even my mother's finest brews, and are
tasteless, odorless, cureless every one.

Yet even in my most desperate need to do a man to death,
I would not stoop to taint the Falernian. I am still civilized.

I feed my father the rest of the good wine. My poor bones creak and pop when I may finally stand.

The poet sees me in a new light, now, and he is curious. Dark Modred, black Morgan's son, little twisty toad-back who crept from the blazing sun of his father's splendid court to follow after mysteries, that is the mask he holds up to cover my face. (Merlin, my master, also delighted in books, but apart from the slander of his begetting—nun's child, devil's seed—he is reputed wise, kind, a maker of marvels. The old pimp.) Why should a creature like me take such pains over this dribble-and-dirt befouled shell of an old man? Let him wonder.

"What—what happened to him, my lord?" the poet asks. It is as direct as he dares come at the matter.

This is all to the good, his asking. If he had not, I would have had to twitch the conversation this way and that until I brought him 'round to pose that very question. I dislike such games; I relish being spared them. I must ask Mother whether my stars are especially fortunate today.

But Mother will keep. I have a poet with whom to deal. "Do you not know who this man is?" I counter-ask. He shakes his head, a fearful emptiness in his eyes. He cannot tell whether he will be punished for not knowing. I have a certain reputation in these lands—no worse than most, but considering whose womb bore me, certain small demerits of morality tend to become exaggerated as my doings pass from lip to lip.

I tell him the true name of who it is sits with clouded eye between us. The marsh wind whirls the too-sweet reek of old man's urine through the room beneath the breath of my terse, plain revelation. The poet's fear blossoms as I speak, a rose of ice. He shakes his head like a hoof-stunned hound. Oh, poet! Poor heart-struck poet, do you dream that if you shake the words away into the night, the fact will follow? No, I speak the truth. Modred is a weak-boned imp, half fey in the blood, called coward because I did not cherish steel over study, but I am no liar. Not yet.

I reach into the soft blue lambskin pouch at my belt and let my dark fingers unwrap from around the mystery I now would show him. An arrowhead so small, so black, so primitively shaped you could not imagine it being able to serve a weapon's purpose unless the full force of otherworldly magic lash it to the fletched shaft and guide it to the mark. I have found many of these toys in my rambles. So have other men. We differ only in what we make of such finds. I am wise enough to know that I cannot guess to what end this tiny chip of flint was made.

But "Elfshot!" gasps the poet. He is of the other sort of man, I see. He looks from the flint to my father, then to me. As I said, he knows the tales. The hidden folk whose land we stole, the malice that is as vital to elfin hearts as blood to human, the wicked weaponry with which they stalk us on the sly, all this is as familiar ground to him as his mother's hearthside.

The healthy ploughman whose arm suddenly falls useless has been stricken by the villainous archery of the Fey. The deep-chested warrior who wakes one morn to find his legs won't bear him is their victim too. The tender lady whose laughter once made all men glad, yet who now lies abed, a muttering crone before her time, has likewise been elfshot to the heart. There is no other explanation. The truth is, no explanation at all exists, but we flee the ignorant dark more eagerly than we flee the foolish lie.

Elfshot. I nod and sigh, giving my consent to the first falsehood. "He has been so since his vanishment. We found him wandering near the Saxon lands. It was fortunate that they did not find him first."

The poet's grief destroys his face. "Mount Badon," he says, "now this." My father's most famous victory over the barbarous tribes has become a staple of every poet's offerings. The best changes rung upon that theme are those which seduce the listeners into believing that they themselves stood shield-by-shield with Arthur at Badon and slew their boar-helmed hundreds.

"I can't believe it." The poet is cast adrift on hostile waters. I have done worse than cheat him of a hero; I have cut down a dream. "I thought our king was loved by the folk of Faerie." He might say more—might casually mention the tales they tell of my mother's fey blood, now mine—but he would not be so discourteous. All things of Faerie by custom shun the touch of iron, and within these walls all the iron blades answer to me.

"Well, they are the Seeliefolk who love him," I explain. "But, then, the Unseelie are another elfin nation altogether, capricious, malign, and not to be trusted."

"Oh yes, oh yes," he says, as if he'd suckled nonsense of that stripe from his mother's breast.

"You can see why I keep him here," I say. "If his old foes discovered this—"

"But the realm is secure." The poet looks uncertain. "Isn't it? Lord Bedwyr reigns—"

"Bless his reign with many days," I say, and no man who knows me can doubt my sincerity. I never craved kingship. This, too, my father held to my account of failings. "But our lord holds only the borderlands. The rest of the realm is broken up under the care of many of Arthur's best knights. Good men, all, but in your wanderings have you ever heard it said that they would rally without question to Bedwyr's aid, if the Saxons pressed?"

The poet makes many annoying small disclaimers as to the reliability of his sources, coupled with the modest assertion that he is too lowly placed a person to learn much of how the great conduct their affairs—the better to escape any blame should the information he gives me prove false. In the end he confirms what my spies have already told me: Each lordling for himself; Bedwyr stands alone.

"My father gave his life to the making of the realm," I say. *His life and others*, I think. *With their consent or without it. My life, too, if I had let him, or been worth the trouble to bully into his dream.* But done is done. Any man who asks the dead if they were content to perish as they did gets no answer to his folly. "If we do not now find a way to destroy all chance of this—" I wave at the figure in the chair "— becoming known, a day will come when the tribes learn the truth."

The poet still shakes his head and puts the knuckles of one finger to his mouth, like a little boy. "What difference will it make, my lord? He does the land no good the way he is, but still he does it no harm either.''

I whirl to lash the thickwit savagely across his wagging jaws. The effort winds me and brands pain along the back of my hand. I doubt the poet will feel the throb of my blow for long, but that means nothing. Our finest acts lie in the ghosts of power they summon up, not in themselves. My father would understand.

"Silence!" I bark. "Prove your ignorance to me again and I'll have my men deal with you. I don't need the services of a fool."

The poet cringes and swears that it shall be as my lordship wishes.

Now I might explain my purpose to him, but to what good? He fears me too much for me to gauge whether he truly comprehends what I need to do or if he is only saying so to shield himself from a black wizard gone mad. That is too bad. I had wished for someone to share more of this with me than merely the execution.

"Come," I command. I hobble from the chamber. The poet follows, no fine-bred questing-hound but a tame hedgehog chumbling in my wake. My men-at-arms stand just outside the door. I signal that they are to escort us. This means the brawnier one is to carry me. I am scooped up in his arms as if I were a babe. His grip on my shoulder is strong, and I see the glimmer of the old, gold ring with which I bought this man's devotion.

We pass through the keep and out into the open air. The second man-at-arms has run ahead. I gave the orders for this day weeks ago. All should have come to pass by now, save for the fact that my men could not find me the proper poet. The dying of the year reaps the roads of gay summer folk— the singers, the tumblers, the pipers and the rest. I think they go to ground with the bear-keeper and his beast, drowsing through the winter on the memory of music.

I glance over my man's shoulder at the poet we have found at last. He is very wan and the fear of death still shimmers in the whites of his eyes like the reflection of a scythe-blade on water.

The horses are waiting. Once mounted, I am as good as any man. My most trusted people gather to my stirrup. They are only nine—I could risk no more—and they must suffice. Guinhwyfar prattled how her white god reached the ears of a world with just twelve men to bear his tidings. My nine will do: I have only a realm to reach.

The poet mounts his steed with difficulty. He is unused to it and will be sore before this task is done. But after, when his true labor begins, I think he will spend time enough in the saddle to grow accustomed to the pain.

I tell my people, "You know your purposes. Be blessed in their accomplishment." The saddle beneath me creaks as I turn and show them the poet. "Remember him," I say. "You will hear more of him in time." They nod. They know that if they do not hear what I have promised, or hear it all recounted hobblewise and clumsy, their duty is to hunt him down or face the wrath of my avenging spirit.

They believe in ghosts! Silly folk, but mine, and useful. And who am I to laugh at those who fear what cannot be seen or touched? I am worse than they. They stand in terror of the unseen; I have come to worship it.

The poet and I ride from the keep. One of my men rides with us the three-days' journey to my mother's house. I need him to guard the poet and to attend my wants on the road.

When the poet learns where we are going, there is no holding him from his verses: *Black Morgan has left the halls of stone where once she ruled the mountains! Black Morgan has stepped down from her aerie with silver wings sweeping back the midnight of her hair!* Here is a man bound for disappointment.

Mother's house takes up the least ruinous wing of an old Roman villa. She dwells there happily, rooting in the tousled garden like a mole, speaking to the dozen cats who prowl her beds of herbs and wail like strayed changelings at the moon. Mother is fond of cats and herbs and seeing things through to a proper ending. When she was tired of queenship, she left it with a calm, sensible grace, and told her successor that if any were sent to follow after her and bother her with trifling ravel-end matters of government, she would loose the full

power of the Fey upon them. She has been undisturbed in the
old villa ever since.

It is her love for ending things with grace that bought me
her cooperation in this. My messenger raced ahead of our
small party to bring her the good news about the poet. She
is mounted and waiting for us at the place where the lichened
corpse of a toppled garden god marks the western edge of her
demesne. Deeply hooded, her face is invisible, but I can see
jewels brightening the brown hands she extends for the poet's
homage. A basket rides pillion behind her. Does it mew? Oh,
Mother!

Two more days' ride and we will be there. I feel the shell
around my shoulders start to crack. Mother keeps her counsel
and her place by the nightly fire my man builds up for her
use alone. To his credit, the poet does not seek to intrude
upon black Morgan's midnight privacies. He eats his food
and drinks his wine and does his business against the trees in
peace, under the vigilant eyes of my human falcon.

And now we lie down for our rest this last night of all. So
near the lake, I marvel that I cannot hear the water lapping
against the shore. I lie on two thicknesses of sheepskin, but
still the cold seeps through the fleeces, knotting my limbs.
The stars scrape silver scars across the sky. I watch them
wheel their way to dawn and pity myself a little that I shall
see them no more.

*Modred?* I wake to cat's eyes burning green. My mother's
voice comes from the brown striped puss that sits so primly
near my head. The cat does not speak—it is simply her vessel—and no one can hear its words but the one of her choos-
ing. *Son, are you sure?*

I close my eyes and fill Mother's cat with all the thought
I have given to tomorrow. If I could spare her the pain, I
would, but the pain is a part of what I have decided, what I
have become. There have been days when I imagined I was
gone and all that was left was a Modred-shape molded of
pain. Not all my art will let me figure myself as a being apart
from the fire eating me by inches, alive. Let her know—not
because I want to burden her with my agony, but so that she

will understand why it was easy for me to choose the path of sacrifice.

Yes, she will understand, my mother. She must, already understanding so much. I have gazed into her eyes and seen the secrets of the dreaming seed, the mysteries of the dying and undying year. Her pastes and potions are only the simplest trappings of the true powers she draws out of the earth. The peasants can never grasp her as what she is, but they nod, very sage and knowing, when we name her sorceress and fey. Before we part, I pray she will find the means and time to reassure me that my pain, too, has its place in the cycle.

The cat goes to carry my message back to Mother. I suppose she had to ask if I were sure. This is no common way I've chosen to make my offering. Least of all she understands why I've chosen to involve my father in this manner. For her to fathom that, she must be reborn someone's son.

Soon I hear her rise from her separate fire and come to ours. My good guard feigns sleep prettily. I soon have cause to be grateful for his skill. When Mother rouses the poet and he cries out loudly enough to shake ripe chestnuts from the trees, the guard just grumbles and rolls over, much to the poet's amazement. Mother has the wit to spin him a story of spells that hold men senseless at her pleasure and all is well.

Her cape rustles over the dead leaves as she draws the poet away. She is telling him of how lonely she has been, cut off from human society by a cruel son's mandate, little better than a thrall within the boundaries I have set for her. The cold air gusts from the folds of her cloak as she settles down beside her fire. I hear the poet crunching leaves under his skinny rump as he joins her.

There will be wine. This time it will not be the Falernian. In moments, his head will grow heavy but he will not sleep. That would not suit our purpose at all. He will blink his eyes and swear he is alert, merely bedazzled by black Morgan's legendary beauty. She is all charm, my royal dam—not false appeal like Guinhwyfar's superficial wiles, but the true art which envious minds call witchery. By the time she asks him to sing her the song of Camlann, the potion has him fast.

"Lady, what song is this?" he whispers. Does he wonder why his lips are half-numb?

"The song of my greatest sorrow," Mother says. "The song of the last great battle." I do not dare to turn my body enough so that I can see them where they sit by her fire. Still, my mind paints her mimicking the pose of that nameless Roman matron whose features grace her sleeping-chamber wall: neck bent, but never to a yoke, head bowed to Fate, but never in surrender.

And then the words, the story that has been my secret portion in all this, the tale I've spun from strands of heart's blood ever since the day they brought that husk, my father, home. I feel a flutter in my chest, a startlement to know that the story over which I lavished so many hours of care could be told in so little time.

I expect by now the poet's brow is furrowed deeper than a mountain gorge. "Lord Modred . . . dead?" He bats at clouds that storm his brain. "But isn't he—?" He must be pointing at this fire now.

"How can that be when you yourself sang of the grim battle where he fell?" Regal indignation often cows more peaceable souls away from the truth they know. The poet stammers out apologies. Mother softens and warms, rewarding him with gentler words for his compliance.

The poet walks through mists that snare his mind as Mother pours more words into his ears, words she claims were always his. Even I, with a mind unfettered by drugged wine—I, who know first to last that the verses are mine—I find myself near to believing them as they fall from her mouth.

Against my eyelids I can see a strong-limbed Modred lusting for his father's queen. I plot, I pace, I bring false accusation against sweet Guinhwyfar's innocence. My treachery's unmasked, I rally my men to me and challenge my lord and sire on the battlefield of Camlann. Many good men fall to serve my wickedness. When truce is called, unhappy chance sends a serpent from the grass to sting a worthy fighter's heel—the poet cannot help but compare the subtle worm to me—the man draws steel, the peace is breached, battle rejoins. This time there can be no truce until my father and I stand face to face and Arthur—sun-king, bear-king, righteous champion—takes back the life he gave in an ill hour with a spear-thrust through my heart.

I do not die without some last harm done. Arthur is wounded by my sword, the great king lies near death. I hear the poet sobbing as Mother recounts the final verses of the song. I fancy that he never knew he had such talent in him! He is still sobbing as the wine's last effect takes hold and shifts him subtly into a shallow slumber. I crawl away from the fire so as not to wake him from this fragile doze.

I have to leave my staff behind. My knees shriek as I drag them over stones and roots, deeper into the lakeside wood. The smell of freezing earth is enough to make me drunk with a last cowardly desire to live until the spring's first greening. I will not tarry too long in worship over the perfection of each blade of grass, the pattern of loveliness written in each fallen leaf, the web my breath casts over the frosty air, for fear that these small, precious beauties make me a traitor to myself. Somewhere birds are singing dawnlight carols to a dying autumn sun whose rebirth I won't see.

For once I understand the strange Gethsemane tale Guinhwyfar used to tell at court. Before this, it always struck me odd that Jesus, being a god, didn't just rise up from among the Roman soldiers come to take him to his death and roar, "*Enough!* I will not submit to this!" I even asked her why he didn't burst into flame and devour them all with his divine splendor, the way Jupiter did to poor stupid Semele in the old story. Her answer was that thin-lipped, condescending smirk and the assurance that I could never hope to understand these Christian mysteries.

Well, if this hard road I follow ever ends, she'll learn how wrong she was. Her Jesus god has come to make me his brother. I understand him now. Will she ever?

They are waiting for me not too far off. It's a relief to see them. For awhile it seemed to me that I would never find them, yet here they are! Four of my trusted servants bide to meet me, to lift me from the dirt and bear me into the rough tent they have pitched in sight of the water. One lifts the leather flap and as I enter hands me the golden staff which is

to be part of my regalia today. I'm just glad to have something strong to lean on again.

Guinhwyfar rises from her stool in a white rage when she
sees me. For an instant I fear she may fly at me to scratch
out my eyes. Then she recalls the drab nun's garb she wears,
and realizes she does not dress for passion these days. A rage
would ruin the waxen image she has made of herself, and so
she folds her ivory hands into an attitude of prayer and lifts
her lilting voice, politely requesting that her god smite me
down into Hell.

I leave her to her devotions. There is too much to see to
and too little time.

He is ready. He sits in the very siege that was his place
while he dwelled under my roof. They have dressed him in
an assortment of silks and armor such as no practical fighting
man would wear. The gold crown is on his head and the
gilded sword at his belt. They have even loaned him a captured Saxon long-ax for the occasion. (Father always decried
the long-ax as better suited for chopping wood than flesh, but
I must admit he does look superb.) His hair has been washed
and combed, his beard trimmed, the stubble scraped from his
neck and the tufts of wiry gray plucked from his ears and
nostrils. They really shouldn't have gone to so much trouble.
No one who matters will come close enough to see that Arthur's ears are clean.

"Welcome back, Father," I murmur, and lift the sword-
worn right hand from his knee. Yes, the ring is there, just as
I commanded. I turn the hand palm upmost and breathe a kiss
against the calloused flesh.

Guinhwyfar is shocked when I summon a man to assist me
to disrobe in her presence. There's no help for it: This tent is
the only place I've got. She flings herself to her knees, amber
beads clicking furiously between her fingers, and keeps her
eyes on the ground. Is it for modesty's sake, or simply because she finds it makes her ill to gaze on anything untoward,
misshapen, less than beautiful?

I regret the inconvenience I have put her to, this cold perfection of a queen—everything I have done to her and with
her has left its mark like dog piss on snow: The false message

that her lost lord was found and called for her by name, which was the ruse to bring her to my keep; the offer of my own men to escort her safely back to her convent, which was the means by which we kidnapped her and brought her here out of all hope of rescue; the enforced captivity in this rude tent, shared with the man whose bed she used to share, which was—

Well, which was some pure, true cruelty on my part, I confess. But she deserved it.

She deserted him! When the first tremors came, the hairline cracks flawing the golden mirror of a king's majesty, the first hints that slivers of the Arthur-oak were being nibbled away from the heartwood out, she burst into religion and fled. Who was there for him then as he slipped by inches deeper into the dark? Was her name on his lips when dusk charmed dire ghosts from his wandering mind? Her name . . . or Lancelot's perhaps; not mine. Yet both of them abandoned him to meet his wraiths alone. Where could I better study cruelty?

I think the truth is that I've done Guinhwyfar a favor, closeting her here with Father these few days. The Christians teach that it is good for the soul to confront the face of its sins. Or perhaps they don't. If I've been mistaken, it's too late now to do anything other for Guinhwyfar than say I'm sorry.

If she needs more than that, too bad.

All is ready now, except Guinhwyfar. I explain what's wanted of her and she balks. I expected this. I've had horses like her, the kind that roll their eyes until the white shows every time you urge them to do something to which they're not inclined. A little windfall apple by way of persuasion works wonders.

The windfall I show Guinhwyfar lies inside a gorgeous casket, set with gems, a treasure of itself. The quantity of gold it contains will buy her the establishment of her own abbey, herself the comfortably invisible crown of abbess. The warrior who carries it in keeping is my man, but he is also a Christian. She knows him, and trusts the holy oath he takes to deliver the treasure to her as soon as she has done my bidding.

She crosses her hands over her bosom and lets her head droop as she tells us, quite solemnly, that she will do whatever I say. *Not* because she covets that gold—oh, never!—but again, for Christian charity.

And so, with Christian charity paid, we may begin. Two of my men come to escort our lord from the tent. A tiring-woman arrives to give Guinhwyfar the silver-shot royal robes she must wear, and the diamond-kissed crown. I am depraved enough to steal a backward glance at Father's queen as she picks up each piece of her ordained dress. I gloat as yearning vanity strives against compulsive holiness in that birchtwig face.

The sun is a pale blotch of watered gold on the horizon. The mists are rising gray and white from the lake waters. The heavy barge is moored securely to the near shore, linked by other, more slender lines to the island. When they hear me give the signal, those who wait invisible among the dry brown reeds of Ynys-witrin, they will draw the vessel home.

Mother is already seated in the prow, her cloak cast aside, herself a blazon of jewels over black silk. When Guinhwyfar joins us, I don't think she'll like seeing a woman twice her age outshine her so extravagantly.

"Don't you think you're wearing a few too many necklaces for a woman in mourning?" I tease her.

"A *queen* in mourning, puppy," she corrects me. Her eyes sparkle with laughter. "Our rules are different. I thought you knew how much I hate black." Then without warning she rises from her place and crushes me to her bosom. "My babe." The words are husky and torn. "Oh, my beloved son."

She lets me go the moment she sees Guinhwyfar approach. We shall have no other parting. The white queen asks a few last frightened questions about the isle to which she is bound. She has heard stories, it seems, stories that have nothing to do with the adventures of her god and his followers. Can the Fey be trusted to keep faith? Don't they often steal fair mortal women? What guarantee does she have that the tall elfin knights of Ynys-witrin won't ravish her away?

I suppose it would be rude to offer her a mirror for an

answer. Besides, she wouldn't know at all what I mean.

There is a bier amidships on the barge, a luxurious contrivance draped in sable damask bought for a fortune at the Londinium market. Pillars of gold hold up an embroidered canopy of black Gaza-cloth, diaphanous as smoke. While Guinhwyfar fusses with her skirt, complains that there is water oozing up through the carpets on the bottom of the barge, shows a soaked slipper to anyone who cares, I go to help my father.

He steps into the barge with a strength I hardly recognize after such a lengthy absence. Impatiently he shakes off the hands of my men as they try to lift him aboard. But when I extend my own hand, he stares at it awhile, then brushes it with his own in a purely ceremonial gesture of homage given and received.

"What now, my son?" he asks, and there are phantoms of the hero and the man asleep beneath those words. I show him the bier and the gilded steps by which he must mount to the top. "For me?" A corner of his mouth twitches. Is it laughter? "I thought I was well," he says.

Then the glimmer vanishes. He stands like deadwood beside the steps until my men carry him up and help him to lie down with his head on the cushions and his crown on his breast. He lies peacefully, a king-doll. When they come down again, I pull myself up the stairs to have a last look at his face.

"Where is he?" I whisper to wrinkles and emptiness and dust. And again, until tears threaten to choke off all breath, "Where is he? What have you done with my father?"

Under the bier there is plenty of room for someone of my size to sit. With such a spectacle as this funerary barge to fill the eye, who will notice if the damask draperies are drawn aside on this side or that? In the shadows, I feel around until I find the hunting horn I'll need to get us started.

Before I take breath for the blast, I pause to think if I have forgotten anything. My lands and my possessions are all distributed and disposed among my loyal people. I am dressed with suitable pomp for what awaits me. Mother has made a place of refuge within her villa walls for the nameless, witless old man who will come to live with her, and pet the cats, and tend the herb beds on his better days. She has few visitors, but if anyone asks they will hear of how this good man stood with Arthur at Mount Badon.

I guess that's everything.

The echoing call of the hunting horn of Faerie must wake a lonesome poet where he sleeps beside a fire gone cold. (All signs of other fires, other folk have been swept away by Mother's art.) He will hark to the sound and stumble from his campsite through the bracken to where a lake gleams green as glass. His head still rings with the grand verses he made the other night about the fall of Arthur, Britain's king, at Camlann. How wonderful to know that he could compose a tale so grand, so tragic! How strange that he has no other memory of Camlann than his own verses. Modred dead, Arthur sorely wounded, a battle at which so many knights perished—and no idea at all from whom he heard the news. But—but it must have happened, or why would he make a song about it?

It happened. Oh yes, it happened as his song assures him it did, for as he stands trembling among the lakeside reeds, he sees a sight that strikes his small heart mute.

*The water laps the shore, the birds of morning sing. There is no other sound to mark the passing of the king. White queen, black queen attend him as he sails across the holy lake to Ynys-witrin's halls. In majesty he departs, yet not to death but sleep he goes. The hands of Faerie heal his hurts; he shall return to conquer Britain's foes.*

The words resound inside my head. Poet, if you are there, I wish I had the power to free them from my mind, to pour them into your hands like water. Let them spill away or hold them to your heart, but make the words you choose to take their place worthy of the man whose passing you witness here.

Arthur goes to his rest, but does not die. Do you see? Will your words make the others see it too—the people of the land, the little lordlings, the barbarous tribes? Arthur waits dreaming like the grain in the winter furrow, but he will come again, the green king, the sun-king, the bear-king rising from a sleep like death, renewed. He does not, will not, can not die!

My father cannot die.

I lift the curtain and see a solitary figure standing in the mists along the lakeside. The wind blows from that quarter and I imagine I can still detect my poet's perfume of stale beer. One hand goes up to touch brow, belly, breast and breast in the Christians' sign. He kneels where the reeds lisp secrets. Then the isle's curve hides us from his sight, and he from mine.

He will stay where he is, as he is, only for as long as the marvel has power to keep him from feeling the cold. Then he will stand, go to his horse and ride away. (A horse? Where did he get—? But here it is, and with his meager gear lashed behind the saddle. He will ride first and question Fortune after.)

Wherever he stops for the night, he will sing the tale of Camlann and Arthur's passing, because it is a very fine tale and he remembers that it is his to sing. In the drinking houses they will look at him as if he is mad—*What battle? We heard of no battle!*—but only for a time.

Because there will come sturdy men, fighting men, nine armed men out of the marshlands. Singly they will seek out every drinking house and market, every lord's keep and manor in the realm. They will share the tale of their greatest battle as payment for a night's shelter and a mug of ale. *Oh, but I was at Camlann, where Arthur fell! Surely you remember Camlann of blood, dark Camlann, Camlann of Modred's death, of Arthur's doom?*

The peasants will not dare to contradict men like these— *Arthur's fall! Well, so that's what became of him. We heard nothing for so long that I wondered. Of course I remember!*— and the lords will half recall a poet who passed through their lands not so long ago and sang of just that battle. Before long, other poets will take up the tale, and the lords will be remembering how *they* were at glorious Camlann, at their true king's side. Maybe one of them will even be bold enough to claim that he stood with his lord in the lakeside dawn and saw the last of Arthur as the queens bore him away.

The barge bumps against the island's bank. I emerge from

under the bier to greet my small, dark kindred. Mother has
anticipated me ashore. The Fey cluster at her skirts, snap-eyed
and merry as a revel of fieldmice. Still aboard, Guinhwyfar
scans the isle in vain for any hope of the tall, elegant knights
of Elfland. Poor cheated queen! I'm afraid all your ravish-
ments must remain the stuff of romance.

They swarm up the steps to Arthur's bier and bring my
father down. Guinhwyfar draws her gown aside from the taint
of his touch as they pass her by. I lean over her shoulder to
murmur, "It's not leprosy; it's worse. And if it's meant to
find you, lady, the sorrow of it is you'll never know it has
until too late." She stares at me with huge, shallow eyes, lips
wobbling from the insult I've done to her pride. I know she
slips my face over the image of the serpent in the garden tale
when I add, "Even through convent walls, king's daughter;
even though you've been a queen."

She folds her long white hands over her lily face and her
shoulders shake. I have seen her strike this pose too many
times at court to give it more than a passing bow, as to an
old friend recognized. Let her tears be genuine, for once, even
if they're only shed for herself.

There is a clamor on shore. The people of the isle fall back,
drop to their knees. Only Mother has the right to stand, to
greet the one who comes as an equal. As she moves forward,
away from Father's side, I must scurry to take her place and
let him lean on me.

Father's head moves slowly from side to side, mouth
agape. Does he know where he is? Does he recall this place,
these people? Does he wonder why we've brought him here?
There is a winey smell of apples in the air, and the sweet bite
of smoke from the burning wood of orchard trees past their
bearing years. The earth has taught the Fey to waste nothing.

"Ynys-witrin." I send the whisper up to reach his ear.
"The Lady's isle." I see his nostrils flare to catch the scent,
but the memory flits through his mind and darts off into the
rising sun.

And now she comes, the Lady. Pale Guinhwyfar melts like
curd in a furnace before her majesty, black Morgan my
mother cannot aspire to equal her sister queen for beauty.

Small and dark like the folk she rules, her darkness glows more brave, more brilliant than any daystar queen or sovereign moon-mistress. Guinhwyfar once dazzled, Morgan smolders, but Vivian the Lady of this isle burns with flame that is all light, immortal.

The formalities are all family matters. It does not take long for Guinhwyfar to be sent back to the shore where my men await her. A few minutes more and Mother and Father too are taken from my sight. His hand clung to mine an instant when they came to lead him away to the boat on the far side of the island, but I don't think it was because he knew who I am or what awaits me. Mother went without a word—we have already said all that needs saying—and if I can bear to add the pain of truth to the burden I already carry, then I admit I said goodbye to my father years ago.

It is just Modred and the Fey.

"You've chosen this?" Queen Vivian eyes my princely robes, weighing their expense as if that were a gauge of my sincerity. "It's no good to either of us if you've been forced. The offering won't count, but you'll be just as dead."

"I've come of my own will," I say, "in return for favors given. Is that free enough? Will it do?"

An ember of the poet's earlier confusion glints in her eyes. "What we did for you, you could have done yourself on the shores of some other lake. The barge and its trappings are not beyond your means. You command men and slaves enough to bring this off without a bit of our aid."

Lady, there is no need for your puzzlement. I haven't asked you to understand me, just to kill me. I will tell you nothing that you do not need to know.

She sighs, and apple blossoms drop from her lips. Where they star the grass between us, hyacinth bells spring up in flourishes of unseasonable fragrance. "He never loved you. You were a disappointment to him."

"That's old news."

"Then why all this? Why purchase him so majestic a leave-taking? He could have remained what he was—an old man stricken weak-minded—and you could have remained—"

Alive? I will not say it, for I might laugh in her face.

"Have you a use for me or not, Lady?" I put the question softly, knowing her reply.

There is a last shadow of regret that flashes in her ancient eyes before she makes the sign her people await. I hear the rumbling roar of the great oak they have felled and hollowed and fitted back together again. They trundle the mighty trunk down to the waterside and stand around it, staring at me. That unpolished hull is to be my passage to eternity.

The rites which my old master Merlin told me they practice on this isle are true, it appears. That wild winter when he disappeared—I wonder if it was to journey here and give himself up as the year's-wane offering? I suppose he might've simply frozen to death in a ditch somewhere, but I'd rather not know that. I glance out over the lake, as if I could hope to see Merlin's oak still drifting beneath the calm water.

"Thank you for your courtesy," I say to the crowd as I lean my hands on the open trunk. "For bringing this to me instead of the other way around. It's been a tiring day, I couldn't walk another step, and I don't think any of you could carry me." I am all smiles.

I climb into the tree unaided, only my golden staff to help me lever uncooperative limbs over the barky lip. The interior is smooth as riverstones, the bottom made soft by a mattress filled with sweet-scented herbs and blossoms. Every move I make as I settle onto my back presses more fragrance from it.

The Lady bends over me. In all my life I never could have hoped to have one so beautiful bring her lips so near to mine. If I steal a kiss, will it harm the sacrifice? Then she says, "To do so much for him when he never did the half for you . . . to let him drift into their legends even at the cost of your life here, and your fame in the times to come . . . they will remember you as a villain, Modred."

Her mouth is unresisting as I take my first and only kiss from a lovely woman. My lips curve up. "But they will remember me."

She imagines I have given her the answer to the riddle. She's wrong. The Modred they'll remember in the tales is good at duping queens. It's only fair I get in a little practice.

She gestures, and her servants serve me a wine that smells of summer mornings. There may be a potion concealed by the taste, a brew to make the sacrifice remain tractable or else a kinder draught to hurry me on my way. In either case, I'm grateful, and the wine itself is almost as fine as the Falernian.

She lifts her hands, and the cutaway slab of the oak rises with no hands laid on it. It lowers itself to a perfect landing, groove fitting snugly into groove, slicing away my last glimpse of the light. The whole tree rocks itself free of the earth and floats, it seems, by the power of the Lady's word. I sense too much air beneath me and not enough in here to keep me company for long. Then the sound of water caresses the walls of my coffin and the first cold trickles send spidery fingers in through cracks I cannot see.

However long I've left of life and breath, I feel neither sorrow, self-pity, nor longing for a chance to backtrack the hasty road that's brought me here. I took it willingly for his sake, for the realm's and—let me be honest, dying—most of all, for mine.

No glamour of Fey, no book of wizardry, no skill with the sword or power of cloistered prayer can hope to equal what I have done this day. With words alone I've made my hero-father into the undying heart of this land, made him its ever-living guardian soul. With words alone I've given him a son he might be proud to love. The poets who come after my tame bard will all sing of how dearly Arthur loved his traitor-son, and so it will be. So it must: Without great love there can be no great treachery.

As long as men sing Arthur, they must sing Modred too. Behind me I leave pain and loneliness, but with me I bring to birth a dream as grand as any of my father's. I perish to lie down with princes. I rise to live forever among kings.

# THE DRAGON LINE

## Michael Swanwick

*"The Dragon Line" was purchased by Gardner Do-
zois, and appeared in the June 1989 issue of* Asimov's,
*with an illustration by N. Taylor Blanchard. Michael
Swanwick has published a long string of stories in Asimov's, under two different editors, and has always
been one of our most popular writers—being, for instance, the only writer ever to have two different novels
serialized in our pages. He has several times been a
finalist for the Nebula Award, as well as for the World
Fantasy Award and for the John W. Campbell Award,
and has won the Theodore Sturgeon Award and the*
Asimov's *Readers Award poll. In 1992, his novel* Sta-
tions of the Tide *won him a Nebula Award as well, and
last year he won the World Fantasy Award for his story
"Radio Waves." His other books include his first novel,*
In The Drift, *which was published in 1985, a novella-
length book,* Griffin's Egg, *and 1987's popular novel*

53

Vacuum Flowers. *His critically acclaimed short fiction
has been assembled in* Gravity's Angels *and in a collection of his collaborative short work with other writers,* Slow Dancing Through Time. *His most recent book
is a new novel,* The Iron Dragon's Daughter, *which was
a finalist for the World Fantasy Award and the Arthur
C. Clarke Award. He's just completed a new novel,*
Jack Faust. *Swanwick lives in Philadelphia with his
wife, Marianne Porter, and their son Sean.*

*Here he takes us down some Mean Streets in modern-
day Philadelphia for an encounter among the oil refineries and tank farms with some very ancient Magic . . .*

At the light, Shikra shoved the mirror up under my nose, and
held the cut-down fraction of a McDonald's straw while I did
up a line. A winter flurry of tinkling white powder stung
through my head to freeze up at the base of the skull, and
the light changed, and off we went. "Burn that rubber, Boss-
man," Shikra laughed. She drew up her knees, balancing the
mirror before her chin, and snorted the rest for herself.

There was an opening to the left, and I switched lanes,
injecting the Jaguar like a virus into the stream of traffic,
looped around, and was headed back toward Germantown. A
swirling white pattern of flat crystals grew in my left eye,
until it filled my vision. I was only seeing out of the right
now. I closed the left and rubbed it, bringing tears, but still
the hallucination hovered, floating within the orb of vision. I
sniffed, bringing up my mouth to one side. Beside me, Shikra
had her butterfly knife out and was chopping more coke.

"Hey, enough of that, okay? We've got work to do."

Shikra turned an angry face my way. Then she hit the window controls and threw the mirror, powder and all, into the
wind. Three grams of purest Peruvian offered to the Goddess.

"Happy now, shithead?" Her eyes and teeth flashed, all
sinister smile in mulatto skin, and for a second she was beautiful, this petite teenaged monstrosity, in the same way that a
copperhead can be beautiful, or a wasp, even as it injects the
poison under your skin. I felt a flash of desire and of tender,

paternal love, and then we were at the Chemical Road turnoff, and I drifted the Jag through three lanes of traffic to make the turn. Shikra was laughing and excited, and I was too.

It was going to be a dangerous night.

Applied Standard Technologies stood away from the road, a compound of low, sprawling buildings afloat on oceanic lawns. The guard waved us through and I drove up to the Lab B lot. There were few cars there; one had British plates. I looked at that one for a long moment, then stepped out onto the tarmac desert. The sky was close, stained a dull red by reflected halogen lights. Suspended between vastnesses, I was touched by a cool breeze, and shivered. How fine, I thought, to be alive.

I followed Shikra in. She was dressed all in denim, jeans faded to white in little crescents at the creases of her buttocks, trade beads clicking softly in her cornrowed hair. The guards at the desk rose in alarm at the sight of her, eased back down as they saw she was mine.

Miss Lytton was waiting. She stubbed out a half-smoked cigarette, strode briskly forward. "He speaks modern English?" I asked as she handed us our visitors' badges. "You've brought him completely up to date on our history and technology?" I didn't want to have to deal with culture shock. I'd been present when my people had dug him, groggy and corpseblue, sticky with white chrysalid fluids, from his cave almost a year ago. Since then, I'd been traveling, hoping I could somehow pull it all together without him.

"You'll be pleased." Miss Lytton was a lean, nervous woman, all tweed and elbows. She glanced curiously at Shikra, but was too disciplined to ask questions. "He was a quick study—especially keen on the sciences." She led us down a long corridor to an unmanned security station, slid a plastic card into the lockslot.

"You showed him around Britain? The slums, the mines, the factories?"

"Yes." Anticipating me, she said, "He didn't seem at all perturbed. He asked quite intelligent questions."

I nodded, not listening. The first set of doors sighed open, and we stepped forward. Surveillance cameras telemetered our images to the front desk for reconfirmation. The doors behind us closed, and those before us began to cycle open. "Well, let's go see."

The airlock opened into the secure lab, a vast, overlit room filled with white enameled fermentation tanks, incubators, autoclaves, refrigerators, workbenches, and enough glass plumbing for any four dairies. An ultrafuge whined softly. I had no clear idea what they did here. To me AST was just another blind cell in the maze of interlocking directorships that sheltered me from public view. The corporate labyrinth was my home now, a secure medium in which to change documentation, shift money, and create new cover personalities on need. Perhaps other ancient survivals lurked within the catacombs, mermen and skinchangers, prodigies of all sorts, old Grendel himself; there was no way of telling.

"Wait here," I told Shikra. The lab manager's office was set halfway up the far wall, with wide glass windows overlooking the floor. Miss Lytton and I climbed the concrete and metal stairs. I opened the door.

He sat, flanked by two very expensive private security operatives, in a chrome swivel chair, and the air itself felt warped out of shape by the force of his presence. The trim white beard and charcoal grey Saville Row pinstripe were petty distractions from a face as wide and solemn and cruel as the moon. I shut my eyes and still it floated before me, wise with corruption. There was a metallic taste on my tongue.

"Get out," I said to Miss Lytton, the guards.

"Sir, I—"

I shot her a look, and she backed away. Then the old man spoke, and once again I heard that wonderful voice of his, like a subway train rumbling underfoot. "Yes, Amy, allow us to talk in privacy, please."

When we were alone, the old man and I looked at each other for a long time, unblinking. Finally, I rocked back on my heels. "Well," I said. After all these centuries, I was at a loss for words. "Well, well, well."

He said nothing.

"Merlin," I said, putting a name to it.

"Mordred," he replied, and the silence closed around us again.

The silence could have gone on forever for all of me; I wanted to see how the old wizard would handle it. Eventually he realized this, and slowly stood, like a thunderhead rising up in the western sky. Bushy, expressive eyebrows clashed together. "Arthur dead, and you alive! Alas, who can trust this world?"

"Yeah, yeah, I've read Malory too."

Suddenly his left hand gripped my wrist and squeezed. Merlin leaned forward, and his face loomed up in my sight, ruthless grey eyes growing enormous as the pain washed up my arm. He seemed a natural force then, like the sun or wind, and I tumbled away before it.

I was on a nightswept field, leaning on my sword, surrounded by my dead. The veins in my forehead hammered. My ears ached with the confusion of noises, of dying horses and men. It had been butchery, a battle in the modern style in which both sides had fought until all were dead. This was the end of all causes: I stood empty on Salisbury Plain, too disheartened even to weep.

Then I saw Arthur mounted on a black horse. His face all horror and madness, he lowered his spear and charged. I raised my sword and ran to meet him.

He caught me below the shield and drove his spear through my body. The world tilted and I was thrown up into a sky black as wellwater. Choking, I fell deep between the stars where the shadows were aswim with all manner of serpents, dragons, and wild beasts. The creatures struggled forward to seize my limbs in their talons and claws. In wonder I realized I was about to die.

Then the wheel turned and set me down again. I forced myself up the spear, unmindful of pain. Two-handed, I swung my sword through the side of Arthur's helmet and felt it bite through bone into the brain beneath.

My sword fell from nerveless fingers, and Arthur dropped

his spear. His horse reared and we fell apart. In that last instant our eyes met and in his wondering hurt and innocence I saw, as if staring into an obsidian mirror, the perfect image of myself.

"So," Merlin said, and released my hand. "He is truly dead, then. Even Arthur could not have survived the breaching of his skull."

I was horrified and elated: He could still wield power, even in this dim and disenchanted age. The danger he might have killed me out of hand was small price to pay for such knowledge. But I masked my feelings.

"That's just about fucking enough!" I cried. "You forget yourself, old man. I am still the Pen-dragon, *Dux Bellorum Britanniarum* and King of all Britain and America and as such your liege lord!"

That got to him. These medieval types were all heavy on rightful authority. He lowered his head on those bullish shoulders and grumbled, "I had no right, perhaps. And yet how was I to know that? The histories all said Arthur might yet live. Were it so, my duty lay with him, and the restoration of Camelot." There was still a look, a humor, in his eye I did not trust, as if he found our confrontation essentially comic.

"You and your fucking Camelot! Your bloody holy and ideal court!" The memories were unexpectedly fresh, and they hurt as only betrayed love can. For I really had loved Camelot when I first came to court, an adolescent true believer in the new myth of the Round Table, of Christian chivalry and glorious quests. Arthur could have sent me after the Grail itself, I was that innocent.

But a castle is too narrow and strait a space for illusions. It holds no secrets. The queen, praised for her virtue by one and all, was a harlot. The king's best friend, a public paragon of chastity, was betraying him. And everyone knew! There was the heart and exemplar of it all. Those same poetasters who wrote sonnets to the purity of Lodegreance's daughter smirked and gossiped behind their hands. It was Hypocrisy Hall, ruled over by the smiling and genial Good King Cuckold. He knew all, but so long as no one dared speak it aloud, he did not care. And those few who were neither fools nor lackeys, those who spoke openly of what all knew, were exiled or killed. For telling the truth! That was Merlin's holy and Christian court of Camelot.

Down below, Shikra prowled the crooked aisles dividing the workbenches, prying open a fermenter to take a peek, rifling through desk drawers, elaborately bored. She had that kind of rough, destructive energy that demanded she be doing something at all times.

The king's bastard is like his jester, powerless but immune from criticism. I trafficked with the high and low of the land, tinsmiths and rivergods alike, and I knew their minds. Arthur was hated by his own people. He kept the land in ruin with his constant wars. Taxes went to support the extravagant adventures of his knights. He was expanding his rule, croft by shire, a kingdom here, a chunk of Normandy there, questing after Merlin's dream of a Paneuropean Empire. All built on the blood of the peasantry; they were just war fodder to him.

I was all but screaming in Merlin's face. Below, Shikra drifted closer, straining to hear. "That's why I seized the throne while he was off warring in France—to give the land a taste of peace; as a novelty, if nothing else. To clear away the hypocrisy and cant, to open the windows and let a little fresh air in. The people had prayed for release. When Arthur returned, it was my banner they rallied around. And do you know what the real beauty of it was? It was over a year before he learned he'd been overthrown."

Merlin shook his head. "You are so like your father! He too was an idealist—I know you find that hard to appreciate—a man who burned for the Right. We should have acknowledged your claim to succession."

"You haven't been listening!"

"You have a complaint against us. No one denies that. But, Mordred, you must understand that we didn't know you were the king's son. Arthur was . . . not very fertile. He had slept with your mother only once. We thought she was trying to blackmail him." He sighed piously. "Had we only known, it all could have been different."

I was suddenly embarrassed for him. What he called my

complaint was the old and ugly story of my birth. Fearing the proof of his adultery—Morgawse was nominally his sister, and incest had both religious and dynastic consequences—Arthur had ordered all noble babies born that feast of Beltaine brought to court, and then had them placed in an unmanned boat and set adrift. Days later, a peasant had found the boat run aground with six small corpses. Only I, with my unhuman vigor, survived. But, typical of him, Merlin missed the horror of the story—that six innocents were sacrificed to hide the nature of Arthur's crime—and saw it only as a denial of my rights of kinship. The sense of futility and resignation that is my curse descended once again. Without understanding between us, we could never make common cause.

"Forget it," I said. "Let's go get a drink."

I picked up 476 to the Schuylkill. Shikra hung over the back seat, fascinated, confused, and aroused by the near-subliminal scent of murder and magic that clung to us both. "You haven't introduced me to your young friend." Merlin turned and offered his hand. She didn't take it.

"Shikra, this is Merlin of the Order of Ambrose, enchanter and master politician." I found an opening to the right, went up on the shoulder to take advantage of it, and slammed back all the way left, leaving half a dozen citizens leaning on their horns. "I want you to be ready to kill him at an instant's notice. If I act strange—dazed or in any way unlike myself—slit his throat immediately. He's capable of seizing control of my mind, and yours too if you hesitate."

"How 'bout that," Shikra said.

Merlin scoffed genially. "What lies are you telling this child?"

"The first time I met her, I asked Shikra to cut off one of my fingers." I held up my little finger for him to see, fresh and pink, not quite grown to full size. "She knows there are strange things astir, and they don't impress her."

"Hum." Merlin stared out at the car lights whipping toward us. We were on the expressway now, concrete crash-guards close enough to brush fingertips against. He tried again. "In my first life, I greatly wished to speak with an

African, but I had duties that kept me from traveling. It was one of the delights of the modern world to find I could meet your people everywhere, and learn from them.'' Shikra made that bug-eyed face the young make when the old condescend; I saw it in the rear-view mirror.

''I don't have to ask what you've been doing while I was . . . asleep,'' Merlin said after a while. That wild undercurrent of humor was back in his voice. ''You've been fighting the same old battles, eh?''

My mind wasn't wholly on our conversation. I was thinking of the *bons hommes* of Languedoc, the gentle people today remembered (by those few who do remember) as the Albigensians. In the heart of the thirteenth century, they had reinvented Christianity, leading lives of poverty and chastity. They offered me hope, at a time when I had none. We told no lies, held no wealth, hurt neither man nor animal—we did not even eat cheese. We did not resist our enemies, nor obey them either, we had no leaders and we thought ourselves safe in our poverty. But Innocent III sent his dogs to level our cities, and on their ashes raised the Inquisition. My sweet, harmless comrades were tortured, mutilated, burnt alive. History is a laboratory in which we learn that nothing works, or ever can. ''Yes.''

''Why?'' Merlin asked. And chuckled to himself when I did not answer.

The Top of Centre Square was your typical bar with a view, a narrow box of a room with mirrored walls and gold foil insets in the ceiling to illusion it larger, and flaccid jazz oozing from hidden speakers. ''The stools in the center, by the window,'' I told the hostess, and tipped her accordingly. She cleared some businessmen out of our seats and dispatched a waitress to take our orders.

''Boodles martini, very dry, straight up with a twist,'' I said.

''Single malt Scotch. Warm.''

''I'd like a Shirley Temple, please.'' Shikra smiled so sweetly that the waitress frowned, then raised one cheek from her stool and scratched. If the woman hadn't fled it might have gotten ugly.

Our drinks arrived. "Here's to progress," Merlin said, toasting the urban landscape. Silent traffic clogged the far-below streets with red and white beads of light. Over City Hall the buildings sprawled electric-bright from Queen Village up to the Northern Liberties. Tugs and barges crawled slowly upriver. Beyond, Camden crowded light upon light. Floating above the terrestrial galaxy, I felt the old urge to throw myself down. If only there were angels to bear me up.

"I had a hand in the founding of this city."

"Did you?"

"Yes, the City of Brotherly Love. Will Penn was a Quaker, see, and they believed religious toleration would lead to secular harmony. Very radical for the times. I forget how many times he was thrown in jail for such beliefs before he came into money and had the chance to put them into practice. The Society of Friends not only brought their own people in from England and Wales, but also Episcopalians, Baptists, Scotch-Irish Presbyterians, all kinds of crazy German sects—the city became a haven for the outcasts of all the other religious colonies." How had I gotten started on this? I was suddenly cold with dread. "The Friends formed the social elite. Their idea was that by example and by civil works, they could create a pacifistic society, one in which all men followed their best impulses. All their grand ideals were grounded in a pragmatic set of laws, too; they didn't rely on good will alone. And you know, for a Utopian scheme it was pretty successful. Most of them don't last a decade. But. . . ." I was rambling, wandering further and further away from the point. I felt helpless. How could I make him understand how thoroughly the facts had betrayed the dream? "Shikra was born here."

"Ahhh." He smiled knowingly.

Then all the centuries of futility and failure, of striving for first a victory and then a peace I knew was not there to be found, collapsed down upon me like a massive barbiturate crash, and I felt the darkness descend to sink its claws in my shoulders. "Merlin, the world is dying."

He didn't look concerned. "Oh?"

"Listen, did my people teach you anything about cybernetics? Feedback mechanisms? Well, never mind. The Earth—" I gestured as if holding it cupped in my palm "—is like a living creature. Some say that it is a living creature, the only one, and all life, ourselves included, only component parts. Forget I said that. The important thing is that the Earth creates and maintains a delicate balance of gases, temperatures, and pressures that all life relies on for survival. If this balance were not maintained, the whole system would cycle out of control and . . . well, die. Us along with it." His eyes were unreadable, dark with fossil prejudices. I needed another drink. "I'm not explaining this very well."

"I follow you better than you think."

"Good. Now, you know about pollution? Okay, well now it seems that there's some that may not be reversible. You see what that means? A delicate little wisp of the atmosphere is being eaten away, and not replaced. Radiation intake increases. Meanwhile, atmospheric pollutants prevent reradiation of greater and greater amounts of infrared; total heat absorption goes up. The forests begin to die. Each bit of damage influences the whole, and leads to more damage. Earth is not balancing the new influences. Everything is cycling out of control, like a cancer.

"Merlin, I'm on the ropes. I've tried everything I can think of, and I've failed. The political obstacles to getting anything done are beyond belief. The world is dying, and I can't save it."

He looked at me as if I were crazy.

I drained my drink. " 'Scuse me," I said. "Got to hit up the men's room."

In the john I got out the snuffbox and fed myself some sense of wonder. I heard a thrill of distant flutes as it iced my head with artificial calm, and I straightened slightly as the vultures on my shoulders stirred and then flapped away. They would be back, I knew. They always were.

I returned, furious with buzzing energy. Merlin was talking quietly to Shikra, a hand on her knee. "Let's go," I said. "This place is getting old."

• • •

We took Passayunk Avenue west, deep into the refineries, heading for no place in particular. A kid in an old Trans Am, painted flat black inside and out, rebel flag flying from the antenna, tried to pass me on the right. I floored the accelerator, held my nose ahead of his, and forced him into the exit lane. Brakes screaming, he drifted away. Asshole. We were surrounded by the great tanks and cracking towers now. To one side, I could make out six smoky flames, waste gases being burnt off in gouts a dozen feet long.

"Pull in there!" Merlin said abruptly, gripping my shoulder and pointing. "Up ahead, where the gate is."

"Getty Gas isn't going to let us wander around in their refinery farm."

"Let me take care of that." The wizard put his forefingers together, twisted his mouth and bit through his tongue; I heard his teeth snap together. He drew his fingertips apart—it seemed to take all his strength—and the air grew tense. Carefully, he folded open his hands, and then spat blood into the palms. The blood glowed of its own light, and began to bubble and boil. Shikra leaned almost into its steam, grimacing with excitement. When the blood was gone, Merlin closed his hands again and said, "It is done."

The car was suddenly very silent. The traffic about us made no noise; the wheels spun soundlessly on the pavement. The light shifted to a melange of purples and reds, color Dopplering away from the center of the spectrum. I felt a pervasive queasiness, as if we were moving at enormous speeds in an unperceived direction. My inner ear spun when I turned my head. "This is the wizard's world," Merlin said. "It is from here that we draw our power. There's our turn."

I had to lock brakes and spin the car about to keep from overshooting the gate. But the guards in their little hut, though they were looking straight at us, didn't notice. We drove by them, into a busy tangle of streets and accessways servicing the refineries and storage tanks. There was a nineteenth-century factory town hidden at the foot of the structures, brick warehouses and utility buildings ensnarled in metal, as if caught midway in a transformation from City to Machine.

Pipes big enough to stand in looped over the road in sets of three or eight, nightmare vines that detoured over and around the worn brick buildings. A fat indigo moon shone through the clouds.

"Left." We passed an old meter house with gables, arched windows and brickwork ornate enough for a Balkan railroad station. Workmen were unloading reels of electric cable on the loading dock, forklifting them inside. "Right." Down a narrow granite block road we drove by a gothic-looking storage tank as large as a cathedral and buttressed by exterior struts with diamond-shaped cutouts. These were among the oldest structures in Point Breeze, left over from the early days of massive construction, when the industrialists weren't quite sure what they had hold of, but suspected it might be God. "Stop," Merlin commanded, and I pulled over by the earth-and-cinder containment dike. We got out of the car, doors slamming silently behind us. The road was gritty underfoot. The rich smell of hydrocarbons saturated the air. Nothing grew here, not so much as a weed. I nudged a dead pigeon with the toe of my shoe.

"Hey, what's this shit?" Shikra pointed at a glimmering grey line running down the middle of the road, cool as ice in its feverish surround. I looked at Merlin's face. The skin was flushed and I could see through it to a manically detailed lacework of tiny veins. When he blinked, his eyes peered madly through translucent flesh.

"It's the track of the groundstar," Merlin said. "In China, or so your paperbacks tell me, such lines are called *lung mei*, the path of the dragon."

The name he gave the track of slugsilver light reminded me that all of Merlin's order called themselves Children of the Sky. When I was a child an Ambrosian had told me that such lines interlaced all lands, and that an ancient race had raised stones and cairns on their interstices, each one dedicated to a specific star (and held to stand directly beneath that star) and positioned in perfect scale to one another, so that all of Europe formed a continent-wide map of the sky in reverse.

"Son of lies," Merlin said. "The time has come for there

to be truth between us. We are not natural allies, and your cause is not mine.'' He gestured up at the tank to one side, the clusters of cracking towers, bright and phallic to the other. ''Here is the triumph of my Collegium. Are you blind to the beauty of such artifice? This is the living and true symbol of Mankind victorious, and Nature lying helpless and broken at his feet—would you give it up? Would you have us again at the mercy of wolves and tempests, slaves to fear and that which walks the night?''

''For the love of pity, Merlin. If the Earth dies, then mankind dies too!''

''I am not afraid of death,'' Merlin said. ''And if I do not fear mine, why should I dread that of others?'' I said nothing. ''But do you really think there will be no survivors? I believe the race will continue beyond the death of lands and oceans, in closed and perfect cities or on worlds built by art alone. It has taken the wit and skill of billions to create the technologies that can free us from dependence on Earth. Let us then thank the billions, not throw away their good work.''

''Very few of those billions would survive,'' I said miserably, knowing that this would not move him. ''A very small elite, at best.''

The old devil laughed. ''So. We understand each other better now. I had dreams, too, before you conspired to have me sealed in a cave. But our aims are not incompatible; my ascendancy does not require that the world die. I will save it, if that is what you wish.'' He shrugged as he said it as if promising an inconsequential, a trifle.

''And in return?''

His brows met like thunderstorms coming together; his eyes were glints of frozen lightning beneath. The man was pure theatre. ''Mordred, the time has come for you to serve. Arthur served me for the love of righteousness; but you are a patricide and cannot be trusted. You must be bound to me, my will your will, my desires yours, your very thoughts owned and controlled. You must become my familiar.''

I closed my eyes, lowered my head. ''Done.''

He owned me now.

•  •  •

We walked the granite block roadway toward the line of cool silver. Under a triple arch of sullen crimson pipes, Merlin abruptly turned to Shikra and asked, "Are you bleeding?"

"Say what?"

"Setting an egg," I explained. She looked blank. What the hell did the kids say nowadays? "On the rag. That time of month."

She snorted. "No." And, "You afraid to say the word menstruation? Carl Jung would've had fun with you."

"Come." Merlin stepped on the dragon track, and I followed, Shikra after me. The instant my feet touched the silver path, I felt a compulsion to walk, as if the track were moving my legs beneath me. "We must stand in the heart of the groundstar to empower the binding ceremony." Far, far ahead, I could see a second line cross ours; they met not in a cross but in a circle. "There are requirements: We must approach the place of power on foot, and speaking only the truth. For this reason I ask that you and your bodyguard say as little as possible. Follow, and I will speak of the genesis of kings.

"I remember—listen carefully, for this is important—a stormy night long ago, when a son was born to Uther, then King and bearer of the dragon pennant. The mother was Igraine, wife to the Duke of Tintagel, Uther's chief rival and a man who, if the truth be told, had a better claim to the crown than Uther himself. Uther begot the child on Igraine while the duke was yet alive, then killed the duke, married the mother, and named that son Arthur. It was a clever piece of statecraft, for Arthur thus had a twofold claim to the throne, that of his true and also his nominal father. He was a good politician, Uther, and no mistake.

"Those were rough and unsteady times, and I convinced the king his son would be safest raised anonymously in a holding distant from the strife of civil war. We agreed he should be raised by Ector, a minor knight and very distant relation. Letters passed back and forth. Oaths were sworn. And on a night, the babe was wrapped in cloth of gold and taken by two lords and two ladies outside of the castle, where

I waited disguised as a beggar. I accepted the child, turned, and walked into the woods.

"And once out of sight of the castle, I strangled the brat." I cried aloud in horror.

"I buried him in the loam, and that was the end of Uther's line. Some way farther in was a woodcutter's hut, and there were horses waiting there, and the wetnurse I had hired for my own child."

"What was the kid's name?" Shikra asked.

"I called him Arthur," Merlin said. "It seemed expedient. I took him to a priest who baptized him, and thence to Sir Ector, whose wife suckled him. And in time my son became king, and had a child whose name was Mordred, and in time this child killed his own father. I have told this story to no man or woman before this night. You are my grandson, Mordred, and this is the only reason I have not killed you outright."

We had arrived. One by one we entered the circle of light.

It was like stepping into a blast furnace. Enormous energies shot up through my body, and filled my lungs with cool, painless flame. My eyes overflowed with light: I looked down and the ground was a devious tangle of silver lines, like a printed circuit multiplied by a kaleidoscope. Shikra and the wizard stood at the other two corners of an equilateral triangle, burning bright as gods. Outside our closed circle, the purples and crimsons had dissolved into a blackness so deep it stirred uneasily, as if great shapes were acrawl in it.

Merlin raised his arms. Was he to my right or left? I could not tell, for his figure shimmered, shifting sometimes into Shikra's, sometimes into my own, leaving me staring at her breasts, my eyes. He made an extraordinary noise, a groan that rose and fell in strong but unmetered cadence. It wasn't until he came to the antiphon that I realized he was chanting plainsong. It was a crude form of music—the Gregorian was codified slightly after his day—but one that brought back a rush of memories, of ceremonies performed to the beat of wolfskin drums, and of the last night of boyhood before my mother initiated me into the adult mysteries.

He stopped. "In this ritual, we must each give up a portion of our identities. Are you prepared for that?" He was matter-of-fact, not at all disturbed by our unnatural environment, the consummate technocrat of the occult.

"Yes," I said.

"Once the bargain is sealed, you will not be able to go against its terms. Your hands will not obey you if you try, your eyes will not see that which offends me, your ears will not hear the words of others, your body will rebel against you. Do you understand?"

"Yes." Shikra was swaying slightly in the uprushing power, humming to herself. It would be easy to lose oneself in that psychic blast of force.

"You will be more tightly bound than slave ever was. There will be no hope of freedom from your obligation, not ever. Only death will release you. Do you understand?"

"Yes."

The old man resumed his chant. I felt as if the back of my skull were melting and my brain softening and yeasting out into the filthy air. Merlin's words sounded louder now, booming within my bones. I licked my lips, and smelled the rotting flesh of his cynicism permeating my hindbrain. Sweat stung down my sides on millipede feet. He stopped.

"I will need blood," said Merlin. "Hand me your knife, child."

Shikra looked my way, and I nodded. Her eyes were vague, half-mesmerized. One hand rose. The knife materialized in it. She waved it before her, fascinated by the colored trails it left behind, the way it pricked sparks from the air, crackling transient energies that rolled along the blade and leapt away to die, then held it out to Merlin.

Numbed by the strength of the man's will, I was too late realizing what he intended. Merlin stepped forward to accept the knife. Then he took her chin in hand and pushed it back, exposing her long, smooth neck.

"Hey!" I lunged forward, and the light rose up blindingly. Merlin chopped the knife high, swung it down in a flattening curve. Sparks stung through ionized air. The knife giggled and sang.

I was too late. The groundstar fought me, warping up underfoot in a narrowing cone that asymptotically fined down to a slim line yearning infinitely outward toward its unseen patron star. I flung out an arm and saw it foreshorten before me, my body flattening, ribs splaying out in extended fans to either side, stretching tautly vectored membranes made of less than nothing. Lofted up, hesitating, I hung timeless a nanosecond above the conflict and knew it was hopeless, that I could never cross that unreachable center. Beyond our faint circle of warmth and life, the outer darkness was in motion, mouths opening in the void.

But before the knife could taste Shikra's throat, she intercepted it with an outthrust hand. The blade transfixed her palm, and she yanked down, jerking it free of Merlin's grip. Faster than eye could follow, she had the knife in her good hand and—the keen thrill of her smile!—stabbed low into his groin.

The wizard roared in an ecstasy of rage. I felt the skirling agony of the knife as it pierced him. He tried to seize the girl, but she danced back from him. Blood rose like serpents from their wounds, twisting upward and swept away by unseen currents of power. The darkness stooped and banked, air bulging inward, and for an instant I held all the cold formless shapes in my mind and I screamed in terror. Merlin looked up and stumbled backward, breaking the circle.

And all was normal.

We stood in the shadow of an oil tank, under normal evening light, the sound of traffic on Passayunk a gentle background surf. The groundstar had disappeared, and the dragon lines with it. Merlin was clutching his manhood, blood oozing between his fingers. When he straightened, he did so slowly, painfully.

Warily, Shikra eased up from her fighter's crouch. By degrees she relaxed, then hid away her weapon. I took out my handkerchief and bound up her hand. It wasn't a serious wound; already the flesh was closing. For a miracle, the snuffbox was intact. I crushed a crumb on the back of a thumbnail, did it up. A muscle in my lower back was trembling. I'd been up days too long. Shikra shook her head when I offered her some, but Merlin extended a hand and I gave him the box. He took a healthy snort and shuddered.

"I wish you'd told me what you intended," I said. "We could have worked something out. Something else out."

"I am unmade," Merlin groaned. "Your hireling has destroyed me as a wizard."

It was as a politician that he was needed, but I didn't point that out. "Oh come on, a little wound like that. It's already stopped bleeding."

"No," Shikra said. "You told me that a magician's power is grounded in his mental somatype, remember? So a wound to his generative organs renders him impotent on symbolic and magical levels as well. That's why I tried to lop his balls off." She winced and stuck her injured hand under its opposite arm. "Shit, this sucker stings!"

Merlin stared. He'd caught me out in an evil he'd not thought me capable of. "You've taught this . . . chit the inner mysteries of my tradition? In the name of all that the amber rose represents, why?"

"Because she's my daughter, you dumb fuck!"

Shocked, Merlin said, "When—?"

Shikra put an arm around my waist, laid her head on my shoulder, smiled. "She's seventeen," I said. "But I only found out a year ago."


We drove unchallenged through the main gate, and headed back into town. Then I remembered there was nothing there for me anymore, cut across the median strip, and headed out for the airport. Time to go somewhere. I snapped on the radio, tuned it to 'XPN and turned up the volume. Wagner's valkyries soared and swooped low over my soul, dead meat cast down for their judgment.

Merlin was just charming the pants off his greatgranddaughter. It shamed reason how he made her blush, so soon after trying to slice her open. "—make you Empress," he was saying.

"Shit, I'm not political. I'm some kind of anarchist, if anything."

"You'll outgrow that," he said. "Tell me, sweet child, this dream of your father's—do you share it?"

"Well, I ain't here for the food."

"Then we'll save your world for you." He laughed that enormously confident laugh of his that says that nothing is impossible, not if you have the skills and the cunning and the will to use them. "The three of us together."

Listening to their cheery prattle, I felt so vile and corrupt. The world is sick beyond salvation; I've seen the projections. People aren't going to give up their cars and factories, their VCR's and Styrofoam-packaged hamburgers. No one, not Merlin himself, can pull off that kind of miracle. But I said nothing. When I die and am called to account, I will not be found wanting. "Mordred did his devoir"—even Malory gave me that. I did everything but dig up Merlin, and then I did that, too. Because even if the world can't be saved, we have to try. We have to try.

I floored the accelerator.

For the sake of the children, we must act as if there is hope, though we know there is not. We are under an obligation to do our mortal best, and will not be freed from that obligation while we yet live. We will never be freed until that day when Heaven, like some vast and unimaginable mall, opens her legs to receive us all.

*The author acknowledges his debt to the unpublished "Mordred" manuscript of the late Anna Quindsland.*

# THE QUIET MONK

## Jane Yolen

*"The Quiet Monk" was purchased by Gardner Dozois,
and appeared in the March 1988 issue of* Asimov's,
*with an illustration by Anthony Bari. One of the most
distinguished of modern fantasists, Jane Yolen has been
compared to writers such as Oscar Wilde and Charles
Perrault, and has been called "the Hans Christian An-
derson of the twentieth century." Primarily known for
her work for children and young adults, Yolen has produced more than sixty books, including novels, collections of short stories, poetry collections, picture books,
biographies, and a book of essays on folklore and fairy
tales. She has received the Golden Kite Award and the
World Fantasy Award, and has been a finalist for the
National Book Award. In recent years, she has also
been writing more adult-oriented fantasy, work which
has appeared in collections such as* Tales of Wonder,
Neptune Rising: Songs and Tales of the Undersea Folk,

*Dragonfield and Other Stories, and* Merlin's Booke,
*and in novels such as* Cards of Grief, Sister Light, Sister
Dark, *and* White Jenna. *Here, in one of her too infrequent* Asimov's *appearances, she shows us that relics
can linger on long after the living thing they represent
is gone—even relics of love.*

## Glastonbury Abbey, in the year of Our Lord, 1191

He was a tall man, and his shoulders looked broad even under
the shapeless disguise of the brown sacking. The hood hid
the color of his hair and, when he pushed the hood back, the
tonsure was so close cropped, he might have been a blonde
or a redhead or gray. It was his eyes that held one's interest
most. They were the kind of blue that I had only seen on
midsummer skies, with the whites the color of bleached muslin. He was a handsome man, with a strong, thin nose and a
mouth that would make all the women in the parish sure to
shake their heads with the waste of it. They were a lusty lot,
the parish dames, so I had been warned.

I was to be his guide as I was the spriest of the brothers,
even with my twisted leg, for I was that much younger than
the rest, being newly come to my vocation, one of the few
infant oblates who actually joined that convocation of saints.
Most left to go into trade, though a few, it must be admitted,
joined the army, safe in their hearts for a peaceful death.

Father Joseph said I was not to call the small community
"saints," for sainthood must be earned not conferred, but my
birth father told me, before he gave me to the abbey, that by
living in such close quarters with saintly men I could become
one. And that he, by gifting me, would win a place on high.
I am not sure if all this was truly accomplished, for my father
died of a disease his third wife brought to their marriage bed,
a strange wedding portion indeed. And mostly my time in the
abbey was taken up not in prayer side by side with saints but
on my knees cleaning the abbot's room, the long dark halls,
and the *dortoir*. Still, it was better than being back at home
in Meade's Hall where I was the butt of every joke, no matter
I was the son of the lord. His eighth son, born twisted ankle

to thigh, the murderer of his own mother at the hard birthing. At least in Glastonbury Abbey I was needed, if not exactly loved.

So when the tall wanderer knocked on the door late that Sunday night, and I was the watcher at the gate, Brother Sanctus being abed with a shaking fever, I got to see the quiet monk first.

It is wrong, I know, to love another man in that way. It is wrong to worship a fellow human even above God. It is the one great warning dunned into infant oblates from the start. For a boy's heart is a natural altar and many strange deities ask for sacrifice there. But I loved him when first I saw him for the hope I saw imprinted on his face and the mask of sorrow over it.

He did not ask to come in; he demanded it. But he never raised his voice nor spoke other than quietly. That is why we dubbed him the Quiet Monk and rarely used his name. Yet he owned a voice with more authority than even Abbot Giraldus could command, for *he* is a shouter. Until I met the Quiet Monk, I had quaked at the abbot's bluster. Now I know it for what it truly is: fear masquerading as power.

"I seek a quiet corner of your abbey and a word with your abbot after his morning prayers and ablutions," the Quiet Monk said.

I opened the gate, conscious of the squawking lock and the cries of the wood as it moved. Unlike many abbeys, we had no rooms ready for visitors. Indeed we never entertained guests anymore. We could scarce feed ourselves these days. But I did not tell *him* that. I led him to my own room, identical to all the others save the abbot's, which was even meaner, as Abbot Giraldus reminded us daily. The Quiet Monk did not seem to notice, but nodded silently and eased himself onto my thin pallet, falling asleep at once. Only soldiers and monks have such a facility. My father, who once led a cavalry, had it. And I, since coming to the abbey, had it, too. I covered him gently with my one thin blanket and crept from the room.

●　●　●

In the morning, the Quiet Monk talked for a long time with Abbot Giraldus and then with Fathers Joseph and Paul. He joined us in our prayers, and when we sang, his voice leaped over the rest, even over the sopranos of the infant oblates and the lovely tenor of Brother John. He stayed far longer on his knees than any, at the last prostrating himself on the cold stone floor for over an hour. That caused the abbot much distress, which manifested itself in a tantrum aimed at my skills at cleaning. I had to rewash the floor in the abbot's room where the stones were already smooth from his years of penances.

Brother Denneys—for so was the Quiet Monk's name, called he said after the least of boys who shook him out of a dream of apathy—was given leave to stay until a certain task was accomplished. But before the task could be done, permission would have to be gotten from the pope.

What that task was to be, neither the abbot nor Fathers Joseph or Paul would tell. And if I wanted to know, the only one I might turn to was Brother Denneys himself. Or I could wait until word came from the Holy Father, which word—as we all knew full well—might take days, weeks, even months over the slow roads between Glastonbury and Rome. If word came at all.

Meanwhile, Brother Denneys was a strong back and a stronger hand. And wonder of wonders (a miracle, said Father Joseph, who did not parcel out miracles with any regularity), he also had a deep pocket of gold which he shared with Brother Aermand, who cooked our meagre meals. As long as Brother Denneys remained at the abbey, we all knew we would eat rather better than we had in many a year. Perhaps that is why it took so long for word to come from the Pope. So it was our small convocation of saints became miners, digging gold out of a particular seam. Not all miracles, Father Joseph had once said, proceed from a loving heart. Some, he had mused, come from too little food or too much wine or not enough sleep. And, I added to myself, from too great a longing for gold.

• • •

Ours was not a monastery where silence was the rule. We had so little else, talk was our one great privilege, except of course on holy days, which there were rather too many of. As was our custom, we foregathered at meals to share the day's small events: the plants beginning to send through their green hosannahs, the epiphanies of birds' nest, and the prayerful bits of gossip any small community collects. It was rare we talked of our pasts. The past is what had driven most of us to Glastonbury. Even Saint Patrick, that most revered of holy men, it was said came to Glastonbury posting ahead of his long past. Our little wattled church had heard the confessions of good men and bad, saints of passing fairness and sinners of surprising depravity, before it had been destroyed seven years earlier by fire. But the stories that Brother Denneys told us that strange spring were surely the most surprising confessions of all, and I read in the expressions of the abbot and Fathers Joseph and Paul a sudden overwhelming greed that surpassed all understanding.

What Brother Denneys rehearsed for us were the matters that had set him wandering: a king's wife betrayed, a friendship destroyed, a repentance sought, and over the many years a driving need to discover the queen's grave, that he might plead for forgiveness at her crypt. But all this was not new to the father confessors who had listened to lords and ploughmen alike. It was the length of time he had been wandering that surprised us.

Of course we applauded his despair and sanctified his search with a series of oratories sung by our choir. Before the church had burned down, we at Glastonbury had been noted for our voices, one of the three famed perpetual choirs, the others being at Caer Garadawg and at Bangor. I sang the low ground bass, which surprised everyone who saw me, for I am thin and small with a chest many a martyr might envy. But we were rather fewer voices than we might have been seven years previously, the money for the church repair having gone instead to fund the Crusades. Fewer voices—and quite a few skeptics, though the abbot, and Fathers Paul and Joseph, all of whom were in charge of our worldly affairs, were quick to quiet the doubters because of that inexhaustible pocket of gold.

How long had he wandered? Well, he certainly did not look his age. Surely six centuries should have carved deeper runes on his brow and shown the long bones. But in the end, there was not a monk at Glastonbury, including even Brother Thomas, named after that doubting forebear, who remained unconvinced.

Brother Denneys revealed to us that he had once been a knight, the fairest of that fair company of Christendom who had accompanied the mighty King Arthur in his search for the grail.

"I who was Lancelot du Lac," he said, his voice filled with that quiet authority, "am now but a wandering mendicant. I seek the grave of that sweetest lady whom I taught to sin, skin upon skin, tongue into mouth like fork into meat."

If we shivered deliciously at the moment of the telling, who can blame us, especially those infant oblates just entering their manhood. Even Abbot Giraldus forgot to cross himself, so moved was he by the confession.

But all unaware of the stir he was causing, Brother Denneys continued.

"She loved the king, you know, but not the throne. She loved the man of him, but not the monarch. He did not know how to love a woman. He husbanded a kingdom, you see. It was enough for him. He should have been a saint."

He was silent then, as if in contemplation. We were all silent, as if he had set us a parable that we would take long years unraveling, as scholars do a tale.

A sigh from his mouth, like the wind over an old unused well, recalled us. He did not smile. It was as if there were no smiles left in him, but he nodded and continued.

"What does a kingdom need but to continue? What does a queen need but to bear an heir?" He paused not to hear the questions answered but to draw a deep breath. He went on. "I swear that was all that drove her into my arms, not any great adulterous love for me. Oh, for a century or two I still fancied ours was the world's great love, a love borne on the wings of magic first and then the necromancy of passion alone. I cursed and blamed that witch Morgaine even as I thanked her. I cursed and blamed the stars. But in the end I knew myself a fool, for no man is more foolish than when he is misled by his own base maunderings.'' He gestured downward with his hand, dismissing the lower half of his body, bit his lip as if in memory, then spoke again.

''When she took herself to Amesbury Convent, I knew the truth but would not admit it. Lacking the hope of a virgin birth, she had chosen me—not God—to fill her womb. In that I failed her even as God had. She could not hold my seed; I could not plant a healthy crop. There was one child that came too soon, a tailed infant with bulging eyes, more *mer* than human. After that there were no more.'' He shivered.

I shivered.

We all shivered, thinking on that monstrous child.

''When she knew herself a sinner, who had sinned without result, she committed herself to sanctity alone, like the man she worshipped, the husband she adored. I was forgot.''

One of the infant oblates chose that moment to sigh out loud, and the abbot threw him a dark look, but Brother Denneys never heard.

''Could I do any less than she?'' His voice was so quiet then, we all strained forward in the pews to listen. ''Could I strive to forget my sinning self? I had to match her passion for passion, and so I gave my sin to God.'' He stood and with one swift, practiced movement pulled off his robe and threw himself naked onto the stone floor.

I do not know what others saw, but I was so placed that I could not help but notice. From the back, where he lay full length upon the floor, he was a well-muscled man. But from the front he was as smoothly wrought as a girl. In some frenzy of misplaced penitence in the years past, he had cut his manhood from him, dedicating it—God alone knew where—on an altar of despair.

I covered my face with my hands and wept; wept for his pain and for his hopelessness and wept that I, crooked as I was, could not follow him on his long, lonely road.

• • •

We waited for months for word to come from Rome, but either the Holy Father was too busy with the three quarrelsome kings and their Crusades, or the roads between Glastonbury and Rome were closed, as usual, by brigands. At any rate, no message came, and still the Quiet Monk worked at the abbey, paying for the privilege out of his inexhaustible pocket. I spent as much time as I could working by his side, which meant I often did double and triple duty. But just to hear his soft voice rehearsing the tales of his past was enough for me. Dare I say it? I preferred his stories to the ones in the Gospels. They had all the beauty, the magic, the mystery, and one thing more. They had a human passion, a life such as I could never attain.

One night, long after the winter months were safely past and the sun had warmed the abbey gardens enough for our spades to snug down easily between the rows of last year's plantings, Brother Denneys came into my cell. Matins was past for the night and such visits were strictly forbidden.

"My child," he said quietly, "I would talk with you."

"Me?" My voice cracked as it had not this whole year past. "Why me?" I could feel my heart beating out its own canonical hours, but I was not so far from my days as an infant oblate that I could not at the same time keep one ear tuned for footsteps in the hall.

"You, Martin," he said, "because you listen to my stories and follow my every move with the eyes of a hound to his master or a squire his knight."

I looked down at the stone floor unable to protest, for he was right. It was just that I had not known he had noticed my faithfulness.

"Will you do something for me if I ask it?"

"Even if it were to go against God and his saints," I whispered. "Even then."

"Even if it were to go against Abbot Giraldus and his rule?"

"Especially then," I said under my breath, but he heard.

Then he told me what had brought him specifically to Glastonbury, the secret which he had shared with the abbot and

Fathers Paul and Joseph, the reason he waited for word from Rome that never came.

"There was a bard, a Welshman, with a voice like a demented dove, who sang of this abbey and its graves. But there are many abbeys and many acres of stones throughout this land. I have seen them all. Or so I thought. But in his rhymes—and in his cups—he spoke of Glastonbury's two pyramids with the grave between. His song had a ring of Merlin's truth in it, which that mage had spoke long before the end of our tale: *'a little green, a private peace, between the standing stones.'* "

I must have shaken my head, for he began to recite a poem with the easy familiarity of the mouth which sometimes remembers what the mind has forgot.

*A time will come when what is three makes one:*
*A little green, a private peace, between the standing stones.*
*A gift of gold shall betray the place at a touch.*
*Absolution rests upon its mortal couch.*

He spoke with absolute conviction, but the whole spell made less sense to me than the part. I did not answer him.

He sighed. "You do not understand. The grave between those stone pyramids is the one I seek. I am sure of it now. But your abbot is adamant. I cannot have permission to unearth the tomb without a nod from Rome. Yet I must open it, Martin, I must. She is buried within and I must throw myself at her dear dead feet and be absolved." He had me by the shoulders.

"Pyramids?" I was not puzzled by his passion or by his utter conviction that he had to untomb his queen. But as far as I knew there were no pyramids in the abbey's yard.

"There are two tapered plinths," Brother Denneys said. "With carvings on them. A whole roster of saints." He shook my shoulders as if to make me understand.

Then I knew what he meant. Or at least I knew the plinths to which he referred. They looked little like pyramids. They were large standing tablets on which the names of the abbots of the past and other godly men of this place ran down the side like rainfall. It took a great imagining—or a greater need—to read a pair of pyramids there. And something more. I *had* to name it.

"There is no grave there, Brother Denneys. Just a sward, green in the spring and summer, no greener place in all the boneyard. We picnic there once a year to remember God's gifts."

"That is what I hoped. That is how Merlin spoke the spell. *A little green. A private peace.* My lady's place would be that green."

"But there is nothing there!" On this one point I would be adamant.

"You do not know that, my son. And my hopes are greater than your knowledge." There was a strange cast to his eyes that I could just see, for a sliver of moonlight was lighting my cell. "Will you go with me when the moon is full, just two days hence? I cannot dig it alone. Someone must needs stand guardian."

"Against whom?"

"Against the mist maidens, against the spirits of the dead."

"I can only stand against the abbot and those who watch at night." I did not add that I could also take the blame. He was a man who brought out the martyr in me. Perhaps that was what had happened to his queen.

"Will you?"

I looked down the bed at my feet, outlined under the thin blanket in that same moonlight. My right foot was twisted so severely that, even disguised with the blanket, it was grotesque. I looked up at him, perched on my bedside. He was almost smiling at me.

"I will," I said. "God help me, I will."

He embraced me once, rose, and left the room.

How slowly, how quickly those two days flew by. I made myself stay away from his side as if by doing so I could avert all suspicion from our coming deed. I polished the stone floors along the hall until one of the infant oblates, young Christopher of Chedworth, slipped and fell badly enough to have to remain the day under the infirmarer's care. The abbot

removed me from my duties and set me to hoeing the herb
beds and washing the pots as penance.

And the Quiet Monk did not speak to me again, nor even
nod as he passed, having accomplished my complicity.
Should we have known that all we did *not* do signaled even
more clearly our intent? Should Brother Denneys, who had
been a man of battle, have plotted better strategies? I realize
now that as a knight he had been a solitary fighter. As a lover,
he had been caught out at his amours. Yet even then, even
when I most certainly was denying Him, God was looking
over us and smoothing the stones in our paths.

Matins was done and I had paid scant attention to the psalms
and even less to the antiphons. Instead I watched the moon
as it shone through the chapel window, illuminating the glass
picture of Lazarus rising from the dead. Twice Brother Thomas had elbowed me into the proper responses and three
times Father Joseph had glared down at me from above.

But Brother Denneys never once gave me the sign I
awaited, though the moon made a full halo over the lazar's
head.

Dejected, I returned to my cell and flung myself onto my
knees, a position that was doubly painful to me because of
my bad leg, and prayed to the God I had neglected to deliver
me from false hopes and wicked promises.

And then I heard the slap of sandals coming down the hall.
I did not move from my knees, though the pains shot up my
right leg and into my groin. I waited, taking back all the
prayers I had sent heavenward just moments before, and was
rewarded for my faithlessness by the sight of the Quiet Monk
striding into my cell.

He did not have to speak. I pulled myself up without his
help, smoothed down the skirts of my cassock so as to hide
my crooked leg, and followed him wordlessly down the hall.

It was silent in the dark *dortoir*, except for the noise of
Brother Thomas's strong snores and a small pop-pop-popping
sound that punctuated the sleep of the infant oblates. I knew
that later that night, the novice master would check on the
sleeping boys, but he was not astir now. Only the gatekeeper

was alert, snug at the front gate and waiting for a knock from Rome that might never come. But we were going out the back door and into the graveyard. No one would hear us there.

Brother Denneys had a great shovel ready by the door. Clearly, he had been busy while I was on my knees. I owed him silence and duty. And my love.

We walked side by side through the cemetery, threading our way past many headstones. He slowed his natural pace to my limping one, though I know he yearned to move ahead rapidly. I thanked him silently and worked hard to keep up.

There were no mist maidens, no white robed ghosts moaning aloud beneath the moon, nor had I expected any. I knew more than most how the mind conjures up monsters. So often jokes had been played upon me as a child, and a night in the boneyard was a favorite in my part of the land. Many a chilly moon I had been left in our castle graveyard, tied up in an open pit or laid flat on a new slab. My father used to laugh at the pranks. He may even have paid the pranksters. After all, he was a great believer in the toughened spirit. But I like to think he was secretly proud that I never complained. I had often been cold and the ache settled permanently in my twisted bones, but I was never abused by ghosts and so did not credit them.

All these memories and more marched across my mind as I followed Brother Denneys to the pyramids that bordered his hopes.

There were no ghosts, but there *were* shadows, and more than once we both leaped away from them, until we came at last to the green, peaceful place where the Quiet Monk believed his lost love lay buried.

"I will dig," he said, "and you will stand there as guard."

He pointed to a spot where I could see the dark outlines of both church and housing, and in that way know quickly if anyone was coming toward us this night. So while he dug, in his quiet, competent manner, I climbed up upon a cold stone dedicated to a certain Brother Silas, and kept the watch.

The only accompaniment to the sound of his spade thudding into the sod was the long, low whinny of a night owl on the hunt and the scream of some small animal that signaled the successful end. After that, there was only the soft *thwack-thwack* of the spade biting deeper and deeper into the dirt of that unproved grave.

He must have dug for hours; I had only the moon to mark the passage of time. But he was well down into the hole with but the crown of his head showing when he cried out.

I ran over to the edge of the pit and stared down.

"What is it?" I asked, staring between the black shadows.

"Some kind of wood," he said.

"A coffin?"

"More like the barrel of a tree," he said. He bent over. "Definitely a tree. Oak, I think."

"Then your bard was wrong," I said. "But then, he was a Welshman."

"It is a Druid burial," he said. "That is what the oak means. Merlin would have fixed it up."

"I thought Merlin died first. Or disappeared. You told me that. In one of your stories."

He shook his head. "It is a Druid trick, no doubt of it. You will see." He started digging again, this time at a much faster pace, the dirt sailing backwards and out of the pit, covering my sandals before I moved. A fleck of it hit my eye and made me cry. I was a long while digging it out, a long while weeping.

"That's it, then," came his voice. "And there's more besides."

I looked over into the pit once again. "More?"

"Some sort of stone, with a cross on the bottom side."

"Because she was Christian?" I asked.

He nodded. "The Druids had to give her that. They gave her little else."

The moon was mostly gone, but a thin line of light stretched tight across the horizon. I could hear the first bells from the abbey, which meant Brother Angelus was up and ringing them. If we were not at prayers, they would look for us. If we were not in our cells alone, I knew they would come out here. Abbot Giraldus might have been a blusterer but he was not a stupid man.

"Hurry," I said.

He turned his face up to me and smiled. "All these years waiting," he said. "All these years hoping. All these years of false graves." Then he turned back and, using the shovel as a pry, levered open the oak cask.

Inside were the remains of two people, not one, with the bones intertwined, as if in death they embraced with more passion than in life. One was clearly a man's skeleton, with the long bones of the legs fully half again the length of the other's. There was a helm such as a fighting man might wear lying crookedly near the skull. The other skeleton was marked with fine gold braids of hair, that caught the earliest bit of daylight.

"Guenivere," the Quiet Monk cried out in full voice for the first time, and he bent over the bones, touching the golden hair with a reverent hand.

I felt a hand on my shoulder but did not turn around, for as I watched, the golden skein of hair turned to dust under his fingers, one instant a braid and the next a reminder of time itself.

Brother Denneys threw himself onto the skeletons, weeping hysterically and I—I flung myself down into the pit, though it was a drop of at least six feet. I pulled him off the brittle, broken bones and cradled him against me until his sorrow was spent. When I looked up, the grave was ringed around with the familiar faces of my brother monks. At the foot of the grave stood the abbot himself, his face as red and as angry as a wound.

Brother Denneys was sent away from Glastonbury, of course. He himself was a willing participant in the exile. For even though the little stone cross had the words HIC JACET AR-THURUS REX QUONDAM REXQUE FUTURUS carved upon it, he said it was not true. That the oak casket was nothing more than a boat from one of the lake villages over-turned. That the hair we both saw so clearly in that early morning light was nothing more than grave mold.

"She is somewhere else, not here," he said, dismissing the torn earth with a wave of his hand. "And I must find her."

I followed him out the gate and down the road, keeping pace with him step for step. I follow him still. His hair has gotten grayer over the long years, a strand at a time, but cannot keep up with the script that now runs across my brow. The years as his squire have carved me deeply but his sorrowing face is untouched by time or the hundreds of small miracles he, all unknowing, brings with each opening of a grave: the girl in Westminster whose once blind eyes can now admit light, a Shropshire lad, dumb from birth, with a tongue that can now make rhymes.

And I understand that he will never find this particular grail. He is in his own hell and I but chart its regions, following after him on my two straight legs. A small miracle, true. In the winter, in the deepest snow, the right one pains me, a twisting memory of the old twisted bones. When I cry out in my sleep, he does not notice nor does he comfort me. And my ankle still warns of every coming storm. He is never grateful for the news. But I can walk for the most part without pain or limp, and surely every miracle maker needs a witness to his work, an apostle to send letters to the future. That is my burden. It is my duty. It is my everlasting joy.

*The Tudor antiquary Bale reported that "In Avallon in 1191, there found they the flesh bothe of Arthur and of hys wyfe Guenever turned all into duste, wythin theyr coffines of strong oke, the boneys only remaynynge. A monke of the same abbeye, standyng and behouldyng the fine broydinges of the womman's hear as yellow as golde there still to remayne, as a man ravyshed, or more than halfe from his wyttes, he leaped into the graffe xv fote depe, to have caughte them sodenlye. But he fayled of his purpose. For so soon as they were touched they fell all to powder."*

*By 1193, the monks at Glastonbury had money enough to work again on the rebuilding of their church, for wealthy pilgrims flocked to the relics and King Richard himself presented a sword reputed to be Excalibur to Tancred, the Norman ruler of Sicily, a few short months after the exhumation.*

# INTO GOLD

## Tanith Lee

*"Into Gold" was purchased by Gardner Dozois, and appeared in the March 1986 issue of* Asimov's, *with an illustration by Terry Lee and a cover illustration by Carl Lundgren. Tanith Lee appears less frequently in* Asimov's *than we might wish, but each appearance has been memorable. Tanith Lee is one of the best-known and most prolific of modern fantasists, with over forty books to her credit, including (among many others)* The Birth Grave, Drinking Sapphire Wine, Don't Bite The Sun, Night's Master, The Storm Lord, Sung In Shadow, Volkhavaar, Anackire, Night Sorceries, The Black Unicorn, *and* The Blood of Roses, *and the collections* Tamastara, The Gorgon, Dreams of Dark and Light, *and* The Forests of the Night. *Her short story "Elle Est Trois (La Mort)" won a World Fantasy Award in 1984 and her brilliant collection of retold folk tales,* Red As Blood, *was also a finalist that year, in the Best Collec-*

*tion category. Her most recent books are the collection*
Nightshades *and the novels* Vivia *and* The Blood of
Roses. *Here she takes us to the tumultuous days after
the fall of the Roman Empire, to a remote border out-
post left isolated by the retreat of the Legions, for a
scary and passionate tale of intrigue, love, obsession
. . . and Dark Magic.*

I

Up behind Danuvius, the forests are black, and so stiff with
black pork, black bears, and black-grey wolves, a man alone
will feel himself jostled. Here and there you come on a native
village, pointed houses of thatch with carved wooden posts,
and smoke thick enough to cut with your knife. All day the
birds call, and at night the owls come out. There are other
things of earth and darkness, too. One ceases to be surprised
at what may be found in the forests, or what may stray from
them on occasion.

One morning, a corn-king emerged, and pleased us all no
end. There had been some trouble, and some of the stores
had gone up in flames. The ovens were standing empty and
cold. It can take a year to get goods overland from the River,
and our northern harvest was months off.

The old fort, that had been the palace then for twelve years,
was built on high ground. It looked out across a mile of country strategically cleared of trees, to the forest cloud and a
dream of distant mountains. Draco had called me up to the
roof-walk, where we stood watching these mountains glow
and fade, and come and go. It promised to be a fine day, and
I had been planning a good long hunt, to exercise the men
and give the breadless bellies solace. There is also a pine-nut
meal they grind in the villages, accessible to barter. The
loaves were not to everyone's taste, but we might have to
come round to them. Since the armies pulled away, we had
learned to improvise. I could scarcely remember the first days.
The old men told you, everything, anyway, had been going
down to chaos even then. Draco's father, holding on to a
commander's power, assumed a prince's title which his or-

phaned warriors were glad enough to concede him. Discipline
is its own ritual, and drug. As, lands and seas away from the
center of the world caved in, soldier-fashion, they turned
builders. They made the road to the fort, and soon began on
the town, shoring it, for eternity, with strong walls. Next, they
opened up the country, and got trade rights seen to that had
gone by default for decades. There was plenty of skirmishing
as well to keep their swords bright. When the Commander
died of a wound got fighting the Blue-Hair Tribe, a terror in
those days, not seen for years since, Draco became the Prince
in the Palace. He was eighteen then, and I five days older.
We had known each other nearly all our lives, learned books
and horses, drilled, hunted together. Though he was born elsewhere, he barely took that in, coming to this life when he
could only just walk. For myself, I am lucky, perhaps, I never
saw the Mother of Cities, and so never hanker after her, or
lament her downfall.

That day on the roof-walk, certainly, nothing was further
from my mind. Then Draco said, "*There* is something."

His clear-water eyes saw detail quicker and more finely
than mine. When I looked, to me still it was only a blur and
fuss on the forest's edge, and the odd sparkling glint of things
catching the early sun.

"Now, Skorous, do you suppose . . . ?" said Draco.

"Someone has heard of our misfortune, and considerably
changed his route," I replied.

We had got news a week before of a grain-caravan, but too
far west to be of use. Conversely, it seemed, the caravan had
received news of our fire. "Up goes the price of bread," said
Draco.

By now I was sorting it out, the long rigmarole of mules
and baggage-wagons, horses and men. He traveled in some
style. Truly, a corn-king, profiting always because he was
worth his weight in gold amid the wilds of civilization. In
Empire days, he would have weighed rather less.

We went down, and were in the square behind the east gate
when the sentries brought him through. He left his people out
on the parade before the gate, but one wagon had come up
to the gateway, presumably his own, a huge conveyance, a

regular traveling house, with six oxen in the shafts. Their straps were spangled with what I took for brass. On the side-leathers were pictures of grind-stones and grain done in purple and yellow. He himself rode a tall horse, also spangled. He had a slim, snaky look, an Eastern look, with black brows and fawn skin. His fingers and ears were remarkable for their gold. And suddenly I began to wonder about the spangles. He bowed to Draco, the War-Leader and Prince. Then, to be quite safe, to me.

"Greetings, Miller," I said.

He smiled at this coy honorific.

"Health and greetings, Captain. I think I am welcome?"

"My prince," I indicated Draco, "is always hospitable to wayfarers."

"Particularly to those with wares, in time of dearth."

"Which dearth is that?"

He put one golden finger to one golden ear-lobe.

"The trees whisper. This town of the Iron Shields has no bread."

Draco said mildly, "You should never listen to gossip."

I said, "If you've come out of your way, that would be a pity."

The Corn-King regarded me, not liking my arrogance— though I never saw the Mother of Cities, I have the blood— any more than I liked his slink and glitter.

As this went on, I gambling and he summing up the bluff, the tail of my eye caught another glimmering movement, from where his house wagon waited at the gate. I sensed some woman must be peering round the flap, the way the Eastern females do. The free girls of the town are prouder, even the wolf-girls of the brothel, and aristocrats use a veil only as a sunshade. Draco's own sisters, though decorous and well brought-up, can read and write, each can handle a light chariot, and will stand and look a man straight in the face. But I took very little notice of the fleeting apparition, except to decide it too had gold about it. I kept my sight on my quarry, and presently he smiled again and drooped his eyelids, so I knew he would not risk calling me, and we had won. "Perhaps,'' he said, ''there might be a little consideration of the detour I, so foolishly, erroneously, made.''

''We are always glad of fresh supplies. The fort is not insensible to its isolation. Rest assured.''

''Too generous,'' he said. His eyes flared. But politely he added, ''I have heard of your town. There is great culture here. You have a library, with scrolls from Hellas, and Semitic Byblos—I can read many tongues, and would like to ask permission of your lord to visit among his books.''

I glanced at Draco, amused by the fellow's cheek, though all the East thinks itself a scholar. But Draco was staring at the wagon. Something worth a look, then, which I had missed.

''And we have excellent baths,'' I said to the Corn-King, letting him know in turn that the Empire's lost children think all the scholarly East to be also unwashed.

By midday, the whole caravan had come in through the walls and arranged itself in the market-place, near the temple of Mars. The temple priests, some of whom had been serving with the Draconis Regiment when it arrived, old, old men, did not take to this influx. In spring and summer, traders were in and out the town like flies, and native men came to work in the forges and the tannery or with the horses, and built their muddy thatch huts behind the unfinished law-house— which huts winter rain always washed away again when their inhabitants were gone. To such events of passage the priests were accustomed. But this new show displeased them. The chief Salius came up to the fort, attended by his slaves, and argued a while with Draco. Heathens, said the priest, with strange rituals, and dirtiness, would offend the patron god of the town. Draco seemed preoccupied.

I had put off the hunting party, and now stayed to talk the Salius into a better humor. It would be a brief nuisance, and surely, they had been directed to us by the god himself, who did not want his warlike sons to go hungry? I assured the priest that, if the foreigners wanted to worship their own gods, they would have to be circumspect. Tolerance of every religious rag, as we knew, was unwise. They did not, I thought, worship Iusa. There would be no abominations. I then vowed a boar to Mars, if I could get one, and the dodderer tottered, pale and grim, away.

Meanwhile, the grain was being seen to. The heathen god-offenders had sacks and jars of it, and ready flour besides. It seemed a heavy chancy load with which to journey, goods that might spoil if at all delayed, or if the weather went against them. And all that jangling of gold beside. They fairly bled gold. I had been right in my second thought on the bridle-decorations, there were even nuggets and bells hung on the wagons, and gold flowers; and the oxen had gilded horns. For the men, they were ringed and buckled and roped and tied with it. It was a marvel.

When I stepped over to the camp near sunset, I was on the lookout for anything amiss. But they had picketed their animals couthly enough, and the dazzle-fringed, clink-bellied wagons stood quietly shadowing and gleaming in the west-ered light. Columns of spicy smoke rose, but only from their cooking. Boys dealt with that, and boys had drawn water from the well; neither I nor my men had seen any women.

Presently I was conducted to the Corn-King's wagon. He received me before it, where woven rugs, and cushions stitched with golden discs, were strewn on the ground. A tent of dark purple had been erected close by. With its gilt-tasseled sides all down, it was shut as a box. A disc or two more winked yellow from the folds. Beyond, the plastered colonnades, the stone Mars Temple, stood equally closed and eyeless, refusing to see.

The Miller and I exchanged courtesies. He asked me to sit, so I sat. I was curious.

"It is pleasant," he said, "to be within safe walls."

"Yes, you must be often in some danger," I answered.

He smiled, secretively now. "You mean our wealth? It is better to display than to hide. The thief kills, in his hurry, the man who conceals his gold. I have never been robbed. They think, Ah, this one shows all his riches. He must have some powerful demon to protect him."

"And is that so?"

"Of course," he said.

I glanced at the temple, and then back at him, meaningly. He said, "Your men drove a hard bargain for the grain and the flour. And I have been docile. I respect your gods, Captain. I respect all gods. That, too, is a protection."

Some drink came. I tasted it cautiously, for Easterners often eschew wine and concoct other disgusting muck. In the forests they ferment thorn berries, or the milk of their beasts, neither of which methods makes such a poor beverage, when you grow used to it. But of the Semites one hears all kinds of things. Still, the drink had a sweet hot sizzle that made me want more, so I swallowed some, then waited to see what else it would do to me.

"And your lord will allow me to enter his library?" said the Corn-King, after a host's proper pause.

"That may be possible," I said. I tried the drink again. "How do you manage without women?" I added, "You'll have seen the House of the Mother, with the she-wolf painted over the door? The girls there are fastidious and clever. If your men will spare the price, naturally."

The Corn-King looked at me, with his liquid man-snake's eyes, aware of all I said which had not been spoken.

"It is true," he said at last, "that we have no women with us."

"Excepting your own wagon."

"My daughter," he said.

I had known Draco, as I have said, almost all my life. He was for me what no other had ever been; I had followed his star gladly and without question, into scrapes, and battles, through very fire and steel. Very rarely would he impose on me some task I hated, loathed. When he did so it was done without design or malice, as a man sneezes. The bad times were generally to do with women. I had fought back to back with him, but I did not care to be his pander. Even so, I would not refuse. He had stood in the window that noon, looking at the black forest, and said in a dry low voice, carelessly apologetic, irrefutable, "He has a girl in that wagon. Get her for me." "Well, she may be his—" I started off. He cut me short. "Whatever she is. He sells things. He is accustomed to selling." "And if he won't?" I said. Then he looked at me,

with his high-colored, translucent eyes. "Make him," he said,
and next laughed, as if it were nothing at all, this choice
mission. I had come out thinking glumly, she has witched
him, put the Eye on him. But I had known him lust like this
before. Nothing would do then but he must have. Women had
never been that way for me. They were available, when one
needed them. I like to this hour to see them here and there,
*our* women, straight-limbed, graceful, clean. In the perilous
seasons I would have died defending his sisters, as I would
have died to defend him. That was that. It was a fact, the
burning of our grain had come about through an old griev-
ance, an idiot who kept score of something Draco had done
half a year ago, about a native girl got on a raid.

I put down the golden cup, because the drink was going to
my head. They had two ways, Easterners, with daughters. One
was best left unspoken. The other kept them locked and
bolted virgin. Mercurius bless the dice. Then, before I could
say anything, the Miller put my mind at rest.

"My daughter," he said, "is very accomplished. She is
also very beautiful, but I speak now of the beauty of learning
and art."

"Indeed. Indeed."

The sun was slipping over behind the walls. The far moun-
tains were steeped in dyes. This glamour shone behind the
Corn-King's head, gold in the sky for him, too. And he said,
"Amongst other matters, she has studied the lore of
Khemia—Old Aegyptus, you will understand."

"Ah, yes?"

"Now I will confide in you," he said. His tongue flickered
on his lips. Was it forked? The damnable drink had fuddled
me after all, that, and a shameful relief. "The practice of the
Al-Khemia contains every science and sorcery. She can read
the stars, she can heal the hurts of man. But best of all, my
dear Captain, my daughter has learned the third great secret
of the Tri-Magae."

"Oh, yes, indeed?"

"She can," he said, "change all manner of materials into
gold."

## II

"Sometimes, Skorous," Draco said, "you are a fool."

"Sometimes I am not alone in that."

Draco shrugged. He had never feared honest speaking. He never asked more of a title than his own name. But those two items were, in themselves, significant. He was what he was, a law above the law. The heart-legend of the City was down, and he a prince in a forest that ran all ways for ever.

"What do you think then she will do to me? Turn me into metal, too?"

We spoke in Greek, which tended to be the palace mode for private chat. It was fading out of use in the town.

"I don't believe in that kind of sorcery," I said.

"Well, he has offered to have her show us. Come along."

"It will be a trick."

"All the nicer. Perhaps he will find someone for you, too."

"I shall attend you," I said, "because I trust none of them. And fifteen of my men around the wagon."

"I must remember not to groan," he said, "or they'll be splitting the leather and tumbling in on us with swords."

"Draco," I said, "I'm asking myself why he boasted that she had the skill?"

"All that gold: They didn't steal it or cheat for it. A witch *made* it for them."

"I have heard of the Al-Khemian arts."

"Oh yes," he said. "The devotees make gold, they predict the future, they raise the dead. She might be useful. Perhaps I should marry her. Wait till you see her," he said. "I suppose it was all pre-arranged. He will want paying again."

When we reached the camp, it was midnight. Our torches and theirs opened the dark, and the flame outside the Mars Temple burned faint. There were stars in the sky, no moon.

We had gone to them at their request, since the magery was intrinsic, required utensils, and was not to be moved to the fort without much effort. We arrived like a bridal procession. The show was not after all to be in the wagon, but the

tent. The other Easterners had buried themselves from view.
I gave the men their orders and stood them conspicuously
about. Then a slave lifted the tent's purple drapery a chink
and squinted up at us. Draco beckoned me after him, no one
demurred. We both went into the pavilion.

To do that was to enter the East head-on. Expensive gums
were burning with a dark hot perfume that put me in mind
of the wine I had had earlier. The incense-burners were gold,
tripods on leopards' feet, with swags of golden ivy. The floor
was carpeted soft, like the pelt of some beast, and beast-skins
were hung about—things I had not seen before, some of
them, maned and spotted, striped and scaled, and some with
heads and jewelry eyes and the teeth and claws gilded. Despite all the clutter of things, of polished mirrors and casks
and chests, cushions and dead animals, and scent, there was
a feeling of great space within that tent. The ceiling of it
stretched taut and high, and three golden wheels depended,
with oil-lights in little golden boats. The wheels turned idly
now this way, now that, in a wind that came from nowhere
and went to nowhere, a demon wind out of a desert. Across
the space, wide as night, was an opaque dividing curtain, and
on the curtain, a long parchment. It was figured with another
mass of images, as if nothing in the place should be spare. A
tree went up, with two birds at the roots, a white bird with a
raven-black head, a soot-black bird with the head of an ape.
A snake twined the tree too, round and round, and ended
looking out of the lower branches where yellow fruit hung.
The snake had the face of a maiden, and flowing hair. Above
sat three figures, judges of the dead from Aegyptus, I would
have thought, if I had thought about them, with a balance,
and wands. The sun and the moon stood over the tree.

I put my hand to the hilt of my sword, and waited. Draco
had seated himself on the cushions. A golden jug was to hand,
and a cup. He reached forward, poured the liquor and made
to take it, before—reluctantly—I snatched the vessel. "Let
me, first. Are you mad?"

He reclined, not interested as I tasted for him, then let him
have the cup again.

Then the curtain parted down the middle and the parchment

with it, directly through the serpent-tree. I had expected the
Miller, but instead what entered was a black dog with a collar
of gold. It had a wolf's shape, but more slender, and with a
pointed muzzle and high carven pointed ears. Its eyes were
also black. It stood calmly, like a steward, regarding us, then
stepped aside and lay down, its head still raised to watch.
And next the woman Draco wanted came in.

To me, she looked nothing in particular. She was pleasantly
made, slim, but rounded, her bare arms and feet the color of
amber. Over her head, to her breast, covering her hair and
face like a dusky smoke, was a veil, but it was transparent
enough you saw through it to black locks and black aloe eyes,
and a full tawny mouth. There was only a touch of gold on
her, a rolled torque of soft metal at her throat, and one ring
on her right hand. I was puzzled as to what had made her
glimmer at the edge of my sight before, but perhaps she had
dressed differently then, to make herself plain.

She bowed Eastern-wise to Draco, then to me. Then, in the
purest Greek I ever heard, she addressed us.

"Lords, while I am at work, I must ask that you will please
be still, or else you will disturb the currents of the act and so
impair it. Be seated," she said to me, as if I had only stood
till then from courtesy. Her eyes were very black, black as
the eyes of the jackal-dog, blacker than the night. Then she
blinked, and her eyes flashed. The lids were painted with
gold. And I found I had sat down.

What followed I instantly took for an hallucination, in-
duced by the incense, and by other means less perceptible.
That is not to say I did not think she was a witch. There was
something of power to her I never met before. It pounded
from her, like heat, or an aroma. It did not make her beautiful
for me, but it held me quiet, though I swear never once did
I lose my grip either on my senses or my sword.

First, and quite swiftly, I had the impression the whole tent
blew upward, and we were in the open in fact, under a sky
of a million stars that blazed and crackled like diamonds.
Even so, the golden wheels stayed put, up in the sky now,
and they spun, faster and faster, until each was a solid golden
O of fire, three spinning suns in the heaven of midnight.

(I remember I thought flatly, We have been spelled. So what now? But in its own way, my stoicism was also suspect. My thoughts in any case flagged after that.)

There was a smell of lions, or of a land that had them. Do not ask me how I know, I never smelled or saw them, or such a spot. And there before us all stood a slanting wall of brick, at once much larger than I saw it, and smaller than it was. It seemed even so to lean into the sky. The woman raised her arms. She was apparent now as if rinsed all over by gilt, and one of the great stars seemed to sear on her forehead.

Forms began to come and go, on the lion-wind. If I knew then what they were, I forgot it later. Perhaps they were animals, like the skins in the tent, though some had wings.

She spoke to them. She did not use Greek anymore. It was the language of Khem, presumably, or we were intended to believe so. A liquid tongue, an Eastern tongue, no doubt.

Then there were other visions. The ribbed stems of flowers, broader than ten men around, wide petals pressed to the ether. A rainbow of mist that arched over, and touched the earth with its feet and its brow. And other mirages, many of which resembled effigies I had seen of the gods, but they walked.

The night began to close upon us slowly, narrowing and coming down. The stars still raged overhead and the gold wheels whirled, but some sense of enclosure had returned. As for the sloped angle of brick it had huddled down into a sort of oven, and into this the woman was placing, with extreme care—of all things—long sceptres of corn, all brown and dry and withered, blighted to straw by some harvest like a curse.

I heard her whisper then. I could not hear what.

Behind her, dim as shadows, I saw other women, who sat weaving, or who toiled at the grind-stone, and one who shook a rattle upon which rings of gold sang out. Then the vision of these women was eclipsed. Something stood there, between the night and the Eastern witch. Tall as the roof, or tall as the sky, bird-headed maybe, with two of the stars for eyes. When I looked at this, this ultimate apparition, my blood froze and I could have howled out loud. It was not common fear, but terror, such as the worst reality has never brought me, though sometimes subtle nightmares do.

Then there was a lightning, down the night. When it passed, we were enclosed in the tent, the huge night of the tent, and the brick oven burned before us, with a thin harsh fume coming from the aperture in its top.

"Sweet is truth," said the witch, in a wild and passionate voice, all music, like the notes of the gold rings on the rattle. "O Lord of the Word. The Word is, and the Word makes all things to be."

Then the oven cracked into two pieces, it simply fell away from itself, and there on a bank of red charcoal, which died to clinker even as I gazed at it, lay a sheaf of golden corn. *Golden* corn, smiths' work. It was pure and sound and rang like a bell when presently I went to it and struck it and flung it away.

The tent had positively resettled all around us. It was there. I felt queasy and stupid, but I was in my body and had my bearings again, the sword-hilt firm to my palm, though it was oddly hot to the touch, and my forehead burned, sweatless, as if I too had been seethed in a fire. I had picked up the goldwork without asking her anything. She did not prevent me, nor when I slung it off.

When I looked up from that, she was kneeling by the curtain, where the black dog had been and was no more. Her eyes were downcast under her veil. I noted the torque was gone from her neck and the ring from her finger. Had she somehow managed her trick that way, melting gold on to the stalks of mummified corn—No, lunacy. Why nag at it? It was *all* a deception.

But Draco lay looking at her now, burned up by another fever. It was her personal gold he wanted.

"Out, Skorous," he said to me. "Out, now." Slurred and sure.

So I said to her, through my blunted lips and woollen tongue, "Listen carefully, girl. The witchery ends now. You know what he wants, and how to see to that, I suppose. Scratch him with your littlest nail, and you die."

Then, without getting to her feet, she looked up at me, only the second time. She spoke in Greek, as at the start. In the morning, when I was better able to think, I reckoned I had

imagined what she said. It had seemed to be: "He is safe, for
I desire him. It is my choice. If it were not my choice and
my desire, where might you hide yourselves, and live?"

We kept watch round the tent, in the Easterners' camp, in the
market-place, until the ashes of the dawn. There was not a
sound from anywhere, save the regular quiet passaging of
sentries on the walls, and the cool black forest wind that
turned grey near sunrise.

At sunup, the usual activity of any town began. The camp
stirred and let its boys out quickly to the well to avoid the
town's women. Some of the caravaners even chose to stroll
across to the public lavatories, though they had avoided the
bathhouse.

An embarrassment came over me, that we should be standing there, in the foreigners' hive, to guard our prince through
his night of lust. I looked sharply, to see how the men were
taking it, but they had held together well. Presently Draco
emerged. He appeared flushed and tumbled, very nearly shy,
like some girl just out of a love-bed.

We went back to the fort in fair order, where he took me
aside, thanked me, and sent me away again.

Bathed and shaved, and my fast broken, I began to feel
more sanguine. It was over and done with. I would go down
to the temple of Father Jupiter and give him something—
why, I was not exactly sure. Then get my boar for Mars. The
fresh-baked bread I had just eaten was tasty, and maybe worth
all the worry.

Later, I heard the Miller had taken himself to our library
and been let in. I gave orders he was to be searched on leaving. Draco's grandfather had started the collection of manu-
scripts, there were even scrolls said to have been rescued from
Alexandrea. One could not be too wary.

In the evening, Draco called me up to his writing-room.

"Tomorrow," he said, "the Easterners will be leaving us."

"That's good news," I said.

"I thought it would please you. Zafra, however, is to remain. I'm taking her into my household."

"Zafra," I said.

"Well, they call her that. For the yellow-gold. Perhaps not her name. That might have been *Nefra*—Beautiful . . ."

"Well," I said, "if you want."

"Well," he said, "I never knew you before to be jealous of one of my women."

I said nothing, though the blood knocked about in my head. I had noted before, he had a woman's tongue himself when he was put out. He was a spoiled brat as a child, I have to admit, but a mother's early death, and the life of a forest fortess, pared most of it from him.

"The Corn-King is not her father," he said now. "She told me. But he's stood by her as that for some years. I shall send him something, in recompense."

He waited for my comment that I was amazed nothing had been asked for. He waited to see how I would jump. I wondered if he had paced about here, planning how he would put it to me. Not that he was required to. Now he said: "We gain, Skorous, a healer and deviner. Not just my pleasure at night."

"Your pleasure at night is your own affair. There are plenty of girls about, I would have thought, to keep you content. As for anything else she can or cannot do, all three temples, particularly the Women's Temple, will be up in arms. The Salius yesterday was only a sample. Do you think they are going to let some yellow-skinned harlot devine for you? Do you think that men who get hurt in a fight will want her near them?"

"You would not, plainly."

"No, I would not. As for the witchcraft, we were drugged and made monkeys of. An evening's fun is one thing."

"Yes, Skorous," he said. "Thanks for your opinion. Don't sulk too long. I shall miss your company."

An hour later, he sent, so I was informed, two of the scrolls from the library to the Corn-King in his wagon. They were two of the best, Greek, one transcribed by the hand, it was said, of a very great king. They went in a silver box, with jewel inlay. Gold would have been tactless, under the circumstances.

•  •  •

Next day she was in the palace. She had rooms on the women's side. It had been the apartment of Draco's elder sister, before her marriage. He treated this one as nothing less than a relative from the first. When he was at leisure, on those occasions when the wives and women of his officers dined with them, there was she with him. When he hunted, she went with him, too, not to have any sport, but as a companion, in a litter between two horses that made each hunt into a farce from its onset. She was in his bed each night, for he did not go to her, her place was solely hers: The couch his father had shared only with his mother. And when he wanted advice, it was she who gave it to him. He called on his soldiers and his priests afterwards. Though he always did so call, nobody lost face. He was wise and canny, she must have told him how to be at long last. And the charm he had always had. He even consulted me, and made much of me before everyone, because, very sensibly he realized, unless he meant to replace me, it would be foolish to let the men see I no longer counted a feather's weight with him. Besides, I might get notions of rebellion. I had my own following, my own men who would die for me if they thought me wronged. Probably that angered me more than the rest, that he might have the idea I would forego my duty and loyalty, forget my honor, and try to pull him down. I could no more do that than put out one of my own eyes.

Since we lost our homeland, since we lost, more importantly, the spine of the Empire, there had been a disparity, a separation of men. Now I saw it, in those bitter golden moments after she came among us. He had been born in the Mother of Cities, but she had slipped from his skin like water. He was a new being, a creature of the world, that might be anything, of any country. But, never having seen the roots of me, they yet had me fast. I was of the old order. I would stand until the fire had me, rather than tarnish my name, and my heart.

Gradually, the fort and town began to fill with gold. It was very nearly a silly thing. But we grew lovely and we shone. The temples did not hate her, as I had predicted. No, for she brought them glittering vessels, and laved the gods' feet with

rare offerings, and the sweet spice also of her gift burned
before Mars, and the Father, and the Mother, so every holy
place smelled like Aegyptus, or Judea, or the brothels of Bab-
ylon for all I knew.

She came to walk in the streets with just one of the slaves
at her heels, bold, the way our ladies did, and though she
never left off her veil, she dressed in the stola and the palla,
all clasped and cinched with the tiniest amounts of gold, while
gold flooded everywhere else, and everyone looked forward
to the summer heartily, for the trading. The harvest would be
wondrous too. Already there were signs of astounding frui-
tion. And in the forest, not a hint of any restless tribe, or any
ill wish.

They called her by the name *Zafra*. They did not once call
her "Easterner." One day, I saw three pregnant women at
the gate, waiting for Zafra to come out and touch them. She
was lucky. Even the soldiers had taken no offense. The old
Salius had asked her for a balm for his rheumatism. It seemed
the balm had worked.

Only I, then, hated her. I tried to let it go. I tried to remember she was only a woman, and, if a sorceress, did us
good. I tried to see her as voluptuous and enticing, or as
homely and harmless. But all I saw was some shuttered-up,
close, fermenting thing, like mummy-dusts reviving in a
tomb, or the lion-scent, and the tall shadow that had stood
between her and the night, bird-headed, the Lord of the Word
that made all things, or unmade them. What was she, under
her disguise? Draco could not see it. Like the black dog she
had kept, which walked by her on a leash, well-mannered and
gentle, and which would probably tear out the throat of anyone who came at her with mischief on his mind—Under her
honeyed wrappings, was it a doll of straw or gold, or a viper?

Eventually, Draco married her. That was no surprise. He
did it in the proper style, with sacrifices to the Father, and all
the forms, and a feast that filled the town. I saw her in colors
then, that once, the saffron dress, the Flammeus, the fire-veil
of the bride, and her face bare, and painted up like a lady's,
pale, with rosy cheeks and lips. But it was still herself, still
the Eastern Witch.

And dully that day, as in the tent that night, I thought, So what now?

## III

In the late summer, I picked up some talk, among the servants in the palace. I was by the well-court, in the peach arbor, where I had paused to look at the peaches. They did not always come, but this year we had had one crop already, and now the second was blooming. As I stood there in the shade, sampling the fruit, a pair of the kitchen men met below by the well, and stayed to gossip in their argot. At first I paid no heed, then it came to me what they were saying, and I listened with all my ears.

When one went off, leaving the other, old Ursus, to fill his dipper, I came down the stair and greeted him. He started, and looked at me furtively.

"Yes, I heard you," I said. "But tell me, now."

I had always put a mask on, concerning the witch, with everyone but Draco, and afterwards with him too. I let it be seen I thought her nothing much, but if she was his choice, I would serve her. I was careful never to speak slightingly of her to any—since it would reflect on his honor—even to men I trusted, even in wine. Since he had married her, she had got my duty, too, unless it came to vie with my duty to him.

But Ursus had the servant's way, the slave's way, of holding back bad news for fear it should turn on him. I had to repeat a phrase or two of his own before he would come clean.

It seemed that some of the women had become aware that Zafra, a sorceress of great power, could summon to her, having its name, a mighty demon. Now she did not sleep every night with Draco, but in her own apartments, sometimes things had been glimpsed, or heard—

"Well, Ursus," I said, "you did right to tell me. But it's a lot of silly women's talk. Come, you're not going to give it credit?"

"The flames burn flat on the lamps, and change color," he

mumbled. "And the curtain rattled, but no one there. And Eunike says she felt some form brush by her in the corridor—"

"That is enough," I said. "Women will always fancy something is happening, to give themselves importance. You well know that. Then there's hysteria and they can believe and say anything. We are aware she has arts, and the science of Aegyptus. But demons are another matter."

I further admonished him and sent him off. I stood by the well, pondering. Rattled curtains, secretive forms—it crossed my thoughts she might have taken a lover, but it did not seem in keeping with her shrewdness. I do not really believe in such beasts as demons, except what the brain can bring forth. Then again, her brain might be capable of many things.

It turned out I attended Draco that evening, something to do with one of the villages that traded with us, something he still trusted me to understand. I asked myself if I should tell him about the gossip. Frankly, when I had found out—the way you always can—that he lay with her less frequently, I had had a sort of hope, but there was a qualm, too, and when the trade matter was dealt with, he stayed me over the wine, and he said: "You may be wondering about it, Skorous. If so, yes. I'm to be given a child."

I knew better now than to scowl. I drank a toast, and suggested he might be happy to have got a boy on her.

"She says it will be a son."

"Then of course, it will be a son."

And, I thought, it may have her dark-yellow looks. It may be a magus too. And it will be your heir, Draco. My future Prince, and the master of the town. I wanted to hurl the wine cup through the wall, but I held my hand and my tongue, and after he had gone on a while trying to coax me to thrill at the joy of life, I excused myself and went away.

It was bound to come. It was another crack in the stones. It was the way of destiny, and of change. I wanted not to feel I must fight against it, or desire to send her poison, to kill her or abort her, or tear it, her womb's fruit, when born, in pieces. For a long while I sat on my sleeping-couch and allowed my fury to sink down, to grow heavy and leaden, resigned, defeated.

When I was sure of that defeat, I lay flat and slept.

In sleep, I followed a demon along the corridor in the women's quarters, and saw it melt through her door. It was tall, long-legged, with the head of a bird, or perhaps of a dog. A wind blew, lion-tanged. I was under a tree hung thick with peaches, and a snake looked down from it with a girl's face framed by a flaming bridal-veil. Then there was a spinning fiery wheel, and golden corn flew off clashing from it. And next I saw a glowing oven, and on the red charcoal lay a child of gold, burning and gleaming and asleep.

When I woke with a jump it was the middle of the night, and someone had arrived, and the slave was telling me so.

At first I took it for a joke. Then, became serious. Zafra, Draco's wife, an hour past midnight, had sent for me to attend her in her rooms. Naturally I suspected everything. She knew me for her adversary: She would lead me in, then say I had set on her to rape or somehow else abuse her. On the other hand, I must obey and go to her, not only for duty, now, but from sheer aggravation and raw curiosity. Though I had always told myself I misheard her words as I left her with him the first time, I had never forgotten them. Since then, beyond an infrequent politeness, we had not spoken.

I dressed as formally as I could, got two of my men, and went across to the women's side. The sentries along the route were my fellows too, but I made sure they learned I had been specifically summoned. Rather to my astonishment, they knew it already.

My men went with me right to her chamber door, with orders to keep alert there. Perhaps they would grin, asking each other if I was nervous. I was.

When I got into the room, I thought it was empty. Her women had been sent away. One brazier burned, near the entry, but I was used by now to the perfume of those aromatics. It was a night of full moon, and the blank light lay in a whole pane across the mosaic, coloring it faintly, but in the wrong, nocturnal, colors. The bed, narrow, low, and chaste, stood on one wall, and her tiring table near it. Through the window under the moon, rested the tops of the forest, so black it made the indigo sky pale.

Then a red-golden light blushed out and I saw her, lighting the lamps on their stand from a taper. I could almost swear she had not been there a second before, but she could stay motionless a long while, and with her dark robe and hair, and all her other darkness, she was a natural thing for shadows.

"Captain," she said. (She never used my name, she must know I did not want it; a sorceress, she was well aware of the power of naming.) "There is no plot against you."

"That's good to know," I said, keeping my distance, glad of my sword, and of every visible insignia of who and what I was.

"You have been very honorable in the matter of me," she said. "You have done nothing against me, either openly or in secret, though you hated me from the beginning. I know what this has cost you. Do not spurn my gratitude solely because it is mine."

"Domina," I said (neither would I use her name, though the rest did in the manner of the town), "you're his. He has made you his wife. And—" I stopped.

"And the vessel of his child. Ah, do you think he did that alone?" She saw me stare with thoughts of demons, and she said, "He and I, Captain. He, and I."

"Then I serve you," I said. I added, and though I did not want to give her the satisfaction I could not keep back a tone of irony, "you have nothing to be anxious at where I am concerned."

We were speaking in Greek, hers clear as water in that voice of hers which I had to own was very beautiful.

"I remain," she said, "anxious."

"Then I can't help you, Domina." There was a silence. She stood looking at me, through the veil I had only once seen dispensed with in exchange for a veil of paint. I wondered where the dog had gone, that had her match in eyes. I said, "But I would warn you. If you practice your business in here, there's begun to be some funny talk."

"They see a demon, do they?" she said.

All at once the hair rose up on my neck and scalp.

As if she read my mind, she said:

"I have not pronounced any name. Do not be afraid."

"The slaves are becoming afraid."

"No," she said. "They have always talked of me but they have never been afraid of me. None of them. Draco does not fear me, do you think? And the priests do not. Or the women and girls. Or the children, or the old men. Or the slaves. Or your soldiers. None of them fear me or what I am or what I do, the gold with which I fill the temples, or the golden harvests, or the healing I perform. None of them fear it. But you, Captain, you do fear, and you read your fear again and again in every glance, in every word they utter. But it is yours, not theirs."

I looked away from her, up to the ceiling from which the patterns had faded years before.

"Perhaps," I said, "I am not blind."

Then she sighed. As I listened to it, I thought of her, just for an instant, as a forlorn girl alone with strangers in a foreign land.

"I'm sorry," I said.

"It is true," she said, "you see more than most. But not your own error."

"Then that is how it is." My temper had risen and I must rein it.

"You will not," she said quietly, "be a friend to me."

"I cannot, and will not, be a friend to you. Neither am I your enemy, while you keep faith with him."

"But one scratch on my littlest nail," she said. Her musical voice was nearly playful.

"Only one," I said.

"Then I regret waking you, Captain," she said. "Health and slumber for your night."

As I was going back along the corridor, I confronted the black jackal-dog. It padded slowly towards me and I shivered, but one of the men stooped to rub its ears. It suffered him, and passed on, shadow to shadow, night to ebony night.

Summer went to winter, and soon enough the snows came. The trading and the harvests had shored us high against the cruelest weather, we could sit in our towers and be fat, and watch the wolves howl through the white forests. They came to the very gates that year. There were some odd stories, that wolf-packs had been fed of our bounty, things left for them, to tide them over. Our own she-wolves were supposed to have started it, the whorehouse girls. But when I mentioned the tale to one of them, she flared out laughing.

I recall that snow with an exaggerated brilliance, the way you sometimes do with time that precedes an illness, or a deciding battle. Albino mornings with the edge of a broken vase, the smoke rising from hearths and temples, or steaming with the blood along the snow from the sacrifices of Year's Turn. The Wolf Feast with the races, and later the ivies and vines cut for the Mad Feast, and the old dark wine got out, the torches, and a girl I had in a shed full of hay and pigs; and the spate of weddings that come after, very sensibly. The last snow twilights were thick as soup with blueness. Then spring, and the forest surging up from its slough, the first proper hunting, with the smell of sap and crushed freshness spraying out as if one waded in a river.

Draco's child was born one spring sunset, coming forth in the bloody golden light, crying its first cry to the evening star. It was a boy, as she had said.

I had kept even my thoughts off from her after that interview in her chamber. My feelings had been confused and displeasing. It seemed to me she had in some way tried to outwit me, throw me down. Then I had felt truly angry, and later, oddly shamed. I avoided, where I could, all places where I might have to see her. Then she was seen less, being big with the child.

After the successful birth all the usual things were done. In my turn, I beheld the boy. He was straight and flawlessly formed, with black hair, but a fair skin; he had Draco's eyes from the very start. So little of the mother. Had she contrived it, by some other witch's art, knowing that when at length we had to cleave to him, it would be Draco's line we wished to see? No scratch of a nail, there, none.

Nor had there been any more chat of demons. Or they made sure I never intercepted it.

I said to myself, She is a matron now, she will wear to our ways. She has borne him a strong boy.

But it was no use at all.

She was herself, and the baby was half of her.

They have a name now for her demon, her genius in the shadowlands of witchcraft. A scrambled name that does no harm. They call it, in the town's argot: *Rhamthibiscan*.

We claim so many of the Greek traditions; they know of Rhadamanthys from the Greek. A judge of the dead, he is connectable to Thot of Aegyptus, the Thrice-Mighty Thrice-Mage of the Al-Khemian Art. And because Thot the Ibis-Headed and Anpu the Jackal became mingled in it, along with Hermercurius, Prince of Thieves and Whores—who is too the guide of lost souls—an ibis and a dog were added to the brief itinerary. Rhadamanthys-Ibis-Canis. The full name, even, has no power. It is a muddle, and a lie, and the invocation says: *Sweet is Truth*. Was it, though, ever sensible to claim to know what truth might be?

## IV

"They know of her, and have sent begging for her. She's a healer and they're sick. It's not unreasonable. She isn't afraid. I have seen her close an open wound by passing her hands above it. Yes, Skorous, perhaps she only made me see it, and the priests to see it, and the wounded man. But he recovered, as you remember. So I trust her to be able to cure these people and make them love us even better. She herself is immune to illness. Yes, Skorous, she only thinks she is. However, thinking so has apparently worked wonders. She was never once out of sorts with the child. The midwives were amazed—or not amazed, maybe—that she seemed to have no pain during the birth. Though they told me she wept when the child was put into her arms. Well, so did I." Draco frowned. He said, "So we'll let her do it, don't you agree, let her go to them and heal them. We may yet be able to open this country, make something of it, one day. Anything that is useful in winning them."

"She will be taking the child with her?"

"Of course. He's not weaned yet, and she won't let another woman nurse him."

"Through the forests. It's three days ride away, this village. And then we hardly know the details of the sickness. If your son—"

"He will be with his mother. She has never done a foolish thing."

"You let this bitch govern you. Very well. But don't risk the life of your heir, since your heir is what you have made him, this half-breed brat—"

I choked off the surge in horror. I had betrayed myself. It seemed to me instantly that I had been made to do it. *She* had made me. All the stored rage and impotent distrust, all the bitter frustrated *guile*—gone for nothing in a couple of sentences.

But Draco only shrugged, and smiled. He had learned to contain himself these past months. Her invaluable aid, no doubt, her rotten honey.

He said, "She has requested that, though I send a troop with her to guard her in our friendly woods, you, Skorous, do not go with them."

"I see."

"The reason which she gave was that, although there is no danger in the region at present, your love and spotless commitment to my well-being preclude you should be taken from my side." He put the smile away and said, "But possibly, too, she wishes to avoid your close company for so long, knowing as she must do you can barely keep your fingers from her throat. Did you know, Skorous," he said, and now it was the old Draco, I seemed somehow to have hauled him back, "that the first several months, I had her food always tasted. I thought you would try to see to her. I was so very astounded you never did. Or did you have some other, more clever plan, that failed?"

I swallowed the bile that had come into my mouth. I said, "You forget, Sir, if I quit you I have no other battalion to go to. The Mother of Cities is dead. If I leave your warriors, I am nothing. I am one of the scores who blow about the world

like dying leaves, soldiers' sons of the lost Empire. If there
were an option, I would go at once. There is none. You've
spat in my face, and I can only wipe off the spit.''

His eyes fell from me, and suddenly he cursed.

"I was wrong, Skorous. You would never have—"

"No, Sir. Never. Never in ten million years. But I regret
you think I might. And I regret she thinks so. Once she was
your wife, she could expect no less from me than I give one
of your sisters.''

*"That bitch,''* he said, repeating for me my error, woman-
like, "her half-breed brat—damn you, Skorous. He's my
son.''

"I could cut out my tongue that I said it. It's more than a
year of holding it back before all others, I believe. Like vomit,
Sir. I could not keep it down any longer.''

"Stop saying *Sir* to me. You call her *Domina.* That's sufficient.''

His eyes were wet. I wanted to slap him, the way you do
a vicious stupid girl who claws at your face. But he was my
prince, and the traitor was myself.

Presently, thankfully, he let me get out.

What I had said was true, if there had been any other life
to go to that was thinkable—but there was not, anymore. So,
she would travel into the forest to heal, and I, faithful and
unshakable, I would stay to guard him. And then she would
come back. Year in and out, mist and rain, snow and sun.
And bear him other brats to whom, in due course, I would
swear my honor over. I had better practice harder, not to call
her anything but *Lady.*

Somewhere in the night I came to myself and I knew. I saw
it accurately, what went on, what was to be, and what I, so
cunningly excluded, must do. Madness, they say, can show
itself like that. Neither hot nor cold, with a steady hand, and
every faculty honed bright.

The village with the sickness had sent its deputation to
Draco yesterday. They had grand and blasphemous names for
*her,* out there. She had said she must go, and at first light
today would set out. Since the native villagers revered her,

she might have made an arrangement with them, some itinerant acting as messenger. Or even, if the circumstance were actual, she could have been biding for such a chance. Or she herself had sent the malady to ensure it.

Her gods were the gods of her mystery. But the Semitic races have a custom ancient as their oldest altars, of giving a child to the god.

Perhaps Draco even knew—no, unthinkable. How then could she explain it? An accident, a straying, bears, wolves, the sickness after all . . . And she could give him other sons. She was like the magic oven of the Khemian Art. Put in, take out. So easy.

I got up when it was still pitch black and announced to my body-slave and the man at the door I was off hunting, alone. There was already a rumor of an abrasion between the Prince and his Captain. Draco himself would not think unduly of it, Skorous raging through the wood, slicing pigs. I could be gone the day before he considered.

I knew the tracks pretty well, having hunted them since I was ten. I had taken boar spears for the look, but no dogs. The horse I needed, but she was forest-trained and did as I instructed.

I lay off the thoroughfare, like an old fox, and let the witch's outing come down, and pass me. Five men were all the guard she had allowed, a cart with traveling stuff, and her medicines in a chest. There was one of her women, the thickest in with her, I thought, Eunike, riding on a mule. And Zafra herself, in the litter between the horses.

When they were properly off, I followed. There was no problem in the world. We moved silently and they made a noise. Their horses and mine were known to each other, and where they snuffed a familiar scent, thought nothing of it. As the journey progressed, and I met here and there with some native in the trees, he hailed me cheerily, supposing me an outrider, a rear-guard. At night I bivouacked above them; at sunrise their first rustlings and throat-clearings roused me. When they were gone we watered at their streams, and once I had a burned sausage forgotten in the ashes of their cookfire.

The third day, they came to the village. From high on the

mantled slope, I saw the greetings and the going in, through the haze of foul smoke. The village did have a look of ailing, something in its shades and colors, and the way the people moved about. I wrapped a cloth over my nose and mouth before I sat down to wait.

Later, in the dusk, they began to have a brisker look. The witch was making magic, evidently, and all would be well. The smoke condensed and turned yellow from their fires as the night closed in. When full night had come, the village glowed stilly, enigmatically, cupped in the forest's darkness. My mental wanderings moved towards the insignificance, the smallness, of any lamp among the great shadows of the earth. A candle against the night, a fire in winter, a life flickering in eternity, now here, now gone forever.

But I slept before I had argued it out.


Inside another day, the village was entirely renewed. Even the rusty straw thatch glinted like gold. She had worked her miracles. Now would come her own time.

A couple of the men had kept up sentry-go from the first evening out, and last night, patrolling the outskirts of the huts, they had even idled a minute under the tree where I was roosting. I had hidden my mare half a mile off, in a deserted bothy I had found, but tonight I kept her near, for speed. And this night, too, when one of the men came up the slope, making his rounds, I softly called his name.

He went to stone. I told him smartly who I was, but when I came from cover, his sword was drawn and eyes on stalks.

"I'm no forest demon," I said. Then I asked myself if he was alarmed for other reasons, a notion of the scheme Draco had accused me of. Then again, here and now, we might have come to such a pass. I needed a witness. I looked at the soldier, who saluted me slowly. "Has she cured them all?" I inquired. I added for his benefit, "Zafra."

"Yes," he said. "It was—worth seeing."

"I am sure of that. And how does the child fare?"

I saw him begin to conclude maybe Draco had sent me after all. "Bonny," he said.

"But she is leaving the village, with the child—" I had

never thought she would risk her purpose among the huts, as she would not in the town, for all her hold on them. "Is that tonight?"

"Well, there's the old woman, she won't leave her own place, it seems."

"So Zafra told you?"

"Yes. And said she would go. It's close. She refused the litter and only took Carus with her. No harm. These savages are friendly enough—"

He ended, seeing my face.

I said, "She's gone already?"

"Yes, Skorous. About an hour—"

Another way from the village? But I had watched, I had skinned my eyes—pointlessly. Witchcraft could manage anything.

"And the child with her," I insisted.

"Oh, she never will part from the child, Eunike says—"

"Damn Eunike." He winced at me, more than ever uncertain. "Listen," I said, and informed him of my suspicions. I did not say the child was half East, half spice and glisten and sins too strange to speak. I said *Draco's son.* And I did not mention sacrifice. I said there was some chance Zafra might wish to mutilate the boy for her gods. It was well known, many of the Eastern religions had such rites. The solider was shocked, and disbelieving. His own mother—? I said, to her kind, it was not a deed of dishonor. She could not see it as we did. All the while we debated, my heart clutched and struggled in my side, I sweated. Finally he agreed we should go to look. Carus was there, and would dissuade her if she wanted to perform such a disgusting act. I asked where the old woman's hut was supposed to be, and my vision filmed a moment with relief when he located it for me as that very bothy where I had tethered my horse the previous night. I said, as I turned to run that way, "There's no old woman there. The place is a ruin."

We had both won at the winter racing, he and I. It did not take us long to achieve the spot. A god, I thought, must have guided me to it before, so I knew how the land fell. The trees were densely packed as wild grass, the hut wedged between, and an apron of bared weedy ground about the door where once the household fowls had pecked. The moon would enter there, too, but hardly anywhere else. You could come up on it, cloaked in forest and night. Besides, she had lit her stage for me. As we pushed among the last phalanx of trunks, I saw there was a fire burning, a sullen throb of red, before the ruin's gaping door.

Carus stood against a tree. His eyes were wide and beheld nothing. The other man punched him and hissed at him, but Carus was far off. He breathed and his heart drummed, but that was all.

"She's witched him," I said. Thank Arean Mars and Father Jupiter she had. It proved my case outright. I could see my witness thought this too. We went on stealthily, and stopped well clear of the tree-break, staring down.

Then I forgot my companion. I forgot the manner in which luck at last had thrown my dice for me. What I saw took all my mind.

It was like the oven of the hallucination in the tent, the thing she had made, yet open, the shape of a cauldron. Rough mud brick, smoothed and curved, and somehow altered. Inside, the fire burned. It had a wonderful color, the fire, rubies, gold. To look at it did not seem to hurt the eyes, or dull them. The woman stood the other side of it, and her child in her grasp. Both appeared illumined into fire themselves, and the darkness of garments, of hair, the black gape of the doorway, of the forest and the night, these had grown warm as velvet. It is a sight often seen, a girl at a brazier or a hearth, her baby held by, as she stirs a pot, or throws on the kindling some further twig or cone. But in her golden arm the golden child stretched out his hands to the flames. And from her moving palm fell some invisible essence I could not see but only feel.

She was not alone. Others had gathered at her fireside. I was not sure of them, but I saw them, if only by their great height which seemed to rival the trees. A warrior there, his metal face-plate and the metal ribs of his breast just glimmering, and there a young woman, garlands, draperies and long curls, and a king who was bearded, with a brow of thunder and eyes of light, and near him another, a musician with wings starting from his forehead—they came and went as the fire danced and bowed. The child laughed, turning his head to see them, the deities of his father's side.

Then Zafra spoke the Name. It was so soft, no sound at all. And yet the roots of the forest moved at it. My entrails churned. I was on my knees. It seemed as though the wind came walking through the forest, to fold his robe beside the ring of golden red. I cannot recall the Name. It was not any of those I have written down, nor anything I might imagine. But it was the true one, and he came in answer to it. And from a mile away, from the heaven of planets, out of the pit of the earth, his hands descended and rose. He touched the child and the child was quiet. The child slept.

She drew Draco's son from his wrapping as a shining sword is drawn from the scabbard. She raised him up through the dark, and then she lowered him, and set him down in the holocaust of the oven, into the bath of flame, and the fires spilled up and covered him.

No longer on my knees, I was running. I plunged through black waves of heat, the amber pungence of incense, and the burning breath of lions. I yelled as I ran. I screamed the names of all the gods, and knew them powerless in my mouth, because I said them wrongly, knew them not, and so they would not answer. And then I ran against the magic, the Power, and broke through it. It was like smashing air. Experienced—inexperiencable.

Sword in hand, in the core of molten gold, I threw myself on, wading, smothered, and came to the cauldron of brick, the oven, and dropped the sword and thrust in my hands and pulled him out—

He would be burned, he would be dead, a blackened little corpse, such as the Semite Karthaginians once made of their children, incinerating them in line upon line of ovens by the shores of the Inner Sea—

But I held in my grip only a child of jewel-work, of poreless perfect gold, and I sensed his gleam run into my hands, through my wrists, down my arms like scalding water to my heart.

Someone said to me, then, with such gentle sadness, "Ah
Skorous. Ah, Skorous."

I lay somewhere, not seeing. I said, "Crude sorcery, to turn
the child, too, into gold."

"No," she said. "Gold is only the clue. For those things
which are alive, laved by the flame, it is life. It is immortal
and imperishable life. And you have torn the spell, which is
all you think it to be. You have robbed him of it."

And then I opened my eyes, and I saw her. There were no
others, no Other, they had gone with the tearing. But she—
She was no longer veiled. She was very tall, so beautiful I
could not bear to look at her, and yet, could not take my eyes
away. And she was golden. She was golden not in the form
of metal, but as a dawn sky, as fire, and the sun itself. Even
her black eyes—were of gold, and her midnight hair. And
the tears she wept were stars.

I did not understand, but I whispered, "Forgive me. Tell
me how to make it right."

"It is not to be," she said. Her voice was a harp, playing
through the forest. "It is never to be. He is yours now, no
longer mine. Take him. Be kind to him. He will know his
loss all his days, all his mortal days. And never know it."

And then she relinquished her light, as a coal dies. She
vanished.

I was lying on the ground before the ruined hut, holding
the child close to me, trying to comfort him as he cried, and
my tears fell with his. The place was empty and hollow as if
its very heart had bled away.

The soldier had run down to me, and was babbling. She
had tried to immolate the baby, he had seen it, Carus had
woken and seen it also. And, too, my valor in saving the boy
from horrible death.

As one can set oneself to remember most things, so one can
study to forget. Our sleeping dreams we dismiss on waking.
Or, soon after.

They call her now, the Greek Woman. Or the Semite
Witch. There has begun, in recent years, to be a story she
was some man's wife, and in the end went back to him. It is

generally thought she practiced against the child and the soldiers of her guard killed her.

Draco, when I returned half-dead of the fever I had caught from the contagion of the ruinous hut—where the village crone had died, it turned out, a week before—hesitated for my recovery, and then asked very little. A dazzle seemed to have lifted from his sight. He was afraid at what he might have said and done under the influence of sorceries and drugs. "Is it a fact, what the men say? She put the child into a fire?" "Yes," I said. He had looked at me, gnawing his lips. He knew of Eastern rites, he had heard out the two men. And, long, long ago, he had relied only on me. He appeared never to grieve, only to be angry. He even sent men in search of her: A bitch who would burn her own child—let her be caught and suffer the fate instead.

It occurs to me now that, contrary to what they tell us, one does not age imperceptibly, finding one evening, with cold dismay, the strength has gone from one's arm, the luster from one's heart. No, it comes at an hour, and is seen, like the laying down of a sword.

When I woke from the fever, and saw his look, all imploring on me, the look of a man who has gravely wronged you, not meaning to, who says: But I was blind—that was the hour, the evening, the moment when life's sword of youth was removed from my hand, and with no protest I let it go.

Thereafter the months moved away from us, the seasons, and next the years.

Draco continued to look about him, as if seeking the evil Eye that might still hang there, in the atmosphere. Sometimes he was partly uneasy, saying he too had seen her dog, the black jackal. But it had vanished at the time she did, though for decades the woman Eunike claimed to meet it in the corridor of the women's quarters.

He clung to me, then, and ever since he has stayed my friend; I do not say, my suppliant. It is in any event the crusty friendship now of the middle years, where once it was the flaming blazoned friendship of childhood, the envious love of young men.

We share a secret, he and I, that neither has ever confided

to the other. He remains uncomfortable with the boy. Now the princedom is larger, its borders fought out wider, and fortressed in, he sends him often away to the fostering of soldiers. It is I, without any rights, none, who love her child.

He is all Draco, to look at, but for the hair and brows. We have a dark-haired strain ourselves. Yet there is a sheen to him. They remark on it. What can it be? A brand of the gods—(They make no reference, since she has fallen from their favor, to his mother.) A light from within, a gloss, of gold. Leaving off his given name, they will call him for that effulgence more often, Ardorius. Already I have caught the murmur that he can draw iron through stone, yes, yes, they have seen him do it, though I have not. (From Draco they conceal such murmurings, as once from me.) He, too, has a look of something hidden, some deep and silent pain, as if he knows, as youth never does, that men die, and love, that too.

To me, he is always courteous, and fair. I can ask nothing else. I am, to him, an adjunct of his life. I should perhaps be glad that it should stay so.

In the deep nights, when summer heat or winter snow fill up the forest, I recollect a dream, and think how I robbed him, the child of gold. I wonder how much, how much it will matter, in the end.

# DR. COUNEY'S ISLAND

## Steven Popkes

*"Dr. Couney's Island" was purchased by Gardner Dozois, and appeared in the December 1994 issue of As-imov's, with an illustration by Laurie Harden. Steven Popkes is not a prolific writer by the high-production standards of the genre, but he has contributed a number of memorable stories for the magazine, including "The Color Winter," a Nebula finalist, and his popular no-vella, "The Egg." His well-received first novel* Caliban Landing *appeared in 1987, and was followed by an expansion to novel-length of "The Egg," called* Slow Lightning. *He was also part of the Cambridge Writers' Workshop project to produce science fiction scenarios about the future of Boston, Massachusetts, that cumu-lated in the 1994 anthology* Future Boston.

*Here he shows us that wherever the real Camelot*

*might have been, Camelot is also in our hearts..*

It was damned cold that morning. You never thought Coney Island would ever be that cold. All you ever thought about the Island were the lights, bright like Fourth of July sparklers, and the smell of crowds and spilled beer, hot dogs and sauerkraut. And it was funny, he mused for a long minute, lying on his side on the frozen sand. Funny, you never remembered the smell of the ocean but here it is, as sudden and surprising as flashpowder: salt and the ripe stink of dirty water. What was the ocean more than that?

Merlin rolled himself up and leaned back against the clapboard wall of Dreamland—No it wasn't. Dreamland burned down years ago, burned down, oh the bright lights of that fire!, and was rebuilt by somebody new, died a financial death and was buried in the middle of Steeplechase. Where *was* he? He'd been nearly fifty when that happened. How old was he now?—and looked out over the water. His stomach hurt, a hard, unyielding knot. The flat land and calm sea looked as if they were drawn on paper. It was early morning just before the sun rose and the sun's breezes bit, as small and sharp as small dogs. Merlin huddled in his torn coat at their expectation.

(The beach on the Normandy coast was always cold. A hard wet sandy beach that matched him, hardness for hardness, when he stepped off the boat. A hardness in me at leaving. A hardness in me at being forced to leave. Arthur, I thought. You're on your own.)

He shook his head. He was trying to remember something. The beach. He was somewhere on the beach—near Nathan's down from the boardwalk. They came here last night—who?

Jimmy the Pinhead was lying next to where Merlin had been sleeping. Merlin slapped him on the rump. "Wake up," he said. Then coughed up a fluid mess, spit it on the sand and eyed it curiously. He shivered as the sun flared over the sea. Baths, he thought. I remember the baths—was that ten?

Twenty years ago? Before John McKane died. Warm, they were. Hot. Steamy.

"Wake up, damn it." He kicked Jimmy viciously in the foot.

"Leave a sick man alone," Jimmy groaned and pushed him away.

"We stay here much longer and we won't be sick." Merlin leaned over him and shouted in his ear. "We'll be dead!"

Jimmy put both hands over his ears and sat up. "You're a filthy old man."

"You're right about that."

"You hurt my foot."

"Stop whining or I'll break your head." Merlin shivered again. "We got to get somewhere warm."

"There any more liquor?"

Merlin stood and stretched, coughed again. "Yeah. French champagne. Come on."

He half led, half pushed Jimmy back up over the boardwalk and down the alley towards Asa's place. As the breeze rose Merlin felt even colder and there were moments of sharp panic when he couldn't seem to remember how to breathe—leaning against the closed storefronts.

Jimmy waited for him, patient as a drafthorse. Finally, Merlin brought them into the warm crook created by the space between Asa Moore's flower shop and Bond's Nickel Beer.

"This is warm, Merle," said Jimmy, sniffing the air. "Smells nice, too."

Merlin didn't answer. He huddled with his back against the brick wall of the flower shop, feeling the warmth of the coal furnace seep slowly into him. It loosened some glutinous substances deep in his chest and he was wracked with deep, painful coughs. Blackness edged his vision and everything he saw had showers of colors. Merlin had a sudden image of himself turned inside out. Then, the coughing passed and he felt the cold mentholated air filling his lungs.

(The air in Salem had been sweet, each breath like a labored symphony as I struggled to lift my chest one more time. Trapped with a mountain lying across me. I wanted to cry

out that I was no witch. Cry out that I was, after all—just for
a clean death. Either admission would destroy my children.
Instead, I stayed silent, trying to breathe, wishing I could just
die. I heard a voice ask me to confess—to what? Ravings?
Had I breath and inclination I might have laughed. Had my
body less strength I might have died right then. Neither happened. Only my breath, sucked in against too much weight
and leaving too quickly.)

What was it he was trying to remember?

Someone took his arm, placed it across his shoulder and
hoisted him to his feet.

"Stupid," Asa Moore said as he helped Merlin into his
shop. "You were always stupid. Now no better than when
you were a kid."

The sunlight seemed brighter in the greenhouse in the back
of Asa's shop, reflected from rows of lilies and camellias,
budding now but not yet bloomed. And it was steamy warm
as when John McKane had taken Merlin and other ballot box
enforcers to the baths on the night of the Coolidge election
as a reward for faithfulness.

(Steamy, as when I'd sat with the Emperor and we'd been
talking about what to do with the Senate. "They'd be useful
as goats. Not otherwise," he'd said, and I had agreed.)

Asa took Merlin's head in his hands and brought his face
close.

"It's me, George. Asa Moore."

"I know you. I was just thinking."

Asa let him go. "Good. You get crazier every year."

Merlin shook his head. "I'm not crazy."

"Of course not." Asa spun around and grabbed Jimmy by
the neck. "Damn you, don't touch the flowers!"

Jimmy snatched his hands back and held them under his
arms. "I'm sorry. I was just trying to smell them."

"Go sit over there, next to the furnace."

Jimmy sat on the bench in the corner and in a few moments
was asleep.

Asa snorted. "At least, he's easy."

Merlin nodded, sleepy himself. The smell of the budding camellias had a hypnotic effect on him. "Best pinhead act on the island."

Asa smiled sourly. "Such a great achievement." He rubbed his chest. "It's too much work carrying you in here. My heart isn't what it used to be. I have to work too hard as it is— two thousand carnations. Three hundred lilies. A hundred camellias. Them, I have to take care of. Otherwise, I don't make it through the year. You, I leave to freeze next time."

"Guinevere loved camellias. I did, too, for that matter."

"Shut up with that crap. You can stay here and keep warm but I don't have to listen to that King Arthur crap."

"He's Merlin," said Jimmy, suddenly awake. "He told me."

"Crap!" Asa stood up, short and furious. "His name is George Thomas and he grew up in Gravesend the same as I did, before it had hotels or amusement parks. We fought over the same girl. We worked for McKane together, keeping his tax collectors and prostitutes in line. George's been drinking himself dead since before you were born. I've seen it for forty years right into the middle of this goddamned depression. You think I don't know who he is *now*?"

Chastened, Jimmy huddled back down on the bench.

"And you," Asa said, turning to Merlin. "Don't tell me flowers. You know how I know you're crazy? 'Cause there were no camellias in King Arthur's time—not there. Camellias aren't native to England. A goddamned florist knows these things. They were brought to Europe. Long, long after your great king!"

(Short, like Keaton is short, standing on the field when the house fell down, so convinced of his own skills, of his planning, that when he stood there, serene as a saint, I had to look away. I've seen the last of him, I thought. He's dead, sure. And we all turned away—even his wife, a slight and pretty thing—and heard the crash and turned back and he was standing, looking at us. And in that moment, we could all read his mind as sure as if he'd shouted at us: "Did you get it? Was the camera rolling?'' And all we could think was, ''How did you *do* that?'')

That's not it. It was something else.

''Some other flower, then. Something like camellias. Asa, you don't understand.'' Merlin rubbed his face with his hands, suddenly aware of the smell of his clothes, the ancient sea smell of his skin. How much could Asa know? Merlin remembered listening to pronouncements and whimperings across the night wind when he was a child. Listening, rapt, to everyone still living, to those that had died. Was there any wonder he was confused? ''It's like,'' he groped for words, feeling the leftover remains of alcohol like wool in his thoughts. ''It's like we can all remember each other. Like remembering dreams.''

''Crap!'' shouted Asa, beating the air with his hands. ''You started this crap when McKane went to jail and we had to hide out in Jersey. It was crap then and crap now.''

''He's all the time, fulla' crap,'' came a thin voice behind Asa.

Asa turned around and let his arms fall, rubbed his chest with one hand and nodded. ''Yeah. Hi, Joe.''

Joe Littlefinger stepped down into the greenhouse, smoking a cigar as thick as his wrist. Joe's wrist, like the rest of him, was diminutive. He was slightly over three feet tall, but every inch of him was dressed impeccably: vest, jacket and pants, gold watch chain and derby. He knocked ash off the end of his cigar into one of the lily pots.

Asa reached down and gently plucked the cigar from his hands. ''Later, when you go outside. I have enough problems without you killing my flowers.'' He reached through the door and placed the cigar outside.

Joe nodded, imperturbable. ''Sure, Asa. I'm going up to Doctor Couney's place to look at the kids. Any of you guys want to go along?''

Merlin looked at him. ''They're closed up. No tours until spring.''

Joe shrugged. ''I'm feeling generous today. One of the nurses will let us look at them for a half a buck each.''

"I don't even have that."

"I'll spring for everybody." Joe waved his hand at them.

Asa had flowers to take care of and Jimmy had fallen asleep again. As Merlin followed Joe out the door, Asa grabbed his arm.

"Don't make me bring you in again, George," he said. "You come on in and sleep next to the furnace. You'll die if you stay out there."

"Thanks, Asa."

Asa looked deep into his face, grimaced. "You won't do it. I'll find you huddled next to the wall outside, dead, one day."

Outside, the cold had sharpened but with the sun stronger now, it didn't feel quite so close. Joe retrieved his cigar carefully from the stoop and lit it, puffed it in glorious satisfaction.

"Life's worth living if y'got a good cigar, eh?" Joe tried to blow a smoke ring. The light breeze defeated him and he shrugged.

Doctor Martin Couney's Premature Baby Incubators had once been a featured attraction of Dreamland. But Dreamland was gone and the babies remained, now down the Bowery from Asa's shop. Joe and Merlin walked quickly to get out of the cold.

"Say, Merle," said Joe matter-of-factly as they walked. "Jimmy tells me there's something to this magic stuff of yours."

"There is no such thing as magic," said Merlin shortly. A sudden breeze down the street made him shiver. "I know."

"Not the way he tells it."

"Jimmy's a pinhead."

Joe nodded. "What's the truth, then?"

Merlin shrugged. "I don't know."

"Come on. Don't clam up on me."

"I don't know what it is. We remember each other. That's all. That's all I've ever said. Asa thinks I'm crazy." Merlin stopped in the middle of the road and stared down at Joe. "Do you think I'm crazy?"

Joe inspected the end of his cigar. "I think you were smart

when you were with McKane and then you started drinking too much and talking too much. Now you're a bum.''

Merlin laughed. ''That's honest.'' He stood up straight and looked around him. The sky was a light turquoise and there were gulls flying overhead on sun-gilded wings. He held his arms wide. ''I remember Arthur as a child—when the Romans left England, running off when the King fell. People dying—a thousand men in an hour. Can you imagine that? I ran. I remember the Romans, marching up big, wide roads—better roads than we got here, f'Christ's sake—into France. But we didn't call it France then. I don't remember what we called it. But I remember watching them. I remember marching with them. I remember marching with the Redcoats through Concord—I remember a lot of marching. I think I remember the Pharaohs—but it gets hazy that far back. Like remembering when you were three. I remember—''

''Right, Merle. Come on.'' Joe took the edge of his coat and started to pull him down the street. ''Let's get out of the damned cold.''

''I remember it all.''

''Yeah.'' Joe spit on the ground. ''Right. I should have known. Asa said you grew up together as kids. He says he should have known it then: you're crazy as they come.'' He strode ahead quickly, his feet striking the ground like small hammers.

''I said I remember it.''

''Just like I remember being that son-of-a-bitch Charlie Stratton, too,'' said Joe viciously. ''And his bitch Lavinia. I'm thirty-eight inches. Four too many inches and fifty years too damned late. I could have made meat out of him. He was *so* genteel. I can sing. I can dance. I can play the fucking piano. You know how hard that is with these fingers?'' He held up his stubby hand.

Merlin stared at him, bewildered. ''What are you talking about?''

''I'm talking about show business, knucklehead.'' Joe slapped his arm. '' 'Tom Thumb is my *stage name*,' he said. Like there was something else. I had my name changed. I

don't give a cobbler's piss I was born John Quincy Armont.
I'm Joseph Littlefinger *now*."

"What—"

Joe stopped in front of him and in a sudden unexpected
display of strength grabbed his jacket and pulled Merlin to
his knees. "I'm talking movies! Jimmy said one of these
ghosts of yours makes fucking movies! In California!"

"Christ," moaned Merlin, and started laughing. He fell
backwards into the street, sat down heavily. "You want an
introduction."

"Yes, goddamn it. Stop laughing."

But Merlin was coughing and spitting and laughing on the
ground.

"Stop laughing," Joe said again, took a long pull on his
cigar and breathed out a great cloud of smoke. "It's a stupid
idea."

Merlin gasped for breath and sat up. "Not really. It just
doesn't work that way. I don't know any of these people. I
just remember them—as if things happened to me. I don't
even know their names."

"Right. You're a bum and a drunk and an ancient magician." Joe chuckled wryly. "But even a blind pig in shit will
find an acorn sometime. And like the hedgehog said to the
hairbrush, you can try anything once. Get up. Let's go see
the babies."

Merlin felt obscurely stung to be so blithely cast aside.
"Maybe I can figure out who he is. He works with Buster
Keaton."

"Never mind."

"We're all related somehow—maybe we had the same an-
cestor somewhere."

"Adam No-navel, no doubt."

"Look, I didn't ask to have this happen to me," Merlin
shouted at him. "Did I? I *liked* John McKane. I was happy
working for him. This stuff eats away at you. It's not my
fault."

Joe gently took his arms. " 'Suffer the fools,' they say.
Come on, Merle. John McKane's been dead for thirty years.
Coney's answer to Boss Tweed died before I was born. And

Midget City was never what it was cracked up to be. It's been a whole new world for forty years."

"You think I'm crazy."

"Who isn't? I come up to your waist. Makes me a little crazy, too."

Merlin still felt sore. "Then, how come you're always inviting me along?"

Joe grinned at him. "How tall am I?"

"How the hell should I know?"

"Exactly," said Joe. "Come on. Let's go see the babies."

(A baby is always small. The hand cradles the child's head easily. Perhaps God shaped men's hands for this purpose and this purpose alone, I thought, holding my son in my arms. All other possible uses for them are but happy accidents. Lie still, little one, I croon. Lie still and sleep. Perhaps some day you will be a great carpenter.)

What was it he was trying to remember?

There were six incubators in the room, large white enamel and glass cabinets, each with its impossibly small infant contents. Here was a little girl, her hands the size of thumbnails. Next to her was a bluish boy, his chest no bigger around than a cup, struggling for breath. The breath goes in, the breath goes out.

The nurse smiled at Joe and looked dubiously at Merlin, but let them both in when Joe gave her an additional quarter. They walked past the different children until Joe stopped before one small, swollen-eyed child.

"You have to meet Billy," he whispered. "Billy Watterson, meet Merlin the Magician. Merle, meet Billy."

"Hello, Billy," whispered Merlin. Billy was no more than skin covering cords and veins. He was smaller than the others, no bigger than a Nathan frank. Merlin pressed his face against the glass so he could hear the boy's tiny breath. Straining, he heard the faintest rustle of leaves, the mere ghost of breathing.

"I like the tyke," said Joe softly. "He's less than two pounds—but Couney says you can't tell what he really weighed when he was born. They lose weight so fast, he said.''

"Mister Billy Watterson, welcome to Coney Island."

They stood together in silence for a long time.

"You know," Joe said slowly. "This is his island."

"Billy?"

"No. This is Doctor Couney's island." Joe put his hand on the glass and leaned forward to see if the baby would respond. The baby seemed too intent on breathing to pay attention. "You and I are just so much air. McKane died. Tweed died. Dreamland died. Luna Park's dying. Steeplechase will die someday. And no one will remember them or us. But they'll remember Martin Couney and these little incubators. And the babies that live here and grow up, strong and tall. People will remember them and forget us."

Merlin shook his head. "No. It won't be like that. They'll remember the lights and the rides and the spectacles and the fat ladies and the strong men and the beaches and the crowds and Nathan's hot dogs and the freak shows. But Couney and his babies they'll forget."

"You're a drunken bum," Joe snarled at him softly. "What the hell do you know?"

Merlin grinned and tapped his skull. "Crazy, too. Merlin has second sight, doesn't he?"

The nurse came in suddenly. She pointed at Merlin. "You have to leave. Doctor Couney knows Joe, but he doesn't know you. He doesn't like to have his nursery cluttered with smelly, drunken bums. Now get out of here."

"Who's smelly?" chuckled Merlin.

"Go on," Joe pushed him. "I'll catch up to you later."

Outside, the air had warmed and it was almost noon. He wandered over behind Nathan's to rummage in the backalley cans for lunch. He was lucky. There was a half pound of moldy cheese and some buns only partly soggy. Sometimes he wondered if the cooks at Nathan's were leaving food out on purpose. He walked back up Twelfth Street and back under the boardwalk to eat. Merlin scraped the cheese against the corner of a brick piling and tossed the wet portion of the bread out to the gulls. In a small protected area, the sun shone on him and reflected from the walls and he was almost cozily warm. He savored the cheese and the bread and the resulting full stomach, and drowsily asked the air for a bottle of wine. The air was unmoved and he fell asleep.

Some long time later, he felt a rough hand shaking him rudely awake. Merlin sat up, blinked several times and rubbed the gum from his eyes. It was Joe, sitting on the sand. Wordlessly, Joe handed a bottle of cheap brandy over to him.

"What's the occasion?" asked Merlin. "Not that there needs to be one."

"We are drinking," said Joe ponderously, "to the late William Watterson."

It was a moment before Merlin knew who Joe was talking about. "Oh, no," he said when he understood.

Joe nodded. His clothes were dirty from walking under the boardwalk and there were deep gouges in the leather of his shoes. Joe did not seem to notice. "Mister Watterson, after a valiant effort at the very basics of living, quit this mortal coil about an hour ago. Doctor Couney tried to persuade the young man to stay but to no avail. Mister Watterson was adamant. This was no world for him."

All Merlin could think of was the tiny sound of the baby's breathing, imagining the faint, almost imperceptible cough, the deepening strain and then a deep sigh and silence. He rubbed his face with his hand, then tipped the bottle up and drank. "To young Billy."

"To young Billy. We hardly knew you," echoed Joe as he took back the bottle. "Christ, Merle. He was so little and he tried so *hard*. I never knew anything so small could work so hard just at breathing." Joe looked as if he was going to weep, as if, for a moment, he was a child himself. "The kid deserved a rattle, or a ball—or at least a tit, like a normal kid. Not a glass box and a little coffin. The best we can give him is a good drunk."

(As I lay on the bed, each breath was life bubbling to me through the fluid in my lungs. I was drowning—hadn't I heard once that drowning was an easy way to die? The man who wrote that was lost in an opium dream. "Gladly live, gladly die . . .'' Did I write that? I never dreamed the last moments would be so hard. The body doesn't die easily. It dies hard—it fights for every breath, every heartbeat. Until, like coal burning, the ashes overwhelm it.)

That was almost it.


Merlin found tears on his own cheeks and wiped them away. He sniffed and that brought on another coughing attack, each building from within to an explosive climax, like nitroglycerin in his lungs, priming the next until there was no breath at all, just one long ragged wheeze.

Joe held him as he fought for breath. "Don't die on me now, Merle," Joe moaned. "I just couldn't take it. I swear, I just couldn't take it."

The cold air finally filled his lungs and he breathed carefully, as a thirsty man is careful with water. When he could, Merlin sat up and drank some of the brandy, feeling the warmth in his throat soothe his lungs, put a fire in his belly and a rubbery strength in his arms and legs.

"I left Jimmy over at Asa's shop. I got to go over and check on him. Asa's always scared he'll break something." Merlin stood up and dizzily leaned against the piling.

"Yeah." Joe drained the bottle and threw it viciously against the piling. The glass exploded and Joe stared at the wet spot. "Poor little son-of-a-bitch. I'm going to go home and get so drunk I can't sit in a chair." He looked up to Merlin. "You come on by if you don't want to sleep under the boardwalk. You always were good drinking company. Good company all around."

Merlin looked down at the sudden compliment. "Yeah. We'll see. I don't know where I'll end up."

"You think about it. It gets damned cold out here." Joe straightened his suit, pulled a cigar out of his pocket and lit it. The fetid smell almost made Merlin throw up.

Joe tipped his hat to Merlin and started walking down the beach towards Steeplechase. Merlin watched him for a moment, then ducked back under the boardwalk to Twelfth Street towards Asa's shop.

•   •   •

(It was a measure of my stature as a physician that I would be called to treat someone such as Harry Houdini. The escape artist had proven difficult to treat not because of the injury—which was, in fact, terminal—but because of Houdini's personality, which I found abrasive and made worse by his great pain. Still, it was hard not to feel pity as the man was pulled inexorably towards death. Houdini's pact with his wife, to come back after death, struck me as pitiful.

"There is no magic," Houdini whispered when we were alone. He looked about the room as if his wife would hear him.

"I know," I said, remembering everyone who remembered me. "More than you do.")

I know I'm looking for something. I know that. Desperately, completely. I want to know what it is.

He met Jimmy on the Bowery next to where the corner of Dreamland used to be.

"Hi, Merle," Jimmy said affably. He jerked his head towards Asa's flower shop. "He didn't look too good, so I thought I'd go home."

Merlin stared for a moment towards the shop, then searched Jimmy's slack face. "How'd he look?"

"Real tired, Merle." Jimmy shrugged. "I thought Gunther'd give me some wine if I came back on my own. He was real pissed the last time he found me under the boardwalk with you."

"Okay. You go on." He pushed Jimmy up the street. "I was just coming to get you."

"You have any wine?" asked Jimmy wistfully.

"Not a drop. But Joe does."

Jimmy nodded. "I'll go see him."

With that, he turned and walked steadily up the street, placing his feet with careful exactness. Merlin, watching him, was reminded of the time he and Jimmy had gotten drunk and the pinhead had fallen and broken his knee. Jimmy must have decided to be more careful from that, or had it pointed out to him. It wasn't clear if Jimmy was smart enough to figure it out for himself.

Asa had fallen asleep in his chair in the shop. His broad
face lay on his chest like a deflated child's ball and snored
faintly through his nose. His face was gray and chalky and
he looked shrunken in his sleep, as if pulling away from a
deep and abiding pain. Asa's heart had been troubling him
for over ten years and Merlin knelt next to him and peered
closely, trying to see if Asa's heart had begun to fail at last.

(Arthur had already heard the songs being sung about him as
he lay on the bed. The King looked bad. His face was white
and the continual, constant pain had given his voice a whimpering quaver that I hated. He hated it more than I, especially
the craven sound that lurked in it when he asked for drugs.

"I never wanted to die," he said through clenched teeth.
"Always, I feared it."

"No man is different," I said and leaned close to him,
cradled his head against my breast. Once he had taken pleasure in that touch but now it was mere consolation.

"You cannot cure me, eh? Not even of the pain?" He tried
to chuckle but it sounded bitter. "You are not much of a
witch."

"No, my love," I said, looking down into his eyes. "I
never was."

"Give me another damned potion then."

I held his head as he sipped it.

"It is spring," he said after a moment, as if that were some
great surprise. "Can you smell the camellias?"

He did not speak again and soon after we laid him amidst
the flowers he loved.)

"Maybe they weren't camellias," Merlin muttered under his
breath. "Just because I remember them there doesn't mean
they weren't there, does it?" Or did it? He remembered the
smell strongly, as strongly as he could smell it here, now, in
the greenhouse. A mistake in memory, maybe? Did that turn
the whole tapestry of mind into rotting cloth?

The flower smell in the greenhouse was overpowering. Asa
did not rouse as Merlin watched him. For the space of a
hundred breaths, Merlin remembered his own life, not the

others. Remembered he and Asa growing up in Gravesend, growing corn and squash, watching as the first hotels were built down on the beach, watching Norton build his bar and gambling den and begin the building of Coney Island. He remembered the whores on Sheepshead Bay and the night John Y. McKane tried to keep his empire against the entire state of New York by protecting the ballot boxes with a mob of Irish thugs. Merlin had been there, had wielded a club against the state-appointed voting supervisors. So had Asa. And hiding up in Harlem for two months waiting to get caught as McKane's trial dragged on and on. Impatient, running from New York into New Jersey, waiting again, following the trial, following the hearsay up and down the coast, trying to find out if it was safe to go home. He remembered working with Asa bucking hay on a horse farm, telling him one day in a moment of weakness about the voices and flinching away at the confusion in Asa's voice. Then, later, when they were both drunk, trying to explain. He'd been trying ever since.

His memories since McKane were faded like old cotton, the past bright as flowers. Even so, Asa was always there. Asa and his carnations, caught up in the idea down in Jersey and coming home to make it happen. Marrying, birthing, dying, all those things mixed together in Asa's life and Merlin watched it from under the boardwalk, like some ancient bridge-confined troll, watching people glitter through the planks, the light of the world reduced to slits. Asa slept. His breathing was labored. Stealthily, Merlin unbuttoned Asa's shirt and rested his hand on the bare skin. A warm smell compounded of earth and sweat escaped from the cloth.

Now, he prayed. If there is no magic, there can be no harm done in this. But if there is—and my life says there might be—heal this heart. Take my own heart for his. I never thought there was a God as the priests told me. Prove me wrong this once.

Out beyond him, residing in the ether like small eddies in a great river, he felt them there, dead and living. He listened to them for a sign, a hint of what to do. All he heard was the sound of the sea. It was as if he were standing in the water with high tide rushing past him, eyes closed, hands in the ocean, overwhelmed, and when the tide had turned, he looked down in his hands to see what had been left him.

(At last, I felt something give inside of me. The breath went out, the last of the good Salem air, and did not come back. And for a long, suspended moment, as I waited for it to return, knowing it would not, I realized that which had given way was life, and with the life the pain. There was no pain in dying. There was only the pain of holding onto life. I must remember this, I thought in sudden fever. I must remember.)

I remembered now.

Merlin pulled his hand away from Asa's chest and carefully and gently replaced the cloth. He sat back and watched him for a long time.

Asa roused and blearily looked around the room. His gaze fell on Merlin. "Hey there." He straightened up. "I wasn't feeling too good so I sat down. I didn't mean to take a nap. What time is it?"

Merlin shrugged. "I don't know. It's late. It'll be dark soon. How do you feel now?"

Asa stretched experimentally. "Better, I think. I don't feel any pain, anyway. For me that's good news. But then, it comes and goes. You don't look so good."

Merlin shrugged again. "There's nothing new in that." He stood up and swayed a moment, felt his heart stab with a sudden pain.

"Are you okay?" Asa stood up and steadied him.

Merlin nodded. Smiled. "Yeah. I'm fine. I think I'll go down to the beach. I like the water."

Asa scowled. "You'll end up getting drunk down there and freezing to death. If it doesn't happen tonight, it'll happen later. Come on back here. Where it's warm."

Merlin shook his head.

"Christ! All those famous people you say you remember. Isn't there one ordinary person that has some sense?"

He chuckled, suddenly weary. "I'm a bum at Coney Island,

Asa. What do you want me to do? What the hell else have I got?''

Asa softened. "Come on back. It's cold out there."

He looked at Asa, watched the small face as wrinkled as an old apple. "Maybe you're right, Asa."

Asa took him by the arms. "You aren't a young man, George. Come back here and stay warm."

George. He tasted the word. It had been a long time since he had thought of himself with that name. "Maybe I will. But I still want to go down to the beach for a while."

"You wouldn't disappoint an old man, would you?"

"Not if I can help it."

The wind died as the sun faded behind Steeplechase. The longest shadow was that of the parachute drop, two hundred feet tall, a long, skeletal umbrella. Dark now against the light. Lit again, Merlin knew, in only a few months.

He stood in the middle of the beach and watched the boardwalk turn charcoal black until there were only the silhouettes of things: the roller coaster, the shuttered freak shows, the Ferris wheel. Behind them, he could see at that moment, the lost towers, minarets and battlements of Luna Park and Dreamland, and behind them, again, the lost palaces and castles of Africa and Araby. Behind them, at last, he could see the memories of his own life, all of them, and adding to them now his own.

Pain shot through him, lancing his life like a scalpel across a boil. He coughed so long and hard that there was thunder in his ears and he forgot how to breathe.

There is no pain in dying, he remembered, proud that this salient fact had stayed with him. And he held this thought as the dark came toward him.

That night, across the cold ether of the world, there were the faint and intermittent sounds of mourning and remembered death. And, if one were quick, the smell of camellias.

# SON OF THE
# MORNING

## Ian McDowell

*"Son of the Morning" was purchased by Shawna Mc-Carthy, and appeared in the December 1983 issue of* Asimov's, *with an illustration by Val Lindahn. Ian Mc-Dowell has made only a handful of science fiction sales to date, most of them to* Asimov's, Amazing, *or* The Magazine of Fantasy and Science Fiction. *In the fantasy and horror fields he has been somewhat more prolific, with sales to* The Pendragon Chronicles, The Camelot Chronicles, Borderlands II, Book of the Dead III, *and* Love in Vein: Tales of Gothic Vampirism, *among other markets. He has a MFA in creative writing from the University of North Carolina at Greensboro.*

*As can be seen from his list of credits, McDowell has long been fascinated with the Matter of Britain and the Arthurian legends. In the poignant story that follows,*

*he takes us to the early part of the story, for a look at*
*the dire consequences that arise from the violation of*
*a young boy's faith . . .*

I sat on the cold cliff and squinted out across the water, absentmindedly trying to drop stones on the heads of the squawking terns that nested on the tiny beach so very far below. I'd been waiting for a long time—my nose felt full of icicles and my backside was almost frozen numb. It was all a rather silly vigil: sea voyages being what they are, Arthur might not make landfall for the better part of a week. Still, I waited there, naively expecting to see the speck of his ship approaching over the dark swells. Time is nothing but an inconvenience when you're fourteen years old.

It was all so exciting. My uncle Arthur was coming to our island to do battle with a giant he'd driven out of his own realms the year before. My Da, King Lot of Orkney, had sent a rather sharp letter to his brother-in-law when Cado (that was the monster's name) turned up on our shores and started terrorizing the peasantry. Not being one to leave such things half done, Arthur responded with a promise to come to Orkney and settle Cado's hash just as soon as he was able.

Lot hadn't given much thought to Cado when his depredations were confined to the Pictish and Dalriadan Scottish peasantry, but that changed when the giant swam the eighteen miles or so of stormy water between those territories and our island and announced his presence on our shores by wiping out three entire farmsteads down on Scapa Bay. And although royal search parties had found the remains of over two dozen gnawed skeletons, they'd not come across a single skull. Cado evidently had the charming habit of collecting his victims' heads:

I thought about all of this as I sat on the cliff at Brough's head. I'd never been particularly worried about the monster, for he had confined himself to the less-settled end of the island—and what were a few rustic peasants more or less? And I enjoyed the embarrassment that my father suffered for being unable to cope with the menace, for I harbored little love for Lot. Still, I looked forward to Arthur's coming. His battle with Cado was sure to be more exciting than a mainland boar hunt. And I did love my uncle. I loved him very much.

Suddenly I spotted it, the tiny speck that could only be a distant ship. I rubbed my salt-stung eyes, but it stayed out there; not wishful thinking but the hoped-for reality. Beyond the toy-like sail, dark clouds tumbled low across a sky as cold and gray as old, unpolished iron. The ship seemed to be riding before a storm. Evidently, they'd decided to chance the weather and make for Orkney rather than turn back to the mainland coast they'd surely been hugging during their long trip up from Cornwall.

I leapt up with a whoop and started scrambling back away from the cliff. The jagged stones, wet and black and speckled with bird dung, gave me poor footing, and several times I stumbled and fell before reaching the sand and turf. Over the rise bulked Lot's palace, squatting there in the lee that gave it some scant protection from the sea and wind. It might not have been much by mainland standards, but it was the grandest building in all the Orkneys. A twenty-foot ditch and two earthworks encircled a horseshoe-shaped two-story stone and timber hall. I dashed across the plank bridge that spanned the ditch and waved up at the soldiers manning the outer earthwork. Those that weren't busy playing dice, sleeping on the job, or relieving themselves waved back.

Mother's tower was on the opposite side of the inner court-yard from the Great Hall. Picking my way through milling clusters of chattering serfs, grunting pigs, squawking chickens, honking geese, and other livestock, I skirted the deepest mud and the piles of fresh excrement until I arrived at the tower's slab-sided foundation. The brass knocker stuck out its tongue and leered at me. "Who goes there?" it demanded in a tinny soprano.

"Mordred mac Lot, Prince of Orkney," I snapped, trying to sound smart and military. The door made no response. "Open up, dammit, I said I'm the Prince!"

The knocker rolled its eyes nonsensically. "I heard you the first time," it trilled, "and I don't care if you're the Prince of Darkness himself, I'm not opening this door until you've wiped your filthy feet!"

It was futile to argue with something that wasn't even really alive. I scraped the heels of my boots against the doorstep while muttering a few choice curses. When I was finished, the door swung wide without further comment. But I knew that it was snickering at me behind my back.

The stairs were steep and winding, which was one reason why King Lot never came here, though they didn't bother Mother, who had the constitution of a plow horse. The room at the top was high and narrow and all of gray stone. It had one window, large and square, with an iron grille and heavy oaken shutters. A ladder connected with a trap door that opened up onto the roof. In one corner was a brick hearth with a chimney flue, not so much a fireplace as an alcove for the black iron brazier that squatted there like a three-legged toadstool. Flanking the alcove were imported cedar shelves lined with animal skulls, a few precious books, rather more scrolls, netted bunches of dried herbs, and small clay jars containing rendered animal fats and various esoteric powders. In the center of the floor was an inlaid tile mosaic depicting a circle decorated with runic and astrological symbols. Off to one side of the mosaic stood a low marble table where Mother sacrificed white doves, black goats, and the occasional slave who'd become too old, sick, or just plain lazy to be worth his keep.

Today it was a goat. Queen Morgawse was bent over the spread-eagled carcass, absorbed in the tangle of entrails that she carefully and genteelly probed with the tip of her silver-bladed sacrificial dagger. From the expression on her sharp, high-cheekboned face, I knew she'd found a particularly interesting set of omens in the cooling guts.

"Hullo, Mother."

She looked up, straightening to her full, considerable height. I may have gotten her black hair and green eyes (I'd seemingly inherited nothing of Lot's appearance, thank the gods), but that impressive stature had all gone to my older brother Gawain, though he'd added to it a broad beefiness that contrasted with her willow slimness. She was dressed in her standard magical attire: an ankle-length black gown that left her arms bare. On her head was a silver circlet, and her long, straight hair was tied back with a blood-red ribbon.

She smiled. "What is it, sweets?"

"Arthur's here. I saw the ship."

She frowned. "Is he now? And me such an untidy mess." She wiped her bloody hands on the linen cloth she'd laid out under the goat. "Do me a favor, love. Clean up this mess while I go change to greet our guests. Do you mind?"

"No, Mother."

After giving me a quick kiss on the cheek, she hurried down the stairs, leaving me alone in the room. I bundled the goat into the stained dropcloth and stumbled with it to the window. That side of the tower was built into the earth and timber wall that formed the fourth side of the courtyard square. With a heave I got my burden through the aperture. It landed on the other side of the wall. Immediately a battle for possession of the carcass broke out between a pack of the palace dogs and several of the serfs who had hovels there.

A wet whistling sound came from somewhere above me. "Hello, Young Master. Please give me something to eat."

I looked up at Gloam where he clung to the ceiling directly over the magic circle. "No, I don't have time. Arthur's here."

Gloam resembled nothing so much as a pancake-shaped mass of dough several feet in diameter, his pale surface moist and sweaty with small patches of yeasty slime. Offset from his center was a bruise-like discoloration about the size of a head of lettuce. Only when its round mouth puckered open and its wrinkled lids parted to reveal eyes like rotting oysters did it become recognizable as a face. Gloam wasn't much to look at, but then, few people keep demons for their beauty.

"I know all about Arthur," he gurgled in a voice like bubbles in a swamp. "Your mother and he . . ." He broke off, looking suddenly uncomfortable.

"What was that?" I asked, curious despite myself.

"Oh, nothing, nothing at all. Forget I even said it."

I sighed impatiently. "Are you trying to trick me, Gloam?"

He darkened to the color of old buttermilk and faded back to his normal pasty hue, always a sign that he was enjoying himself. "No, not at all. I just know something that I'm not allowed to tell you."

"Something about Arthur, I take it."

He whistled and expelled gas. "Well, yes, and rather more than that. Have you ever wondered who your father is?"

My patience was wearing thin. "He's the King of Orkney, you stupid twit."

"Haven't you ever considered the possibility that King Lot might not be your da?"

Hadn't I ever. I suddenly felt a strange gnawing in my guts, as if I'd swallowed something cold and hungry. Not that Lot not being my father would make for any great loss, but if he wasn't, just who was? Finding my voice again, I asked Gloam as much.

"I can't tell you that," he gurgled in reply. "Your mother doesn't want you to find out until after you've reached manhood."

"I'm fourteen, dammit," I snapped in my best regal manner.

"Well, yessss," he mused, "and there was the serving maid with whom you tried to . . ."

"Never mind that!"

"And that *is* one common definition of initiation into manhood," he continued. "Not that you managed it very well."

Enough was enough. "Listen, you stinking, slimy mollusk, if you don't tell me right this very moment what it is that you've been hinting at, I'll . . ."

"Oh, all right," he said before I could come up with an appropriate threat. "But you must find me something to eat first. A dog, perhaps. Or a cat. A child would be best, really. A tender little milk-fed babe."

"Oh, stuff it," I snapped, "I'll go catch you a chicken."

He smiled, never a pleasant sight. "A chicken would be very nice."

So I ended up chasing chickens through the deep mud of the inner courtyard for several frustrating minutes. Finally, I caught a fat rooster. Tying its legs together with a strip torn from the hem of my surtunic, I puffed and panted my way back up the stairs with the protesting cock tucked securely under one arm. It shat on me, of course, but my clothes were already so soiled that it hardly mattered.

I tossed the bird onto the tiled circle. Gloam detached himself from the ceiling with a loud sucking noise and fell on the hapless fowl, his jellyfish-like substance hiding it from view. After a brief struggle, the thing that moved under that white surface lost all recognizable shape and there was only a sort of pale sac that quivered slightly beneath its coat of frothy perspiration. The inflamed face erupted from his upper surface and grinned at me, the toothless mouth slack and drooling.

"Well, out with it, you repulsive greaseball!"

Gloam frowned. "All right, Mordred. Arthur's your father."

I didn't understand. "But he's my uncle!"

"Oh yes, that too."

"Oh." My mind felt blank; I didn't know what to think or feel. "How?"

Gloam sighed. "Your mother will have my arse for this."

"You don't have an arse. Now, tell me how it happened."

His face flushed from dark purple to bluish green. "Fifteen years ago Arthur was little more than a green boy with his first command. No one knew who his father was: he was a landless bastard of a soldier. But he was very handsome. It happened during the Yuletide feast at Colchester, when the King and Queen of Orkney were paying their seasonal visit to Uther's court. Arthur had just had his first taste of battle and it had gone very badly. He drank too much. Your mother was tired of her dry little stick of a king, so she paid a midnight visit to Arthur's tent. It was dark and he never knew that she was the Queen of Orkney, much less that she was his own sister. When they met some years later he thought it was the first time. That's all there is to tell."

Arthur was my father. It was dizzying to go from being the son of a cold and loveless island lord to being the son of the best man in the known world. What would he say if he knew he was my da? My understanding of his Christian morality was dim at best, and, foolish as it sounds, the incest taboo never entered my mind. I'd had no formal schooling in *any* religion, and had no idea what the followers of the crucified carpenter thought about such things.

Arthur had hardly ever spoken of his faith. That was un-
derstandable: he'd come to power in a realm that was at least
half what he'd call pagan, and no doubt he'd had to learn
tact. Certainly, he'd never held being a nonbeliever against
my brother, nor had he tried to repress the worship of Mithras,
the Roman soldier's god, among his mounted troops.

But tolerance of different religions hardly meant that he'd
welcome an illegitimate (and incestuous, but I still wasn't
thinking of that) son with proverbial and literal open arms.
Still, there was the chance he might. I suddenly found myself
wanting that very much. He was unmarried, and according to
gossip had not left behind the usual string of bastards that
would be expected of a thirty-two-year-old bachelor king and
former soldier. Though it was said that he'd shown more than
a passing interest in Guenevere, the reputedly stunning daughter of the Cornish lord Cador Constantius.

The sound of sudden commotion outside broke my reverie.
"That would be Arthur's arrival," commented Gloam dryly,
as he flopped over to the wall and began to climb it, leaving
a sluglike trail across the tiles and flagstones.

I was out of the room and down the steps in a trice, for at
least action would keep me from having to think. Indeed, the
yard was a confusion of babbling serfs, barking dogs, and
clucking chickens, all frantically trying to stay clear of the
muddy wake churned up by the two-dozen riders that came
pounding under the fortified gatehouse. A trim man on a magnificent black gelding rode at their head, snapping off orders
with the practiced ease of long command.

Arthur was dressed for rough travel in an iron-studded
leather jerkin and knee-high doeskin boots. His head was protected by an iron-banded cap of padded leather, lighter than
the conical helmet he'd wear on campaign, and a sopping
cloak was draped around his shoulders and saddle like limp
wings. Obviously, his ship had passed through the storm I'd
seen brewing.

He was of medium height, with broad shoulders and a barrel chest. His brown hair was cut short and his face clean-
shaven in the Roman manner. Although this tended to
emphasize his rather large ears, he was still a handsome man.

For the first time I realized that his slightly beaky nose was almost identical to my own.

He vaulted down from his tall horse and clapped me on the shoulder. With his crooked grin and easy manner, he was still more the soldier than the king.

"Hullo, laddy-buck, you've become quite the man since I saw you last." I started to bow, which was rather hard with him standing so close. "No need for that," he laughed, "we're all bloody royal here."

"Actually, they're always saying Gawain got all the height and I'm the puny one," I replied to his compliment.

"Are they now? Well, a lad's growth is measured in more than the distance from his head to his heels, and that's the truth of it."

I saw no sign of Gawain. "Did you bring my brother with you, sir?"

He shook his head. "His squadron's manning the Wall, keeping an eye on our Picti friends."

Lot's acid bark cut through the brouhaha. "Mordred, get the hell out of the way, you're as filthy as a Pict! Change before supper or eat in the stable: by Mannanan and Lir, I'll have no mud splattered brats in my hall."

I quickly stepped back out of reach as the thin, stooped form of my nominal father came gingerly through the clinging mud. Arthur's formal smile was as cold as the sea wind. "Give you good day, my Lord of Orkney." To me he whispered, "Run along now before your Da starts to foam at the mouth. We can talk later, when we're out of this forsaken gale."

"Gale, hell, this is a slight breeze for this place," grumbled one of his captains who'd overheard the last sentence.

I scurried through the crowd to the entrance of the Great Hall. Brushing past clucking servants, I entered the building, shut the stout oak doors behind me, and crossed the huge room to the stairwell, where I started bounding up the steps two and three at a time. As I ran down the hall to my room, I began stripping off my filthy clothes. Once in my chamber, I tossed the soiled garments out the narrow window, shouting down instructions to the slave whose head they landed on to

have them patched and laundered and to send someone up
with a bucket of hot water. After washing with more than my
usual care, I donned a fresh linen shirt, cross-gartered wool
breeches, a long-sleeved and highnecked undertunic, a short-
sleeved and v-necked surtunic, and calfskin shoes. That done,
I went downstairs to the feast.

Lot sat at the head of the table with his back to the roaring
hearth, Mother at his right and Arthur at his left. The King
of Orkney had dressed for the occasion in a purple robe
trimmed with ermine fur and there was fresh black dye in his
thinning hair. The beard that he wore to conceal his lack of
a chin was more clipped and clean than usual, but the bar-
bering only emphasized its sparse inadequacy.

By contrast, Arthur's garments were of plain wool and bare
of any fashionable embroidery at the neck, sleeves, or hem
of his surtunic. His brown breeches were cross-gartered with
undyed strips of dull leather and he'd changed to a clean but
far from new cloak that was fastened at the shoulder with a
simple bronze brooch. Although he'd been on his throne for
almost three years, he'd never learned to dress like a king.

Mother had saved a place for me on her left. Lot glared
but said nothing as I sat down and Arthur winked. The first
courses were just being served: salads of watercress and
chickweed, heaping piles of raw garlic, leeks, and onions,
hardboiled auk and puffin eggs, and smoked goat cheese.
Usually Lot tended to serve guesting lords niggardly meals
of boiled haddock, salt herring, and the occasional bit of mut-
ton stewed in jellied hamhocks, leading Mother to the fre-
quent observation that we might be better off as Christians,
for they observed their Lent only *once* a year. But he dared
not be stingy with his royal brother-in-law, High King of all
the Britons. This time there'd be real meat to come, and
plenty of it.

Arthur's men and the household warriors sat on sturdy,
roughhewn benches, quaffing tankards of ale and wine while
the palace dogs and a few favored pigs milled about, waiting
patiently for the scraps they knew were soon to come. The
wall tapestries had recently been cleaned, fresh rushes were
strewn on the floor, and the long wooden table was spread

with that ultimate luxury, a snow-white linen tablecloth. More
courses began to arrive: dogfish and grayfish in pies, whale
flesh simmered in wine, smoked plovers and shearwaters, and
a whole roasted ox and boar. Individual servings were shov-
eled out onto trenchers of hard, crusty bread and each man
was given several small clamshells to use as table imple-
ments, though most preferred to stick with their knives and
fingers. Most of the guests did respect the tablecloth and instead wiped their hands on their clothing or on the backs of
passing dogs.

Lot was actually trying to keep up a polite facade. "Of
course, good Artorius," he was saying (he always called Arthur by his formal Latin name), "I'll be more than happy to
help fortify the northern coast of the mainland—assuming, of
course, that you can force a treaty on the Picts."

Arthur nodded. "The Picti are half-naked savages, but
they're natives just the same as us and we could use their
help against the Saxons."

"Ach, I thought you'd finished them for once and all at
Badon Hill, back before you'd even ascended to the throne."

Arthur shook his head. "Not by half, I didn't. Oh, it will
take them a few years to mount a new invasion, but they'll
be back. They can't get it out of their thick heads that this
isn't their land; do you know what they're calling us now?
*Welshmen*, their word for foreigners. Foreigners, in our own
forsaken country! Well, either Briton and Picti will find a way
to stand together, or they'll go down separately under the
Saxon yoke!"

Lot sipped his wine. "Of course, as an outsider, I can see
certain virtues in them that your folk can't. For instance, their
kings are very brave."

Arthur looked at Lot sharply. He knew as well as I did that
the King of Orkney wasn't one to be praising others unless
he had an ulterior motive. "Lord of Orkney," he said softly,
"I came here to rid your land of a dire menace, not to hear
you sing the virtues of my enemies."

"Well spoken," replied Lot easily, "but I was simply re-
marking on a fact. Take old Beowulf Grendelsbane, for instance. He took on the monster that was menacing his people

alone, and with bare hands, besides. Grabbed the beastie by
the arm and pulled it off as easily as I tear the wing off this
bird's carcass.''

"I am familiar with the story," said Arthur dryly. "What's
the point?"

Lot smiled. "Just this. Though you've never said as much,
I do believe that it would please you to see these islands
convert to Christianity."

Arthur nodded warily. "It would do my heart good to see
my nephews and sister living in a Godly household." Mother
cleared her throat and made a point of looking down at her
hands.

"But you must understand," continued Lot, "my people
find it hard to be impressed with your faith when you must
bring with you over a score of armored men to do the sort of
job that Beowulf of the Geats was able to do with his good
right arm."

One of Arthur's men spoke up. "Sire, this is boastful nonsense! That Saxon oaf could never have . . ."

Arthur silenced him with a gesture. He turned back to Lot.
"Lot Mac Connaire, if I go against Cado tomorrow all alone,
taking none of my men with me, and if I bring you back his
head, do I have your word that you will accept Holy Bap-
tism?"

Lot nodded. "If you can manage that, I'll build a church
on every island."

I felt stunned. Such a deed would be appropriate to a clas-
sical hero, but it could hardly be expected of a flesh-and-
blood man. I looked carefully at my father. He was clearly
not a fool. "Uncle Arthur," I said softly, "you are the
greatest warrior in all of Britain. But is this wise?"

He looked at me solemnly. "You're a good lad, Mordred.
Some day you'll be an excellent king. I would see you
brought into the Faith."

I felt uncomfortable under his gaze. "I was thinking of
your realm, sir. Your people need you. Such a risk puts them
in danger, too."

He grinned his lopsided grin. "Well, they'll just have to
cross their fingers and hold their breath, won't they? Don't

be a worrywart, lad, I do know what I'm doing. My God defended Padriac against the serpents of Ireland, and Columba against the dragon of Loch Ness. He protected Daniel in the lion cage and lent needed strength to little Daffyd's good right arm. He will not fail me, not if I'm half the man I must needs be if I'm to call myself a king.''

Mother cleared her throat. ''Tell me, brother, has that kingship become a bore yet, or do you still like the office?''

Arthur laughed. ''It's been far from dull. Before I learned of my paternity, I thought I'd be a simple soldier all my life and that all my difficulties would end once I beat the Saxons. Then came Badon Hill, where I did that very thing, and I dreamed that I might retire in peace and quiet.'' Several of his men snorted at that, but he ignored them. ''Don't laugh; I even had visions of becoming some sort of gentleman farmer, as larky as that sounds. But then Uther opened his deathbed Pandora's box and there were suddenly at least ten thousand voices crying 'Artorius Imperator! We want Arthur for our king!' and who was I to say them nay? My first year on the throne was all fighting. The Picts had to be driven back across the Wall, the Irish were making pirate raids, and every local king with a cohort to his name thought it worth his while to challenge my right to rule. Such a bloody mess you never saw and I imagined I'd be old and dying like Uther before I had it straightened out.''

He motioned for a slave to refill his goblet. ''But that was just the easy part. The fighting's been over for two years this winter and since then I've spent half my days haggling like a fishmonger and the other half wearing as many masks as a dozen troupes of actors. But I can't complain. It's been fun for all of that.''

Mother laughed sweetly. ''I'm sure it has.'' She smiled icily at her husband. ''Isn't it refreshing to listen to a ruler who takes his duties seriously and doesn't look upon his office as his godsgranted excuse for never having to sully himself with a day's honest work?'' Lot's only reply was a belch. His flushed and sweaty face indicated that he was getting very drunk.

Mother turned back to Arthur. "You must have future plans."

He nodded. "Trite as it sounds, peace and prosperity are the first things that come to mind."

"That's a rather vague agenda."

The King of Britain smiled. "Isn't it just? I'm afraid that my ideas of good government are not particularly complex. I'll die happy if I can just maintain a nation ruled by the principles of Roman law and Christian virtue."

Lot hiccuped explosively. "I thought it was Roman Law that nailed your Christian virtue to a bloody tree."

The room went very quiet. More than ever, I was glad that Lot was not my father, but I felt ashamed of him just the same. Arthur's face seemed to freeze over like a winter loch, but he kept his voice calm. "I'll ignore that remark, Lord of Orkney. Some men are always fools and others need a touch of strong drink to bring it out."

Once again, Mother saved the situation. She clapped her hands for Fergus, the court bard. The little Leinsterman strutted out, bowed, and began to pluck his gilded harp. Lot and Arthur's eyes gradually unlocked while they listened to those soothing melodies. Skillful harpsong can calm a Brit that way, and even when drunk Lot was too much the coward to meet Arthur's gaze for long. Arthur's men relaxed and took their hands away from their swordbelts, causing our household guardsmen to breathe sighs of deep relief. Though the numbers were on their side, they knew full well that Arthur's crack troops could carve them up like so many feast-day bullocks. I understand that the Saxons consider it in bad taste to wear steel at the table, and in this regard I've come to suspect that they may be a bit more civilized than we are.

Soon it was time for all to say goodnight. Arthur's men trooped out to the barracks (in deep winter weather they'd have stretched out before the hearth, sharing the floor with the dogs and pigs and the household guard), while Arthur himself had been granted an apartment at the far end of the upper hall. I paid my respects, trudged up the stairs, and settled wearily into bed without bothering to remove my clothing.

I had the oddest dream. I was standing below the crest of a steep hill, where a tall wooden cross loomed against an inky sky. A corpse had been crucified there in the old Roman fashion. After awhile I somehow realized that it was the *Cristos*. Although the birds had had his eyes and lips, I still recognized his face as being Arthur's.

I awoke all drenched with sweat, and found it hard to relax and sleep again.

Despite my lack of rest I managed to rise before dawn and dress in new and heavier woolen clothing, to which I added otter-skin boots with the fur inside, a hooded cloak, and a leathern jerkin with protective bronze scales. Then I strapped on a shortsword and slung a bow and quiver over my shoulder. These might not be much protection against Cado, but only fools take extra chances when such monsters are about. I knew my way well enough to navigate the upper floor and the pitch-black stairwell, but right after reaching the lower landing I tripped over a sleeping boarhound, who put his considerable weight on my chest and began to wash my face with his enormous tongue. After I'd cuffed him in the nose several times, he finally realized that I didn't want to play and released me. There was nothing left of the fire but embers, but those gave me enough light to tiptoe through the sleeping forms until I reached the outer door.

The yard was empty, for all the livestock and the serfs were huddled in the barns, and the mud was frozen solid by the evening chill. The dawn was close at hand, and enough light leaked over the horizon to see by. Squaring off in front of one of the wooden practice posts that stood between the barracks and the stables, I drew my sword and began to hack away. Despite the cold and the usual fierce wind, I'd actually started to work up a sweat when the door to the Great Hall opened and Arthur emerged.

Like me, he'd dressed for travel in a fur-lined cloak and high boots. Instead of the iron-studded leather he'd worn the day before, he was now clad in a mail hauberk: a thigh-length coat of inch-wide steel rings, wherein each metal circlet was tightly interlocked with four others. This was the sophisticated modern gear that, along with the recent introduction of the stirrup, had made his mounted troops the terror of the Saxon infantry. On his head sat a conical helmet with lacquered leather cheekguards and a metal flange that projected down over his nose. The sword at his side was at least half again as long as the traditional German *spatha*, and it had a sharpened point like that of a spear, as well as an efficient double edge. He also carried a sturdy iron-headed cavalry spear and a circular white shield embossed with a writhing red dragon was slung across his back.

He seemed surprised to see me. "Practicing this early?"

"Every day," I gasped between strokes. "Gawain won't be the only warrior in the family."

He leaned on his spear and watched me with a critical eye. "Use the point, not the edge: a good thrust is worth a dozen cuts. That's it, boyo, but remember; a swordsman should move like a dancer, not like a clod-hopping farmer."

Exhausted, I sat down on the cold ground. The post was splintered and notched and my sword was considerably blunted. No matter, it was just a cheap practice weapon.

"I rather foolishly forgot to ask your father for directions to Cado's lair," Arthur was saying.

"I know," I panted. "I'll take you there. Folk say he's made himself a den out of the old burial cairn of Maes Howe, down on the shore of the Loch of Harray."

He shook his head. "It would be too dangerous for you to come along."

I'd known he'd say that. "You need a guide. I know the way, because I used to play down there when I was just a kid." Time for the baited hook. "Don't you want me to witness the power of your God?"

He looked very grave. "Would the deed convince you of the correctness of my Faith?"

No, my faith was in him and not his *Cristos*, but I could hardly say *that*. "It would be something to watch," I said truthfully, "and I'd like very much to see a miracle."

His frown finally worked itself into a grin, as I'd known it would. Even then I must have partially realized just how vain he was of his faith, for all that he tried not to show it. "Saddle up," he said, pointing towards the stable. I readied his horse and mine while he went back into the Great Hall to steal bread and smoked cheese from the kitchen. The sun was only beginning to peek over the horizon when we rode across the plank bridge and skirted the nearby village's earth-and-timber palisade.

We passed fallow fields strewn with dung and seaweed, thatch-roofed stone cottages where the crofters were just rising for their daily toil, and low hills bedecked with grazing sheep. The Royal Cattle ruminated unconcernedly in pastures surrounded by nothing but low dikes of turf and stone. On the mainland the local kings and lordlings considered cattle raids to be good sport and engaged in livestock robbery with the same gleeful abandon that they brought to deer or boar hunts, but our island status protected us from that sort of nuisance.

Keeping in sight of the ocean, we rode between wind-shaped dunes and rolling slopes carpeted with peat and stubby grass. The sun rose slowly into view and shone golden on the water.

There was a whale hunt in progress beyond the tip of Marwick Head. Men in boats chased the herd towards a sand bar while beating pitchers, rattling their oarlocks, and shouting in an attempt to terrify the creatures into beaching themselves. The women and children who waited in the shallows would then attack with harpoons and makeshift weapons that ranged from peatforks to roasting spits. As they died the whales made shrill, whistling cries and strange humming noises that sounded like distant pipes and drums. Ordinarily I would have stopped and made sure the royal share was put aside for the castle household, for whale flesh was always a welcome treat. However, today there wasn't time.

It was over six miles down the coast to the Bay of Skail. We soon passed all signs of human settlement. The tireless wind actually seemed to get fiercer as the morning warmed. My feet itched from the otter fur inside my boots and not being able to scratch made for a decided nuisance. For once, I could smell no sign of rain. The great clouds that raced overhead were as white as virgin snow.

"Arthur," I said, breaking a long silence, "were you glad to find out that Uther was your father?"

He took no offense at what might have been an impertinent question. "Yes, though the old sinner wasn't the sort I might have chosen for my da. Still, I'd been conceived in wedlock, and knowing that took many years' load off my mind."

"Why? Is that important to a Christian?"

"Very. Bastardy is a stain that does not wash off easily. Being born that way just makes the struggle harder."

This was getting rather deep. "What struggle?"

"To keep some part of yourself pure. A man has to look beyond the muck he's born in."

For some reason I wanted to keep making conversation. "Is it hard, then?"

He was looking out at the waves but his gaze was focused on something else entirely.

"Always. I remember my first battle. A fog had rolled in from the coast and hid the fighting. Men would come stumbling out of the mist waving bloody stumps or with their guts about their feet."

I'd never heard war described that way. "But you won, didn't you?"

He nodded. "The first of many 'glorious victories.' I was as green as a March apple and could no more control my men than I can command the sea. They burned three Saxon steadings with the men still in them, British slaves and all. The women they crucified upside down against a row of oak trees, after they'd raped them half to death."

I didn't want to hear this, but he kept on. "There was a celebration at Colchester in honor of our triumph. Your parents were there, I think, though my rank was too low for me to sit at the royal table and so I didn't meet them. I messed with the junior officers, got more drunk than I've ever been since, and committed all the standard soldier's sins. When I sobered up and decided I would live, I made a vow to never again become what I was that day."

Later, we dismounted and devoured the bread and cheese while taking shelter in one of the stone huts of Skara Brae, the ancient remains of a Pictish village that stood half-buried in the sand beside the Bay of Skail. The meal done, Arthur stood beside his gelding and gazed inland, scanning the treeless horizon. Gesturing out at that rolling emptiness, he said, "For all its smallness, there's none that could accuse this island of being the most *crowded* kingdom in the world. Not to worry; some day you'll be lord of more than this."

"What do you mean?"

"The time will come when you take your father's place upon the throne of Orkney."

"I don't know," I said doubtfully. "It's bound to go to Gawain, not me. After all, he's the oldest."

Arthur clapped me on the shoulder. "Not if I have anything to say about it. Your brother's a good man and I love him dearly, but he doesn't have the makings of a king. Too thickheaded. The Saxons will return someday, and when they do I may be too old or too tied down by royal duties to lead the war host into battle. I'll need a good *Dux Bellorum*, and the role of warlord fits your brother like a glove. Lot will proclaim you his heir if he knows what's good for him, and that's the truth of it."

I gave up on all attempts at idle chatter as we rode inland for the Loch of Harray. Arthur remained outwardly calm, but I was beginning to feel the first gnawings of anticipation in my churning stomach. Ach, but I was so sure that I was about to see a deed the like of which had not been witnessed since the days of Hercules himself.

At last we spied Maes Howe. It was a huge green mound over a hundred feet in diameter and as high as a two-story dwelling. Here and there the great gray stones of the cairn's roof poked their way above their covering of grass and soil. I knew from my boyhood explorations that there was an exposed passage on the other side of the barrow that led to a central chamber about fifteen or twenty feet square. If Cado was as large as he was reputed to be, he obviously did not object to cramped living quarters. Of course, giants were probably used to things being too small for them.

Arthur reined in his horse at the edge of the broad but shallow ditch that surrounded the mound. "I assume that this is it, then."

"Aye. The only entrance that I know of is on the other side."

His eyes scanned the great mass of earth and rock. "I think you'd best keep back a ways, so that if I should fail you'll have time to wheel your horse around and escape."

And in that moment Cado walked around from behind the ancient pile.

Arthur and I gasped in unison and I actually came close to shitting in my breeches. The giant was at least eight feet tall and tremendously broad, with ox-like shoulders and a barrel torso. In fact, he was so stumpy that if seen at a distance he might be mistaken for a dwarf. His filthy, mud-colored hair blended with his equally filthy beard and fell to his knees in matted waves. Woven into this tangled mass were the scalps and facial hair of his victims' severed heads, so that he wore over a dozen mummified skulls in a sort of ghastly robe. This served as his only clothing. From the mass of snarled locks and grinning eyeless faces protruded arms and legs as massive as tree trunks, all brown and leathery and pockmarked with scrapes and scratches that had festered into scabby craters. Even at thirty paces his stench was awful, a uniquely nauseating combination of the smells of the sick room, the privy, and the open grave. His appearance alone was so formidable that the weapon he held easily in one gnarled hand, a twenty-foot spear with an arm-length bronze head, seemed virtually superfluous.

Ignoring me, his gaze met Arthur's. "Ho, Centurion," he boomed in surprisingly pure Latin. "How goes the Empire?"

This was the real thing, with no safe gloss of legendary unreality. I found myself wanting to be hunting or fishing or snatching birds' eggs from the cliffs, or doing anything as long as I was far away from here. It was a shameful feeling, and I did my best to ignore it. Arthur at least seemed to be keeping his cool.

"No more Empire, Cado, not for years. And I'm no centurion. You must know that."

Cado squinted at him with red-rimmed eyes the size of goose eggs. "Aye, the Empire's dead. And so are you, *Artorius Imperator*."

Arthur wasn't taken aback. "You know me, then. Good."

Cado snorted. "Oh, I know you well enough, Artorius. How could I not know the man whose soldiers have harried me across the length of Britain. You're mad to come here without them, *Imperator*. Do you wish your son to see you die?"

I was suddenly unable to breathe. How could Cado know? How could he *know*? By the very look in his eyes, I was suddenly sure that he did.

Arthur stiffened. "He is not my son. And I do not intend to die."

Cado's black-lipped mouth spread out in a face-splitting grin, exposing a double row of square yellow teeth that might have done justice to a plow horse. "I think he is, Artorius. I can smell you in his sweat and see you in his face. Like all immortal folk, my kind can sense things that humans cannot. He's your seed, or I'm the Holy Virgin."

Arthur looked at me. Afraid to meet his eyes, I tried to turn away, but I felt frozen by his expressionless gaze. Before I could speak, he turned back to Cado and laughed out loud.

"You can't confuse me with such paltry tricks, monster. And don't make it any harder on yourself with blasphemy. I don't profess to know whether or not you have a soul, but if you do you'd better make your peace with God."

Cado never stopped smiling. "Don't you know where giants come from? We're descended from the ancient *nephilim*, the sons of the unions between the *Elohim* and the daughters of Adam. I need no peace with God—my blood is part divine!"

Arthur lowered his lance and unslung his shield. "More blasphemy, Cado? You might face your ending with somewhat better grace."

Cado growled, a low rumbling that spooked my horse and made him difficult to control. "Tell me one thing," said the giant. "Why have you hounded me these many leagues? What am I to you now that I am no longer hunting in your lands?"

"You know full well what you are," said Arthur grimly.

"Your actions have made you an abomination in the eyes of the Lord."

Cado began to laugh, an ear-splitting sound like a dozen asses braying all at once. "Little man, your puking Lord fathered all abomination. I see his world as it truly is and act accordingly."

Couching his lance, Arthur spurred his horse forward with what might have been a prayer and might have been a muttered curse. The sun gleamed on his polished mail as he emerged from the shadow of a wind-driven sweep of cloud. Lugh and Dagda, but he looked magnificent in that brief moment.

Cado casually lifted his spear and thrust out with the blunt haft, catching Arthur squarely in the midriff before he was close enough to use his lance. Torn from the saddle, he seemed to sit suspended in the air for a brief eternity. As he crashed to the sward, his horse shied past Cado and went galloping away in the direction of the distant loch.

Cado bent over him, reversing his spear so that his spear head just touched Arthur's throat. For a measureless time they seemed locked in that silent tableau. My brain screamed that I should do something, but my body showed no interest in responding. The two combatants were frozen and so was I, and I lost all sense of myself as my awareness shrank to nothing but those still and silent figures.

At last Cado spoke. "Now would be the time to look me in the eye and say 'kill me and be done'—I do believe that that's the standard challenge. But you can't say it, can you?" He laughed even more loudly than before. "They all tell themselves it's victory or death, but in the end they find those two limited alternatives not half so attractive as they'd thought."

Arthur hadn't moved. I was suddenly abnormally aware of my physical sensations: the itchy fur inside my boots, the sting of the cold air upon my raw nose, the spreading warmth at my crotch where I'd pissed my breeches, and the mad pounding of my heart. Arthur was down. He wasn't moving. I knew that I must do something, and it seemed incredibly unfair for such responsibility to have fallen upon my puny shoulders.

I've always been good with horses. Urging my mare forward with my knees, I unslung my bow and drew an arrow from my quiver. The trick was not to think about it, but to act smoothly and mechanically. If I thought about it, I'd fumble. Cado was within range now. He looked up just as I pulled the string back to my ear and let the arrow fly. The feathered shaft seemed to sprout from his left eye socket. I'd already drawn again, but all my instinctive skill left me and the arrow went wild. Not that it mattered. My impossibly lucky first shot had done the job.

Cado stiffened and groaned. He shivered all over, causing the heads in his hair and beard to clack together like dry and hollow gourds. When he fell over backwards it was like a tower going down.

As suddenly clumsy as a six-year-old, I half-fell out of my saddle and ran to Arthur. "Don't be dead," I pleaded like a stupid twit, "please Da, don't be dead."

He groaned. "Too big. Sometimes evil's just too damned big. And I'm too old for this."

"Are you all right?"

He sat up painfully. "Rib's broken, I think, but I can still stand." With my help he did. "My horse has run off."

I pointed to mine. "Take the mare. I'll search for your gelding."

He clapped me on the shoulder. "You're a good lad. I was an arrogant fool today—I hope you can forgive me."

I didn't know what he meant. "Of course," I muttered, cupping my hands and helping him into the saddle. From this vantage point, he surveyed Cado's corpse.

"Like Daffyd and Goliath. The Lord works his will: I'm taught humility and Cado is destroyed."

I looked him in the eye. "Are you saying that your god guided my arrow?"

He shrugged. "Perhaps. Not that it takes any of the credit away from you. I'm very proud, Mordred. I pray that someday the Lord will give me as fine a son as the one he gave to Lot."

I'd been trying to find an opening all day. My heart was in my mouth—this was more frightening than confronting Cado. "Arthur, there is something you must know."

Something in my voice must have warned him, for he looked at me very oddly. "And what would that be?"

No hope for a smooth tongue: I had to be blunt and open. "You're my father."

"What?"

"You're my father."

I knew it then: I'd blundered. His face wore no expression, but the words hung between us in the heavy air. I tried to laugh, but it was a forced, hollow sound. "I was just joking," I stammered, desperately trying to unsay my revelation. "I didn't mean . . ."

He reached out and gripped my shoulder. His clutch was firm, painful. And his eyes were cold and hard as Lot's. "You're lying now. I know that much. And Cado called you my son, too. How could it be true?"

I tried to pull away, but he held me fast. Now my terror was of *him*, of the man himself. This was a side of Arthur that I'd never seen. "Please," I said, "it's all a mistake. I . . ."

He shook me. "What makes you think you are my son? Tell me now, the truth, and all of it."

I could no more refuse that command than I could up and fly away, though I would have been glad to do either. "Mother's familiar told me."

"A demon? And you believed such a creature?"

"I asked Mother, and she said that it was true."

He shook his head. "How? It's impossible. We've never . . ." He broke off then, but his eyes were still commanding.

"It was at Uther's court after your first battle. She came to your tent in disguise."

The silence that followed that statement was as cold and painful as the bitter wind. He mumbled something that might have been a prayer, and his expression resembled that of a man kicked by a horse. His hand slipped from my shoulder.

"It's sin," he said at length, his eyes not meeting mine. "It's mortal sin."

This was worse than I'd feared. Bloody gods, but why couldn't I have kept my foolish mouth shut? "She didn't know you were her brother. It's not her fault."

"No, for she's a pagan, and lost anyway. I'm the one to blame."

"It wasn't your fault either. It wasn't anybody's fault."

He shook his head sadly. "Ach, no, it's always someone's fault. Always." Straightening up, he reined the mare towards Cado's still form. "You knew, monster. You knew what I was. Perhaps you should have killed me." His shoulders slumped, and he looked so *old* as he sat there swaying in the saddle. "But no, then I'd have died in ignorance, unshriven, with no chance at repentance. No wonder that I lost today. My own sin rode beside me."

"Don't talk like that!" I shouted, suddenly angry as well as hurt.

He ignored my protest. "Come up behind me. I won't leave you here, no matter what you are."

*No matter what you are.* Words that have haunted half my life.

"Go on with you," I snapped. "I said I'd find your god-damned horse."

He didn't react visibly to my profanity. He just sat there, slumped in the saddle, the wind tugging at his cloak. His eyes were focused in my direction, but it was as if he was looking through me at something else. At length he spoke. "All right, Mordred, suit yourself." With that he spurred the mare into a gallop. I suppose that in that moment I became the only thing he ever fled from, but that distinction does not make me proud. I stood there, watching him ride away, while the wind whispered in the grass.

"Throw it all away, then!" I shouted when he was well beyond hearing. "Damn you, Da, it wasn't my fault either!"

I never did find his bloody horse.

And so, the end of this testament. Why did I tell him, when even the young fool I was then might have guessed how he'd react? I don't know. It's all very well for Socrates to maunder on about how one should know oneself, but sometimes the water is just so deep and murky that you cannot see the bottom. I didn't hate Arthur, not then, but the love was all dried up. I'd never asked to be made the symbol of his own imagined sin.

It was a long walk home. A storm rolled in from the ocean long before I reached my destination. The rain was curiously warm, as if Arthur's god were pissing on his handiwork. Wrapped in my soggy cloak, I trudged back to Lot and Mother's world.

# SILVER LADY AND THE FORTYISH MAN

## Megan Lindholm

*"Silver Lady and the Fortyish Man" was purchased by
Gardner Dozois, and appeared in the January 1989
issue of* Asimov's, *with an illustration by Laura Lakey.
Lindholm has only appeared in* Asimov's *twice, the
other time being with her novella "A Touch of
Lavender," but both stories were popular with our
readers, and we hope to see more from her in the future. Lindholm is the author of the well-received* The
Wizard of the Pigeons, *one of the most talked-about
fantasy novels of the '80s, as well as the novels* Rein-
deer People *and* Cloven Hooves.

*In the whimsical story that follows, she examines the
kinds of magic that can survive in even the most prosaic
of neighborhoods.*

It was about 8:15 P.M. and I was standing near the register in a Sears in a sub-standard suburban mall the first time the fortyish man came in. There were forty-five more minutes to endure before the store would close and I could go home. The Muzak was playing and a Ronald McDonald display was waving at me cheerily from the children's department. I was thinking about how animals in traps chew their legs off. There was a time when I couldn't understand that type of survival mechanism. Now I could. I was wishing for longer, sharper teeth when the fortyish man came in.

For the last hour or so, salespeople had outnumbered customers in the store. A dead night. I was the only salesperson in Ladies' Fashions and Lingerie and I had spent the last two hours straightening dresses on hangers, zipping coats, putting T-shirts in order by size and color, clipping bras on hangers, and making sure all the jeans faced the same way on the racks. Now I was tidying up all the bags and papers under the register counter. Boredom, not dedication. Only boredom can drive someone to be that meticulous, especially for four dollars an hour. One part boredom to two parts despair.

So a customer, *any* kind of a customer, was a welcome distraction. Even a very ordinary fortyish man. He came straight up to my counter, threading his way through the racks without even a glance at the dresses or sweaters or jeans. He walked straight up to me and said, "I need a silk scarf."

Believe me, the last thing this man needed was a silk scarf. He was tall, at least six foot, and had reached that stage in his life where he buckled his belt under his belly. His dark hair was thinning, and the way he combed it did nothing to hide the fact. He wore fortyish-man clothing, and I won't describe it, because if I did you might think there was something about the way he dressed that made me notice him. There wasn't. He was ordinary in the most common sense of the word, and if it had been a busy night in the store, I'd never even have seen him. So ordinary he'd be invisible. The only remarkable thing about him was that he was a fortyish man in a Sears store on a night when we had stayed open longer than our customers had stayed awake. And that he'd said he needed a silk scarf. Men like him *never* buy silk scarves, not for any reason.

But he'd said he needed a silk scarf. And that was a double miracle of sorts, the customer knowing what he wanted, and I actually having it. So I put on my sales smile and asked, "Did you have any particular color in mind, sir?"

"Anything," he said, an edge of impatience in his voice. "As long as it's silk."

The scarf rack was right by the register, arranged with compulsive tidiness by me earlier in the shift. Long scarves on the bottom rack, short scarves on the top rack, silk to the left, acrylics to the right, solid colors together in a rainbow spectrum on that row, patterns rioting on that hook, all edges gracefully fluted. Scarves were impulse sales, second sales, "wouldn't you like a lovely blue scarf to go with that sweater, miss?" sales. No one marched into a Sears store at 8:15 at night and demanded a silk scarf. People who needed silk scarves at 8:15 at night went to boutiques for them, little shops that smelled like perfumes or spices and had no Hamburglars lurking in the aisles. But this fortyish man wouldn't know that.

So I leaned across the counter and snagged a handful, let my fingers find the silk ones and pull them gently from their hooks. Silk like woven moonlight in my hands, airy scarves in elusive colors. I spread them out like a rainbow on the counter. "One of these, perhaps?" I smiled persuasively.

"Any of them, it doesn't matter, I just need a piece of silk." He scarcely glanced at them.

And then I said one of those things I sometimes do, the words falling from my lips with sureness, coming from god knows where, meant to put the customer at ease but always getting me into trouble. "To wrap your Tarot cards, undoubtedly."

Bingo, I'd hit it. He lifted his eyes and stared at me, as if suddenly seeing me as a person and not just a saleswoman in a Sears at night. He didn't say anything, just looked at me. It was like having cross-hairs tattooed on my forehead. In exposing him, I had exposed myself. Something like that. I cleared my throat and decided to back off and get a little more formal.

"Cash or charge?" I asked, twitching a blue one from the

slithering heap on the counter, and he handed me a ten, and dug for the odd change. I stuffed the scarf in a bag and clipped his receipt on it and that was it. He left, and I spent the rest of my shift making sure that all the coat hangers on the racks were exactly one finger space apart.

I had taken the job in November, hired on in preparation for the Christmas rush, suckered in by the hope that after the new year began I would become full time and get better wages. It was February, and I was still getting less than thirty hours a week and only four dollars an hour. Every time I thought about it, I could feel rodents gnawing at the bottom of my heart. There is a sick despair to needing money so desperately that you can't quit the job that doesn't pay you enough to live on, the job that gives you just enough irregular hours to make job hunting for something better next to impossible. Worst of all was the thought that I'd fashioned and devised this trap myself. I'd leaped into it, in the name of common sense and practicality.

Two years ago I'd quit a job very similar to this one, to live on my hoarded savings and dreams of being a free-lance writer. I'd become a full-time writer, and I loved it. And I'd almost made it. For two years I skimped along, never much above poverty level, but writing and taking photographs, doing a little free-lance journalism to back up the fiction, writing a story here, a story there, and selling them almost often enough to make ends meet.

Almost.

How the hell long can anyone live on *almost?* Buying almost new clothes at the second-hand store, almost fresh bread at the thrift store, almost stylish shoes at the end-of-season sales. Keeping the apartment almost warm, the dripping, rumbling refrigerator keeping food almost cold, telling my friends I was almost there. Almost writing the one really good story that would establish me as a writer to be reckoned with. I still loved it, but I started to notice little things. How my friends always brought food when they came to visit, and my parents sent money on my birthday, and my sister gave me "hand-me-downs" that fit me perfectly, and, once, still had the tags on. This is fine, when you are twenty or so, and just striking out on your own. It is not so good when you are thirty-five and following your chosen career.

One day I woke up and knew that the dream wasn't going to come true. My Muse was a faithless slut who drank all my wine and gave me half a page a day. I demanded more from her. She refused. We quarreled. I begged, I pleaded, I showed her the mounting stacks of bills, but she refused to produce. I gave her an ultimatum, and she ignored me. Left me wordless, facing empty white pages and a stack of bills on the corner of my desk. One of two things happened to me then. I've never decided which it was. Some of my friends told me I'd lost faith. Others said I'd become more practical. I went job-hunting.

In November, I re-entered the wonderful world of retail merchandising, to work a regular nine-to-five job and make an ordinary living, with clockwork paychecks and accounts paid the first time they billed me. I'd leaped back into salesmanship with energy and enthusiasm, pushing for that second sale, persuading women to buy outfits that looked dreadful on them, always asking if they wanted to apply for our charge card. I'd been a credit to the department. All management praised me. But no one gave me a raise, and full time hours were a mirage on the horizon. I limped along, making *almost* enough money to make ends meet. It felt very familiar. Except that I didn't love what I did. I was stuck with it. I wasn't any better off than I had been.

And I wasn't writing anymore, either.

My Muse had always been a fickle bitch, and the moment I pulled on panty-hose and clipped on an ''I AM SEARS'' tag, she moved out, lock, stock, and inspiration. If I had no faith in her power to feed me, then to hell with me, was the sentiment as she expressed it. All or nothing, that was her, like my refrigerator, either freezing it all or dripping the vegetable bin full of water. All or nothing, no half-way meetings. So it was nothing, and my days off were spent, not pounding the keys, but going to the laundromat, where one can choose between watching one's underwear cavort gaily in the dryer window, or watching gaunt women in mis-matched outfits abuse their children. (''That's *it*, Bobby! That's it, I absolutely mean it, you little shit! Now you go stand by that basket and you hold onto it with both hands, and don't you *move* until I tell you you can. You move one step away from that basket and I'm going to whack you. You hear me, Bobby? YOU (Whack!) GET YOUR (Whack!) HANDS ON THAT (Whack!) BASKET! Now shut up or I'll *really* give you something to cry about!'') I usually watched my underwear cavorting through the fluff-dry cycle.

And so I worked at Sears, from nine to one, or from five to nine, occasionally getting an eight hour day, but seldom more than a twenty-four hour week, watching income not quite equal out-go, paying bills with a few dollars and many promises, spacing it out with plastic, and wondering, occasionally, what the hell I was going to do when it all caught up with me and fell apart.

Days passed. Not an elegant way to express it, but accurate. So there I was again, one weekday night, after eight, dusting the display fixtures and waiting for closing time, wondering why we stayed open when the rest of the mall closed at seven. And the fortyish man came in again. I remembered him right away. He didn't look any different from the first time, except that this time he was a little more real to me because I had seen him before. I stood by my counter, feather duster in hand, and watched him come on, wondering what he wanted this time.

He had a little plastic container of jasmine potpourri, from the bath and bedding department. He set it on the counter and asked, ''Can I pay for this here?''

I was absolutely correct as a salesperson. ''Certainly, sir. At Sears, we can ring up purchases from any department at any register. We do our best to make things convenient for our customers. Cash or charge?''

''Cash,'' he said, and as I asked, ''Would you like to fill out an application for our Sears or Discover Charge Card? It makes shopping at Sears even more convenient, and in addition to charging, either card can be used as a check cashing card,'' he set three Liberty Walking silver dollars, circa 1923, on the plastic countertop between us. Then he stood and looked down at me, like I was a rat and he'd just dropped a pre-fab maze into place around me.

"Sure you want to use those?" I asked him, and he nodded without speaking.

So I rang up the jasmine potpourri and dropped the three silver dollars into the till, wishing I could keep them for myself, but we weren't allowed to have our purses or any personal cash out on the selling floor, so there was no way I could redeem them and take them home. I knew someone would nab them before they ever got to the bank, but it wasn't going to be me, and wasn't that just the way my whole life had been going lately? The fortyish man took his jasmine potpourri in his plastic Sears bag with the receipt stapled on the outside of it and left. As he left, I said, "Have a nice evening, sir, and thank you for shopping at our Sears store." To which he replied solemnly, "Silver Lady, this job is going to kill you." Just like that, with the capital letters in the way he said it, and then he left.

Now I've been called a lot of things by a lot of men, but Silver Lady isn't one of them. Mud duck. More of a mud duck, that's me, protective coloring, not too much makeup, muted colors in my clothes, unobtrusive jewelry if any at all. Camouflage. Dress just enough like anyone else so that no one notices you, that's the safest way. In high school, I believed I was invisible. If anyone looked at me, I would pick my nose and examine it until they looked away. They hardly ever looked back. I'd outgrown those tricks a long time ago, of course, but *Silver Lady?* That was a ridiculous thing to call me, unless he was mocking me, and I didn't think he had been. But somehow it seemed *worse* that he had been serious, and it stung worse than an insult, because he had seemed to see in me something that I couldn't imagine in myself. Stung all the sharper because he was an ordinary fortyish man, run of the mill, staid and regular, pot-belly and thinning hair, and it wasn't *fair* that he could imagine more about me than I could about myself. I mean, hell, I'm the writer, the one with the wild imagination, the vivid dreams, the razor-edged visions, right?

So. I worked out my shift, chewing on my tongue until closing time, and it wasn't until I had closed my till, stapled my receipts together, and chained off the dressing room that I noticed the little box on the corner of my counter. Little cardboard jewelry box, silver tone paper on the outside, no bag, no label, no nothing, just the silver stripes and Nordstrom in elegant lettering on the outside. A customer had forgotten it there, and I shoved it into my skirt pocket to turn it in at Customer Convenience on my way out.

I went home, climbed the stairs to my apartment, stepping in the neighbor's cat turd on the way up, got inside, cleaned off my shoe, washed my hands five or six times, and put the kettle on for a cup of tea. I dropped into a chair and got jabbed by the box in my pocket. And the ''oh, shit, here's trouble come knocking'' feeling washed over me in a deep brown wave.

I knew what would happen. Some customer would come looking for it, and no one would know anything about it, but security would have picked me up on their closed circuit camera inside their little plastic bubbles on the ceiling. This was going to be it, the end of my rotten, low-paying little job, and my rent was due in two weeks, and this time the landlord wanted all of it at once. So I sat, holding the little silver box, and cursing my fate.

I opened it. I mean, what the hell, when there's no place left but down, one might as well indulge one's curiosity, so I opened it. Inside were two large earrings, each as long as my thumb. Silver ladies. They wore long gowns and their hair and gowns were swept back from their bodies by an invisible wind that pressed the metallic fabric of their bodices close against their high breasts and whipped their hair into frothy silver curls. They didn't match, not quite, and they weren't intended to be identical. I knew I could go to Nordstrom's and search for a hundred years and I'd never find anything like them. Their faces were filled with serenity and invitation, and they weighed heavy in my hand. I didn't doubt they were real silver, and that someone had fashioned them, one at a time, to be the only ones of their kinds. And I *knew*, like *knowing* about the Tarot cards, that the fortyish man had made them and brought them and left them, and they were for me.

Only I don't have pierced ears.

So I put them back on the cotton in their little box and set them on my table, but I didn't put the lid back on. I looked at them, now and then, as I fixed myself a nutritious and totally adequate Western Family chicken pot pie for dinner and ate it out of the little aluminum pan and followed it with celery with peanut butter on it and raisins on top of the peanut butter.

That evening I did a number of useful and necessary things, like defrosting the refrigerator, washing out my panty-hose, spraying my shoes with Lysol spray, and dribbling bleach on the landing outside my apartment in the hopes it would keep the neighbor's cat away. I also put my bills in order by due date, and watered the stump of the houseplant I'd forgotten to water last week. And then, because I wasn't writing, and the evening can get very long when you're not writing, I did something I had once seen my sister and two of her girlfriends do when I was thirteen and they were seventeen and rather drunk. I took four ice cubes and a sewing needle and went into the bathroom and unwrapped a bar of soap. The idea is, you sandwich your earlobes between the ice cubes and hold them there until they're numb. Then you put the bar of soap behind your earlobe to hold it steady, and you push the sewing needle through. Your earlobes are numb, so it doesn't hurt, but it is weird because you hear the sound the needle makes going through your earlobe. On the first ear. On the second ear, it hurt like hell, and a big drop of blood welled out and dripped down the side of my neck, and I screamed "Oh, SHIT!" and banged my fist on the bathroom counter and broke a blood vessel in my hand, which hurt worse than my ears.

But it was done, and when my ears quit bleeding, I went and got the earrings and stood before the mirror and threaded their wires through my raw flesh. The wires were thin, and they pulled at the new holes in my ears, and it couldn't have hurt more if I'd hung a couple of anvils from my bleeding earlobes. But they looked beautiful. I stood looking at what they did to my neck and the angle of my jaw and the way they made the stray twining of my hair seem artful and deliberate. I smiled, serene and inviting, and almost I could see his Silver Lady in my own mirror.

But like I say, they hurt like hell, and tiny drips of my blood were sliding down the silver wires, and I couldn't imagine sleeping with those things swinging from my ears all night. So I lifted them out and put them back in their box and the wires tinged the cotton pink. Then I wiped my earlobes with hydrogen peroxide, shivering at the sting. And I went to bed wondering if my ears would get infected.

They didn't, they healed, and the holes didn't grow shut, even though I didn't keep anything in them to hold them open. A Friday came when there was a breath of spring in the air, and I put on a pale blue blouse that I hadn't worn in so long that it felt like new again. Just before I left my apartment, I went back, and got the box and went to the bathroom and hung the silver ladies from my ears. I went to work.

Felicia, my department head, complimented me on them, but said they didn't look, quite, well, professional, to wear to work. I agreed she was probably right, and when I nodded, I felt their pleasant weight swinging on my ears. I didn't take them off. I collected my cash bag and went to open up my till.

I worked until six that day, and I smiled at people and they smiled back, and I didn't really give a damn how much I sold, but I sold probably twice as much as I'd ever sold before, maybe because I didn't give a damn. At the end of my shift, I got my coat and purse and collected my week's paycheck and decided to walk out through the mall instead of through the back door. The mall was having 4-H week, and I got a kick out of seeing the kids with their animals, bored cats sitting in cages stuffed full of kitty toys, little signs that say things like, "Hi, my name is Peter Pan, and I'm a registered Lop Rabbit," an incubator full of peeping chicks, and, right in the middle of the mall, someone had spread black plastic and scattered straw on top of it, and a pudgy girl with dark pigtails was demonstrating how to groom a unicorn.

I looked again, and it was a white billy goat, and one that was none too happy about being groomed. I shook my head, and felt the silver ladies swing, and as I turned away, the fortyish man stepped out of the Herb and Tea Emporium with an armful of little brown bags. He swung into pace beside me, smelling like cinnamon, oranges and cloves, and said, "You've just got to see this chicken. It plays tic-tac-toe."

Sure enough, some enterprising 4-H'er had rigged up a board with red and blue lights for the x's and o's, and for a quarter donation, the chicken would play tic-tac-toe with you. It was the fattest old rooster I'd ever seen, its comb hanging rakishly over one eye, and it beat me three times running. Which was about half my coffee money for the week, but what the hell, how often do you get the chance to play tic-tac-toe with a chicken?

The fortyish man played him and won, which brought the rooster up to the bars of the cage, flapping its wings and striking out, and I found myself dragging the fortyish man back out of beak range while the young owner of the rooster tried to calm his bird. We just laughed, and he took my elbow and guided me into a little Mexican restaurant that opens off the mall, and we found a table and sat down. The first thing I said was, "This is ridiculous. I don't even know you, and here I find myself defending you from irate roosters and having dinner with you."

And he said, "Permit me to introduce myself, then. I am Merlin."

I nearly walked out right then.

It's like this. I'm a skeptic. I have this one friend, a very nice woman. But she's always saying things like, "I can tell by your aura that you are troubled today," or talking about how I stunt my spiritual growth by ignoring my latent psychic powers. Once she phoned me up at eleven at night, long distance, *collect*, to tell me she'd just had a psychic experience. She was house-sitting for a friend in a big old house on Whidby Island. She was sitting watching television, when she clearly heard the sound of footsteps going up the stairs. Only from where she was sitting, she could (she says) see the stairs quite clearly and there was no one there. So she froze, and she heard footsteps going along the upstairs hallway and then she heard the bathroom door shut. Then, she said, she heard the unmistakable and noisy splashing of a man urinating. The toilet flushed, and then all was silence. When she got up the nerve to go check the upstairs bathroom, there was no one there. But—THE SEAT WAS UP! So she had phoned me right away to jar me from my skepticism. Every time she comes over, she always has to throw her rune chips for me, and for some reason, they always spell out death and disaster and horrendous bad fortune just around the bend for me. Which may actually prove that she's truly psychic, because that fortune had never been far wrong for me. But it doesn't keep me from kidding her about her ghostly urinator. She's a friend, and she puts up with it, and I put up with psychic-magic-spiritualism jazz.

But the fortyish man I didn't know at all—well, at least not much, and I wasn't going to put up with it from him. That was pushing it too far. There he was, fortyish and balding and getting a gut, and expecting me to listen to him talk weird as well. I mean, okay, I'm thirty-five, but everyone says I look a lot younger, and while only *one* man had ever called me Silver Lady, the rest haven't exactly called me Dog Meat. Maybe I'm not attractive in the standard, popular sense, but people who see me don't shudder and look away. Mostly they just tend not to see me. But at any rate, I *did* know that I wasn't so desperate that I had to latch onto a fortyish man with wing-nut ideas for company. Except that just then the waitress walked past on her way to the next table, laden with two combination plates, heavy white china loaded to the gunnels with enchiladas and tacos and burritos, garnished with dollops of white sour cream and pale green guacamole, with black olives frisking dangerously close to the lip of the plate, and I suddenly knew I could listen to anyone talk about anything a lot more easily than I could go home and face Banquet Fried Chicken, its flaking brown crust covered with thick hoarfrost from my faulty refrigerator. So I did.

We ordered and we ate and he talked and I listened. He told me things. He was not *the* Merlin, but he did know he was descended from him. Magic was not what it had been at one time, but he got by. One quote I remember exactly. "The only magic that's left in the world right now is the magic that we make ourselves, deliberately. You're not going to stumble over enchantment by chance. You have to be open to it, looking for it, and when you first think you might have glimpsed it, you have to *will* it into your life with every machination available to you." He paused. He leaned forward to whisper, "But the magic is never quite what you expect it to be. Almost, but never exactly." And then he leaned back and smiled at me, and I knew what he was going to say next.

He went on about the magic he sensed inside me, and how he could help me open myself up to it. He could feel that I was suppressing a talent. It was smooth, the way he did it. I think that if I had been ten or fifteen years younger, I could have relaxed and gone along with it, maybe even been flattered by it. Maybe if *he* had been five or ten years younger, I would have chosen to be gullible, just for the company. But dinner was drawing to a close, and I had a hunch what was going to come after dinner, so I just sort of shook my head and said that nothing in my life had ever made me anything but a skeptic about magic and ESP and psychic phenomena and all the rest of that stuff. And then he said what I knew he would, that if I'd care to come by his place he could show me a few things that would change my mind in a hurry. I said that I'd really enjoyed talking to him and dinner had been fun, but I didn't think I knew him well enough to go to his apartment. Besides, I was afraid I had to get home and wash my hair because I had the early shift again tomorrow morning. He shrugged and sat back in his chair and said he understood completely and I was wise to be cautious, that women weren't the only ones distressed by so-called "date-rapes." He said that in time I would learn that I could trust him, and someday we'd probably laugh about my first impression of him.

I agreed, and we chuckled a little, and the waitress brought more coffee and he excused himself to use the men's room. I sat, stirring sugar and creamer into my coffee, and wondering if it wouldn't be wiser to skip out now, just leave a little note that I had discovered it was later than I thought and I had to hurry home but that I'd had a lovely time and thank-you. But that seemed like a pretty snakey thing to do to him. It wasn't like he was repulsive or anything, actually he was pretty nice and had very good eyes, dark brown, and a shy way of looking aside when he smiled and a wonderful voice that reminded me of cello strings. I suppose it was that he was fortyish and balding and had a pot-belly. If that makes me sound shallow, well, I'm sorry. If he'd been a little younger, I could probably have warmed up to him. If *I'd* been a little younger, too, maybe I would even have gone to his apartment to be deskepticised. But he wasn't and I wasn't and I wouldn't. But I wasn't going to be rude to him, either. He didn't deserve that. So I sat, toughing it out.

He'd left his packages of tea on the table and I picked one up and read it. I had to smile. Magic Carpet Tea. It smelled like orange spice to me. Earl Grey tea had been re-named Misplaced Dreams Tea. The scent of the third was unfamiliar to me, maybe one of those pale green ones, but it was labeled Dragon's Breath Tea. The fortyish man was really into this psychic-magic thing, I could tell, and in a way I felt a little sorry for him. A grown man, on the slippery-slide down side of his fortieth birthday, clinging to fairy-tales and magic, still hoping something would *happen* in his life, some miracle more wondrous than financing a new car or finding out the leaky hot-water heater is still under warranty. It wasn't going to happen, not to him, not to me, and I felt a little more gentle toward him as I leaned back in my chair and waited for him to return.

He didn't. You found that out a lot faster than I did. I sat and waited and drank coffee, and it was only when the wait-ress re-filled my cup that I realized how long it had been. His coffee was cold by then, and so was my stomach. I knew he'd stuck me with the check and why. I could almost hear him telling one of his buddies, "Hey, if the chick's not going to come across, why waste the bread, man?" Body slammed by humiliation that I'd been so gullible, I wondered if the whole magic thing was something he just used as a lure for women. Probably. And here I'd been preening myself, just a little, all through dinner, thinking that he was still seeing in me the possibility of magic and enchantment, that for him I had some special fey glow.

Well, my credit cards were bottomed out, I had less than two bucks in cash, and my check book was at home. In the end, the restaurant manager reluctantly cashed my paycheck for me, probably only because he knew Sears wouldn't write a rubber check and I could show him my employee badge. Towards the end he was even sympathetic about the fortyish man treating me so badly, which was even worse, because he acted like my poor little heart was broken instead of me just being damn mad and embarrassed. As I was leaving, finally, let me get *out* of here, the waitress handed me the three little paper bags of tea with such a condescending ''poor baby'' look that I wanted to spit at her. And I went home.

The strange part is that I actually cried after I got home, more out of frustration and anger than any hurt, though. I wished that I knew his real name, so I could call him up and let him know what I thought of such a cheap trick. I stood in front of the bathroom mirror, looking at my red eyes and swollen runny nose, and I suddenly knew that the restaurant people had been seeing me more clearly than I or the fortyish man did. Not Silver Lady or even mud duck, but plain middle-aged woman in a blue-collar job with no prospects at all. For a moment it got to me, but then I stood up straight and glared at the mirror. I felt the silver ladies swinging from my ears, and as I looked at them, it occurred to me that they were probably worth a lot more than the meal I had just paid for, and that I had his tea, to boot. So, maybe he hadn't come out of it any better than I had, these earrings hadn't gotten him laid, and if he had skipped out without paying for the meal, he'd left his tea as well, and those specialty shop teas don't come cheap. For the first time, it occurred to me that things didn't add up, quite. But I put it out of my mind, fixed myself a cup of Misplaced Dreams Tea, read for a little while, and then went to bed.

I dreamed about him. Not surprising, considering what he'd put me through. I was in a garden, standing by a silver bench shaded by an arching trellis heavy with a dark green vine full of fragrant pink flowers. The fortyish man was standing before me, and I could see him, but I had the sense that he was disembodied, not really there at all. "I want to apologize," he said, quite seriously. "I never would have left you that way voluntarily. I'm afraid I was magicked away by one of my archrivals. The same one who has created the evil spell that distresses you. He's imprisoned me in a crystal, so I'm afraid I won't be seeing you for a while."

In this dream, I was clad in a gown made of peacock feathers, and I had silver rings on all my fingers. Little silver bells were on fine chains around my ankles. They tinkled as I stepped closer to him. "Isn't there anything I can do to help you?" my dream-self asked.

"Oh, I think not," he replied. "I just didn't want you to think badly of me." Then he smiled. "Silver Lady, you are one of the few who would worry first about breaking the enchantment that binds me, rather than plotting how to break your own curse. I cannot help but believe that the forces that balance all magic will find a way to free us both."

"May you be right, my friend," I replied.

And that was the end of the dream, or the end of as much as I can remember. I awoke in the morning with vague memories of a cat batting at tinkling silver chimes swinging in a perfumed wind. I had a splitting headache. I got out of bed, got dressed, and went to work at Sears.

For a couple of days, I kept expecting him to turn up again, but he didn't. I just kept going along. I told Felicia that I couldn't live on the hours and pay I was getting, and she told me that she was very disappointed with the number of credit applications I was turning in, and that full-time people were only chosen from the most dedicated and enthusiastic part-timers. I said I'd have to start looking for work elsewhere, and she said she understood. We both knew there wasn't much work of any kind to be had, and that I could be replaced with a bored house-wife or a desperate community college student at a moment's notice. It was not reassuring.

In the next three weeks, I passed out twenty-seven copies of my resume to various bored people at desks. I interviewed for two jobs that were just as low-paying as the one I already had. I found a fantastic job that would have loved to hire me, but its funding called for it to be given to a displaced home-maker or a disadvantaged worker. Then I called on a tele-phone interviewing position ad in the paper. They liked my voice and asked me to come in. After a lot of pussyfooting, it turned out to be a job where you answered toll calls from heavy breathers and conversed animatedly about their sexual fantasies. "Sort of an improvisational theater of the erotic," said my interviewer. She had some tapes of some sample calls, and I found myself listening to them and admitting, yes, it sounded easy. Best of all, the interviewer told me, I could work from my own home, doing the dishes or sorting laundry while telling some man how much I'd like to run a warm sponge over his body, slathering every nook and cranny of his flesh with soapsuds until he gleamed, and then, when he was hard and warm and wet, I'd take him and . . . for six to seven dollars an hour. They even had pamphlets that ex-plained sexual practices I might not be familiar with and gave the correct jargon to use when chatting about them. Six to seven dollars an hour. I told the interviewer I'd have to think about it, and went home.

And got up the next day and defrosted the refrigerator again and swept the carpet in the living room because I was out of vacuum bags. Then I did all the mending that I had been putting off for weeks, scrubbed the landing outside my apart-ment door and sprayed it with Cat-B-Gon, and thought about talking on the telephone to men about sex, and how I could do it while I was ironing a shirt or arranging flowers in a vase or wiping cat-turds off my shoe. Then I took a shower and changed and went in to work at Sears for the five to nine evening shift. I told myself that the work wasn't dirty or dif-ficult, that my co-workers were pleasant people and that there was no reason why this job should make me so depressed.

It didn't help.

The mall was having Craft Week, and to get to Sears I had to pass all the tables and people. I wondered why I didn't get busy and make things in the evenings and sell them on the weekends and make ends meet that way. I passed Barbie dolls whose pink crocheted skirts concealed spare rolls of toilet paper, and I saw wooden key-chains that spelled out names, and ceramic butterfly windchimes, and a booth of rubber-stamps, and a booth with clusters of little pewter and crystal sculptures displayed on tables made of old doors set across saw-horses. I slowed a little as I passed that one, for I've always had a weakness for pewter. There were the standard dragons and wizards, and some thunder-eggs cut in half with wizard figures standing inside them. There were birds, too, eagles and falcons and owls of pewter, and one really nice stag almost as big as my hand. For fifty-two dollars. I was looking at it when I heard a woman standing behind me say, "I'd like the crystal holding the wizard, please."

And the owner of the stall smiled at her and said, "You mean the wizard holding the crystal, right?" and the woman said, in this really snotty voice, "Quite."

So the owner wrapped up the little figurine of a wizard holding a crystal ball in several layers of tissue paper, and held it out to the woman and said, "Seventeen-seventy-eight, please," and the woman was digging in her purse and I swear, all I did was try to step out of their way.

I guess my coat caught on a corner of the door or something, for in the next instant everything was tilting and sliding. I tried to catch the edge of the door-table, but it landed on the woman's foot, really hard, as all the crystal and pewter crashed to the floor and scattered across the linoleum like a shattered whitecap. The woman screamed and threw up her hands and the little wrapped wizard went flying.

I'm not sure if I really saw this.

The crystal ball flew out of the package and landed separately on the floor. It didn't shatter or tinkle or crash. It went Poof! with a minute puff of smoke. And the crumple of tissue paper floated down emptily.

"You stupid bitch!" the woman yelled at me, and the owner of the booth glared at me and said, "I hope to hell you have insurance, klutz!"

Which is a dumb thing to say, really, and I couldn't think of any answer. People were turning to stare, and moving toward us to see what the excitement was, and the woman had sort of collapsed and was holding onto her foot, saying, "My god, it's broken, it's broken."

I knew, quite abruptly and coldly, that she wasn't talking about her foot.

Then the fortyish man grabbed me by the elbow and said, "We've got to get out of here!" I let him pull me away, and the funny thing is, no one tried to stop us or chase us or anything. The crowd closed up around the woman on the floor like an amoeba engulfing a tidbit.

Then we were in a pickup truck that smelled like a wet dog, and the floor was cluttered with muddy newspapers and styrofoam coffee cups and wrappers from Hostess Fruit Pies and paper boats from the textured vegetable protein burritos they sell in the Seven-Eleven stores.

Part of me was saying that I was crazy to be driving off with this guy I hardly knew who had stuck me with the bill for dinner, and part of me was saying that I had better get back to Sears, maybe I could explain being this late for work. And part of me just didn't give a shit anymore, it just wanted to flee. And that part felt better than it had in ages.

We pulled up outside a little white house and he turned to me gravely and said, "Thank you for rescuing me."

"This is really dumb," I said, and he said, "Maybe so, but it's all we've got. I told you, magic isn't what it used to be."

So we went inside the little house and he put the tea kettle on. It was a beautiful kettle, shining copper with a white and blue ceramic handle, and the cups and saucers he took down matched it. I said, "You stuck me with the bill at the restaurant."

He said, "My enemies fell upon me in the restroom and magicked me away. I told you. I never would have chosen to leave you that way, Silver Lady. But for your intervention today, I would still be in their powers." Then he turned, holding a little tin cannister in each hand and asked, "Which will you have: Misplaced Dreams or Forgotten Sweetness?"

"Forgotten Sweetness," I said, and he put down both cannisters of tea and took me in his arms and kissed me. And yes, I could feel his stomach sticking out a little against mine, and when I put my hand to the back of his head to hold his mouth against mine, I could tell his hair was thinning. But I also thought I could hear windchimes and scent an elusive perfume on a warm breeze. I don't believe in magic. The idea of willing enchantment into my life is dumb. Dumb. But as the fortyish man had said, it was all we had. A dumb hope for a small slice of magic, no matter how thin. The fortyish man didn't waste his energy carrying me to the bedroom.

I never met a man under twenty-five who was worth the powder to blow him to hell. They're all stuck in third gear.

It takes a man until he's thirty to understand what gentleness is about, and a few years past that to realize that a woman touches a man as she would like him to touch her.

By thirty-five, they start to grasp how a woman's body is wired. They quit trying to kick-start us, and learn to make sure the battery is charged before turning the key. A few, I've heard, learn how to let a woman make love to them.

Fortyish men understand pacing. They know it doesn't have to all happen at once, that separating each stimulus can intensify each touch. They know when pausing is more poignant than continuing, and they know when continuing is more important than a ceramic kettle whistling itself dry on an electric burner.

And afterwards I said to him, "Have you ever heard of 'Lindholm's Rule of Ten'?"

He frowned an instant. "Isn't that the theory that the first ten times two people make love, one will do something that isn't in sync with the other?"

"That's the one," I said.

"It's been disproved," he said solemnly. And he got up and went to the bathroom while I rescued the smoking kettle from the burner.

I stood in the kitchen, and after a while I started shivering, because the place wasn't all that well heated. Putting my clothes back on didn't seem polite somehow, so I called through the bathroom door, "Shall I put on more water for tea?"

He didn't answer, and I didn't want to yell through the door again, so I picked up my blouse and slung it around my shoulders and shivered for a while. I sort of paced through his kitchen and living room. I found myself reading the titles of his books, one of the best ways to politely spy on someone.

*Theories of Thermodynamics* was right next to *The Silmaril-lion*. All the books by Carlos Castenada were set apart on a shelf by themselves. His set of Kipling was bound in red leather. My ass was freezing, and I suspected I had a rug burn on my back. To hell with being polite. I went and got my underwear and skirt and stood in the kitchen, putting them on.

"Merlin?" I called questioningly as I picked up my panty-hose. They were shot, a huge laddered run up the back of one leg. I bunched them up and shoved them into my purse. I went and knocked on the bathroom door, saying, "I'm coming in, okay?" And when he didn't answer, I opened the door.

There was no one in there. But I was sure that was where he had gone, and the only other exit from the bathroom was a small window with three pots of impatiens blooming on the sill. The only clue that he had been there was the used rubber floating pathetically in the toilet. There is nothing less romantic than a used rubber.

I went and opened the bedroom door and looked in there. He hadn't made his bed this morning. I backed out.

I actually waited around for a while, pretending he would come back. I mean, his clothes were still in a heap on the floor. How he could have gotten re-dressed and left the house without my noticing it, I didn't try to figure out. But after an hour or so, it didn't matter how he had done anything. He was *gone*.

I didn't cry. I had been too stupid to allow myself to cry. None of this made sense, but my behavior made the least sense of all. I finished getting dressed and looked at myself in the bathroom mirror. Great. Smeared makeup and nothing to repair it with, so I washed it all off. Let the lines at the corners of my mouth and the circles under my eyes show. Who cared. My hair had gone wild. My legs were white-fleshed and goosebumpy without the pantyhose. The cute lit-tle ankle-strap heels on my bare feet looked grotesque. All of me looked rumpled and used. It matched how I felt, an outfit that perfectly complemented my mood, so I got my purse and left.

The old pickup was still outside. That didn't make sense either, but I didn't really give a damn.

I walked home. That sounds simpler than it was. The weather was raw, I was barelegged and in heels, it was getting dark and people stared at me. It took me about an hour, and by the time I got there I had rubbed a huge blister on the back of one of my feet, so I was limping as well. I went up the stairs, narrowly missing the moist brown pile the neighbor's cat had left for me, unlocked my apartment door and went in.

And I still didn't cry. I kicked off my shoes and got into my old baggy sweatsuit and went to the kitchen. I made myself hot chocolate in a little china pot with forget-me-nots on it, and opened the eight ounce canned genuine all-the-way-from-England Cross and Blackwell plum pudding that my sister had given me last Christmas and I had saved in case of disasters like this. I cut the whole thing up and arranged it on a bone china plate on a little tray with my pot of hot chocolate and a cup and saucer. I set it on a little table by my battered easy chair, put a quilt on the chair and got down my old leather copy of Dumas' *The Three Musketeers*. Then I headed for the bathroom, intending to take a quick hot shower and dab on some rose oil before settling down for the evening. It was my way of apologizing to myself for hurting myself this badly.

I opened the bathroom door, and a stenchful cloud of sulphurous green smoke wafted out. Choking and gasping, I peered in, and there was the fortyish man, clad only in a towel, smiling at me apologetically. He looked apprehensive. He had a big raw scrape on one knee, and a swollen lump on his forehead. He said, "Silver Lady, I never would have left you like that, but. . . ."

"You were teleported away by your arch rival," I finished.

He said, "No, not teleported, exactly, this involved a spell requiring a monkey's paw and a dozen nightshade berries. But they were *last* year's berries, and not potent enough to hold me. I had a spell of my own up my sleeve and. . . ."

"You blasted him to kingdom come," I guessed.

"No." He looked a little abashed. "Actually, it was the

'Incessant Rectal Itch' spell, a little crude, but always effective and simple to use. I doubt that he'll be bothering us again soon.'' He paused, then added, ''As I've told you, magic isn't what it used to be.'' Then he sniffed a few times and said, ''Actually, I've found that Pinesol is the best stuff for getting rid of spell residues. . . .''

So we cleaned up the bathroom. I poured hydrogen peroxide over his scraped knee and he made gasping noises and cursed in a language I'd never heard before. I left him doing that and went into the kitchen and began re-heating the hot chocolate. A few moments later he came out dressed in a sort of sarong he'd made from one of my bed sheets. It looked strangely elegant on him, and the funny thing was, neither of us seemed to feel awkward as we sat down and drank the hot chocolate and shared the plum pudding. The last piece of plum pudding he took, and borrowing some cream cheese from my refrigerator, he buttered a cabalistic sign onto it. Then he went to the door and called, ''Here, kitty, kitty, kitty.''

The neighbor's cat came at once, and the ratty old thing let the fortyish man scoop him up and bring him into my living room, where he removed two ticks from behind its ears and then fed it the plum pudding in small bites. When he had done that, he picked it up and stared long into its yellowish eyes before he intoned, ''By bread and cream I bind you. Nevermore shalt thou shit upon the threshold of this abode.'' Then he put the cat gently out the door, observing aloud, ''Well, that takes care of the curse you were under.''

I stared at him. ''I thought my curse had something to do with me working at Sears.''

''No. That was just a viciously cruel thing you were doing to yourself, for reasons I will never understand.'' He must have seen the look on my face, because after a while he said, ''I told you, the magic is never quite what you think it to be.''

Then he came to sit on the floor beside my easy chair. He put his elbow on my knee and leaned his chin in his hand. ''What if I were to tell you, Silver Lady, that I myself have no real magic at all? That, actually, I climbed out my bathroom window and sneaked through the streets in my towel to meet you here? Because I wanted you to see me as special.''

I didn't say anything.

"What if I told you I really work for Boeing, in Personnel?"

I just looked at him, and he lifted his elbow from my knee and turned aside a little. He glanced at his own bare feet, and then over at my machine. He licked his lips and spoke softly. "I could get you a job there. As a word processor, at about eleven dollars an hour."

"Merlin," I said warningly.

"Well, maybe not eleven dollars an hour to start. . . ."

I reached out and brushed what hair he had back from his receding hairline. He looked up at me and then smiled the smile where he always looked aside from me. We didn't say anything at all. I took his hand and led him to my room, where we once more disproved Lindholm's Rule of Ten. I fell asleep curled around him, my hand resting comfortably on the curve of his belly. He was incredibly warm, and smelled of oranges, cloves, and cinnamon. Misplaced Dreams Tea, that's what he smelled like. And that night I dreamed I wore a peacock feather gown and strolled through a misty garden. I had found something I had lost, and I carried it in my hand, but every time I tried to look at it to see what it was, the mist swirled up and hid my hand from me.

In the morning when I woke up, the fortyish man was gone.

It didn't really bother me. I knew that either he would be back, or he wouldn't, but either way no one could take from me what I already had, and what I already had was a lot more magic than most people get in their lives. I put on my ratty old bathrobe and my silver ladies and went out into the livingroom. His sarong sheet was folded up on the easy chair in the livingroom, and the neighbor's cat was asleep on it, his paws tucked under his chin.

And my Muse was there, too, perched on the corner of my desk, one knee under her chin as she painted her toenails. She looked up when I came in and said, "If you're quite finished

having a temper tantrum, we'll get on with your career now.''
So I sat down at my machine and flicked the switch on and
put my fingers on the home row.

Funny thing. The keys weren't even dusty.

# WAKE-UP CALL

## *Esther M. Friesner*

*"Wake-Up Call" was purchased by Gardner Dozois, and appeared in the December 1988 issue of* Asimov's, *with an illustration by Judith Mitchell. (Esther M. Friesner's "The Three Queens" appears elsewhere in this anthology; see there for biographical notes.)*

*In the very funny story that follows, Friesner shows us that when duty calls, it calls—no matter how long it takes, or how strange a voice it calls in . . .*

"I *know* I heard something this time." Vivian set down her cards and cocked her head towards the closed bedroom door just off the kitchen. She turned to the woman on her left. "Hadn't you best take a peep in there, Fay?"

"Whuffo?" Fay's reply was somewhat garbled by the cigarette dangling from her thickly lipsticked mouth. Vivian could not remember the last time she'd seen Fay without a smoking fag wiggling and bobbing when she spoke.

Across from Vivian, Gwen snickered nastily into her hand. "Always hearing things from in there, *you* are." She tucked a wisp of bleached blonde hair back behind her ear and fanned her cards. "*Last* time it was a loose shutter. Time before, it was just the local brats wheeling their Guy about the parish in a rattly old pram, collecting for the bonfire. Time before that, a mouse'd got in."

"Bloody shame, that." Fay plucked a card from one position in her hand and slid it into another. "Council did halfway decent by us, they'd keep the vermin out." An inch of ash dropped from her cigarette. Gwen edged away from it fastidiously.

"You might use a saucer if an ashtray's too much to ask." She brushed handfuls of invisible ashes from her beige linen sheath skirt and winced as the waistband cut into her growing midriff.

"Get stuffed," Fay replied pleasantly.

"But I *did* hear something," Vivian insisted. "I *did*."

"One club," said Fay.

"Two hearts," Gwen countered.

The basin of water opposite Fay bubbled and seethed. An arm, clothed all in white samite, rose out of the enamelled depths and brandished a hand of cards. It laid these face down on the oilcloth-covered kitchen table, plunged back into the water, and came up again with gemmed rings sparkling brightly on thumb and forefinger.

"Lady bids two diamonds," Fay muttered. The slim white hand at the end of that samite-clothed arm gave her the old thumbs-up. "Stupid cow," Fay added.

This time the Lady's hand used a different finger-sign to communicate her displeasure with her over-critical bridge partner.

"Pass," Vivian said without thinking. She completely missed the venomous glance Gwen shot her. Her watery brown eyes, pink-rimmed and weak, kept darting towards the closed bedroom door. "Look, I really *have* to check. I simply can *not* play an intelligent rubber with these doubts preying on my mind."

"Or any other time," Gwen hissed for Fay's benefit. Fay

snorted prodigiously and stroked her sagging jowls, her attention still focused on her hand. She paid no heed when Vivian scraped her chair backwards and padded away from the table in her ratty Marks and Spencer scuffs.

She paid heed aplenty, though, when Vivian opened the bedroom door and screamed.

"He's gone! He's *gone!*" Vivian reeled against the doorjamb, clutching her seersucker wrap-dress tightly around her scrawny body. "I *knew* it!" she squealed at them all. "I *told* you the time was ripe for this happening, the country in the state it's in and all—crime, devaluation, the Irish, all those peculiar foreigners just *streaming* in, worse than the Saxons ever were. Would you listen? Would *any* of you listen? 'Oh, it's just little Viv again,' you all said. 'Little Viv will have her fancies.' Well, where's the fancy in an empty bed's what *I'd* like to know!" She straightened her shoulders and struck a self-righteous pose, one hand on the doorjamb, one still securing the neck of her wrapper.

Fay stood up and slowly laid her cards on the table, face down. " 'F this is another one of your hysteric attacks, Vivian, I'll take you and stick you headfirst into the crotch of one of your own damned oak trees."

"*Crotch?*" Gwen burst into a fit of dirty-schoolgirl giggles. She scraped one expensively manicured forefinger over the other. "Naughty, naughty. Such language for a royal lady!"

"Oh, stop your gob, you great simpering slug!" Fay was so provoked, she actually let the cigarette drop from her lips. It rolled across the oilcloth and smoldered among the fallen cards until the Lady of the Basin thoughtfully extinguished it with a splash.

Gwen pursed her lips, painstakingly outlined and lovingly tinted a most fashionable and unsuitable shade of maroon. Her over-plucked eyebrows rose. "You're just jealous," she said, "because *I'm* the only one around here who hasn't let herself go to seed while we've been waiting."

"No, just let yourself go down on your back for anything young as crawls out of a pub too tiddled to tell your proper age in a dim light!"

"Doesn't *any*one want to look after where he's got to?" Vivian gazed from one enraged queen to the other, her weak eyes blinking madly.

"Bloody hell, why bother?" Fay picked up her chair and slammed it down on the linoleum for emphasis. "If it's Time, we'll hear of it soon enough. And if it's just another false alarm . . ."

"Last time he was sleepwalking," Gwen said, enjoying the distress her words caused little Viv. "*You* remember, don't you, love? It was during the Battle of Britain. You kept on about how this was It, he couldn't possibly stay asleep through a crisis *this* big, the country needed him, the New Age was coming and you were going to celebrate by going out and getting a marcel wave once the shouting died." Her ungenerous mouth quirked up coldly at the corners. "*I* was the one found him down in the Underground—still asleep, mind—and brought him into the light of day again. Just as well. You'd've looked beastly with a marcel." She patted her chignon. "I'll be the one to know when he really *does* wake. A wife always knows."

"A wife always knows sweet bugger-all," Fay snarled. She shouldered her way past Vivian into the bedroom. The iron-headed single bed was empty, the jewel-encrusted coverlet in disarray on the floor. Briskly, Fay shook it out, her big, capable hands smoothing it back so that the black silk veiled the tell-tale bottom of the funeral barge stowed in segments beneath the bedstead. Then she went back to the kitchen table and lit herself another cigarette.

"That's *it?*" Vivian's gingery eyelashes looked pathetic when she fluttered them in disbelief like that. She had an unfortunate habit of plucking them out when beset by rude tradespeople in the market. "Fay, that's all you're going to *do?*"

"Don't skirl your voice like that, Viv. It gives me the pip. Sweet loving Christ, what do you *expect* of me?"

Vivian waved her hands about helplessly. "I don't know. Something . . . magical?"

"Jesus God, woman, if it's magic you want, you're able to work some yourself. You're a fucking *nymph*, after all."

Fay glowered at Vivian, chin in hand, as the little woman showed no greater reaction than a blush at such foul language.

"Now, Fay . . ." Gwen's voice was all treacly. "You know Viv hasn't been able to use her magic ever since . . . you know." Her goody-goody face, full of compassion and forbearance, just begged for a bashing. Fay's fingers itched to do it.

"Shouldn't've locked the old sod *up* in that damned tree, then, if she was going to go soft about it after!"

"I've tried." Viv wove the neck-ties of her wrap around and over and through her knobbly fingers. She was going to turn teary any moment. "You know I have, Fay. The therapists I've been to, the doctors, the discussion groups, the self-help books from the States—!"

"And hardly any of it on the National Health. Can't see why you don't let him *out* again, then."

"But I *can't* do that! Honestly, not. I have made the effort, you know, but it's no good. It's as if all my powers were tied up in that tree with the dear old fella. You can't imagine the guilt."

"Ballocks," said Fay. "Ballocks to you and your guilt, too." She got up again and fetched a plate of cream buns from the pantry. "I'm going to watch telly. Stuff your bloody guilt, Viv, and make me a mug of tea. Maybe I'll try scaring up a vision of our Arthur after Benny Hill's done. 'Til then, bugger off, the lot of you." She chomped down hard on a round, sticky pastry.

"That is *hardly* the way to address us." Gwen had caught the infirmity of self-righteousness from a presently sniveling Vivian. While the smaller woman went whimpering away to put the kettle on, the erstwhile Lady of Camelot held forth. "We are all queens in our own right. You were never this common in Cornwall. I shudder to think what the gentlemen of the press will make of you: The style of an underpaid char and the vocabulary of a Billingsgate porter. Ugh."

"You *do* outrank Gwen and me, Fay," Vivian mentioned timorously from stoveside. "I was never really a queen, unless you count poor, dear Merlin's flatteries, and Gwen was only Queen of Camelot by marriage, but you—"

"Bugger you *and* Gwen *and* Camelot *and* Merlin *and* the gentlemen of the press while you're at it! Queenship, bah! I bloody well wish I'd never *heard* of the fucking realm of Air and Darkness!" Morgan le Fay went quite scarlet with her diatribe and began to choke on a bite of cream bun. It devolved upon Gwen to hustle her into a chair, the Lady to reach up out of the basin and pound her on the back, and little Vivian to bustle over with a frosty glass of lemon squash.

They were so caught up in ministering to their own that they never heard the back door open, or the approaching jingle and creak of a chain-mail shirt over boiled leather armor. In fact, they didn't even notice that Arthur had returned, until he plopped down heavily in one of the empty chairs.

Fay recovered quickly. "Where the hell have *you* been?"

Cool, imperturbable eyes the color of newly forged steel met her own. Arthur drew a breath, twiddled his fingers in the empty scabbard at his side, and thought better of saying anything. He seized a bun instead, and devoured it.

Gwen made a strong comeback from the shock of seeing him so suddenly with them. *"Darling!"* she trilled, opening her arms wide to receive her long-slumbering lord.

The basin waters churned themselves into a maelstrom as the Lady enthusiastically lifted Excalibur clear of the foam. Arthur made no move to embrace either his wife or his sword. He did not move at all, except for masticating the cream bun slowly and thoughtfully. The Lady held her pose for some time, then tilted the blade towards its whilom master in an inquiring, then an encouraging, then an insistent manner, brandishing it urgently. It was for naught.

"No go, eh, Artie?" Fay chuckled knowingly. She rose, and a glamour fell over her. Her eternal cigarette was gone, as was the dowdy housedress Gwen so deplored. Her still alluring figure was sheathed in crimson silk starred with pearls, and when she reached up to undo the dusting kerchief binding her hair, a cascade of raven curls tumbled to her feet. Her face no longer sagged, but shone with the soft radiance of a star.

"No." His voice was harsh with long disuse.

"What's the cock-up this time?"

"*I* wake; the dream still slumbers." The King of the Britons wiped his crumb-decked beard with the back of his hand. "My people are deaf to the great call. They will not follow me. They hardly *know* me."

Morgan le Fay clucked her tongue. "Comes of not enough central heating and too many boiled sweets, I'll be bound. Never you mind, Artie. They'll be ready for you some day."

Arthur's eyes blazed. "And when will that day come? Soon or late? Too late or never?"

"Now, pet, there'll still be an England for you to rule when you *do* return. Trust old Morgan." Fay put her arm around his shoulders. She had to go on tip-toe to do it, at which discovery she looked a bit surprised.

"He's grown," Viv said in that mouse-hush voice of hers.

"Legends will," Fay remarked over one shoulder as she steered Arthur back into the bedroom. She shut the door behind them.

Viv had a fresh kettle on the boil when Fay emerged, alone. Her gown was rumpled and her hair in tousles. Gwen's eyes narrowed.

"Just *what* were you doing with my Arthur?"

"A lot better than you, likely. How in bloody hell did you *expect* me to get that poor bastard back off to sleep? Warm milk? Nembutal? Another fucking mortal wound? Christ, I want a fag." Morgan le Fay swept her hands over her bosom and was rewarded with the full resurgence of her frowsy *tenue*, dusting kerchief included. She extracted a pack of Players from the pocket of her housedress and lit up gratefully.

She flopped into a kitchen chair as Viv set a fresh mug of tea at her place. She slurped it with gusto while her companions observed her somberly.

"Didn't they *know* who he was?" Vivian was the first to dare break the spell. "They saw him and they didn't *know?*" Her weak eyes swam with sudden tears.

Fay shrugged. A damp, tragic silence fell over the kitchen. The others sat down at the table again. Gwen sighed deeply and repeatedly. Vivian absently plucked out one eyelash after another. Excalibur fell from the Lady's hand and made a rubbery ringing sound when it hit the lino. Fay looked up from her tea to note that the Lady's fingernails were all nibbled down to the quick and the cuticles were in woeful need of trimming.

"Never you mind, girls," Fay said, attempting to lift their collective spirits. "Time'll come some day, and we'll be there to meet it. Chin up." She glanced at the Lady. "Or whatever."

Fay snapped her fingers and a ball of blue fire appeared in front of Vivian, delivered itself of a fresh pack of cards, and vanished. Viv gave a faint smile and broke the seal.

A bedspring groaned. Vivian froze.

"I *heard* something."

"Oh, shut up, Viv—and deal the cards."

# THE DOG'S STORY

## *Eleanor Arnason*

*"The Dog's Story" was purchased by Gardner Dozois,
and appeared in the May 1996 issue of* Asimov's, *with
an illustration by Darryl Elliott. Arnason is not prolific
at short lengths, her only other* Asimov's *story being
her novelette "The Lovers," but each of her appearances in the magazine has been with a complex, sub-
stantial, and satisfying piece of fiction. She's more
prolific at novel length, publishing her first novel,* The
Sword Smith, *in 1978, and following it with novels such
as* Daughter of the Bear King *and* To The Resurrection
Station. *In 1991, she published her best-known novel,
the critically acclaimed* A Woman of the Iron People,
*which won the prestigious James Tiptree Jr. Memorial
Award. Her most recent novel is* Ring of Swords. *In
the vivid and evocative story that follows, she examines
the Matter of Britain from a totally fresh and unexpected perspective, one that's never occurred to any of*

*the hundreds of other writers who have dealt with the*
*legends of Camelot and its High Court . . .*

The wizard Merlin, traveling on his monarch's business, came
to a ford where a knight was raping a maiden. The rape had
just begun, though it had apparently been preceded by a murder. A second man, most likely the girl's companion, lay on
the ground nearby, bloody and unmoving. Three horses wandered loose. Merlin reined his own animal and considered the
scene to make sure that his first impression was correct.

The girl had already lost her long embroidered belt. The
knight held it in one hand, while his other arm assumed the
belt's position around the girl's waist. This seemed clear
enough to Merlin. It isn't easy to rape anyone while garbed
in a knee-length mail shirt. Nor is it easy to pull such a gar-
ment off, while holding a struggling woman. Struggle the
maiden did, screaming like a peacock, a creature that Merlin
had seen—and heard—in King Arthur's menagerie. The
knight was planning to tie the girl up, then undress the two
of them at leisure.

By this time he had noticed Merlin. He gave the wizard a
brief glance, returning to his contest with the girl. An old
man on a palfrey could be no threat. After the girl was tied,
maybe to the tree that shaded the ford and the two contestants,
he'd be free to drive off Merlin or kill him; and then he'd be
able to get back to his pleasure, if pleasure was the right word
here.

Merlin, who'd been a sensualist in his youth, began to feel
anger. This man dishonored all lovers of women and love.
The old man straightened in his saddle and lifted a hand. "A
cur you are," he cried. "A cur you shall be in the future!"

The knight turned as if jerked at the end of a rope. His
armor fell in pieces around him; his clothing vanished; and
for a moment he stood naked: a tall, fair, ruddy man with an
erection. Then he dropped on all fours. A moment after that,
he became a dog. In this form he glanced at the fragments of
his mail and at the girl, who was trying to arrange her torn
garments. He groaned; it was an oddly human sound to be

coming from the dark lips and long curling tongue of a dog; then he ran away.

"You must be a magician," the girl said in the calm voice of one who had experienced too much.

"Evidently." Merlin dismounted and examined the man on the ground. Beyond any question he was dead.

Her brother, the girl told Merlin. They had been on a pilgrimage to a local shrine. On the way back, the false knight had attacked them. Their servants had fled. Her brother had fought and died. "And I was on the road to death when you arrived. What good fortune!"

Merlin kept quiet, knowing the events that occur around wizards are rarely accidental.

They loaded the dead man on Merlin's palfrey, which was not disturbed by blood, and the wizard coaxed the three loose horses, till they approached him, lowering their heads, letting him take their reins. Mounted once again, he and the girl went on.

The name of the false knight was Ewen. He was the younger son of a minor baron: a rough, healthy, violent lad, awkward around women. At the time he met Merlin, he was eighteen years old.

Now a dog, he ran through a forest, one of the many that grew in England in those days. If a person wanted to, he or she could travel the length of the king's realm and never leave the forest shadow, except briefly to cross a road or field. Outlaws used this green route, as did fairies and people grown tired of their obligations.

At first Ewen ran at full speed. Becoming tired, he trotted, then walked, pausing now and then to sniff at something that seemed interesting: a dead bat, folded among last year's fallen leaves, a badger's scat, the mark left by a male fox on a tree. Finally, exhausted, he settled in a patch of ferns and slept.

In the morning, he woke hungry and went looking for food. There was plenty, but he'd not hunted on four feet till now. The pungent aromas of the forest confused him. For some reason—who can understand the mind of a wizard, or the paths that magic follows?—the enchantment had not affected

his vision. He still saw color as a human would. This was no
help; it might even have been a hindrance. In any case, he
couldn't see animals in hiding. When the animals leaped out
of hiding, he chased but did not catch them, being unaccus-
tomed to his new form, though it was a fine body: large,
rangy, fierce of aspect and entirely white except for a pair of
blood red ears. Looking in a pool of still water, he saw himself and fled, horrified.

After several days of hunger, he came to a farm. It was
nothing much: a rough cottage, a couple of outbuildings that
were little more than sheds, and a pen that held pigs.

There was food in the cottage and in the pen. Ewen could
smell it, but the scent of people frightened him, and no one
in his right mind would climb in a pen with pigs. They were
(and are) fierce, strong animals, intelligent enough to know
that humans mean them no good. If they can, they'll kill.

He waited till nightfall and slunk close. The pigs grunted
angrily. The cottage door opened. Ewen slunk away.

In the morning he hunted again, caught an unwary rabbit
and ate it, crunching the bones between powerful jaws. It
wasn't enough. He returned to the farmstead.

This time he investigated the outbuildings. One smelled of
grain and vegetables, things he'd liked when human, but
which did not entice him now. The second hut smelled of
meat. Saliva filled his mouth. His tongue lolled out and
dripped. He nosed the door. Unfastened, it swung open. Even
as a man, he hadn't been much for thinking. Now, as a hungry
dog, he didn't think at all. Instead of considering the possibility of danger, he pushed inside. The night was moonless
and the hut as black as pitch, but he could smell roast pig
above him. Ewen leaped and caught nothing, then leaped a
second time. On the third try, his teeth closed around a bone.
He held on, off the ground and twisting in the darkness. The
bone was one of many, fastened together and hung from the
hut's low roof. They knocked against each other now and
made a loud clattering noise, while Ewen swung below them
like the clapper on a bell.

The hut's door closed. A bar came down with a bang.
"There!" said the farmer. "He's a fine big dog. Someone

must own him, a noble, if looks are anything. Or if not, a noble may buy him.''

Merlin delivered the maiden to her father, along with the corpse of her brother. Then he rode on, leading the false knight's charger. For two days, he traveled along the forest's edge, coming at last to an isolated farm.

The farmer made him welcome. Although nobles often ignored or mistook the old man in plain dark clothing, peasants usually realized he was someone important and dangerous, maybe because they actually looked at him.

The farmer's wife prepared dinner. The farmer told Merlin about the dog he'd captured.

"Can I see him?" the wizard asked.

They went to the hut, and Merlin peered through a crack. It was midsummer. The days were long. Rays of sunlight slanted through the hut, and Merlin had no trouble making out the white hound lying on the floor and gnawing bones.

"He's mine," said Merlin. "I'll pay you for your trouble."

The farmer praised his good fortune and Merlin's.

In the morning, Merlin went out to the hut and opened the door. Ewen raised his head. He'd eaten the few shreds of meat on the pig bones, then cracked the bones and licked out the marrow. Now he was bored and ready to leave.

"The man you killed has a father, who has sworn to hunt you down. He hasn't decided whether to kill you or tie you in his courtyard. It might be satisfying to have his boy's killer as a dog by his door. If I leave you here, he'll get you." Merlin tilted his head, considering. "Maybe I should have made you a wolf. You might have lasted longer in the wild. But you don't have a wolf's nature. Come on." The wizard beckoned. Ewen rose and followed.

In the histories, Camelot is a fine lofty city built of stone. In point of fact, it was made of low wood buildings, narrow dirt streets, yards with manure and midden heaps. The king's fort stood in the center of the town. *It* was stone, good Roman work from the days before the empire had abandoned Britain, though damaged by time, war, and neglect. Arthur was rebuilding. The gaps in the outer walls had been filled by rubble and logs bound with iron; inside the fort, scaffolding stood against most of the surviving buildings; and heaps of stone were piled next to the scaffolding, ready for use.

Merlin rode in the fortress gate, the captured charger following, the white hound running at his side. Before him, in the large front court, men practiced with swords. Among them was Arthur, a big handsome man just entering middle age. His hair was dark and curly, his face fair, his eyes grey. He was the love of Merlin's life, and both men knew it, though it was never mentioned. Their relationship was too complicated already.

Merlin dismounted stiffly. Arthur called a halt to the swordplay, and they embraced. Then the king asked about the new horse and the white dog that was trying to hide behind Merlin, afraid of all these people, especially the king.

"You know I have a way with animals. They'll follow if I tell them to."

"I know that you don't want to tell the story that lies in back of these new acquisitions. The dog is handsome, though a bit timid. Will you give him to me?"

"I'll give you the horse, but not the dog."

The king frowned, then laughed and accepted the horse.

"Not up to my weight, of course, but I'll find some poor young knight in need of a mount."

Merlin excused himself and went to his quarters, the white hound following. Servants brought him water and a brazier full of coals: the weather was cool, the wizard past his prime. He washed all over and put on a clean robe, then settled with a cup of wine, also brought by the king's servants.

"You're wondering why I refused to tell the king about you," Merlin said to the dog. "One can never tell about Arthur. He might insist that I turn you back into a man. He might want to kill you. I doubt that he'd want to have a former knight fighting over scraps of food in his feasting hall." The wizard snapped his fingers. The dog came near. He ran his hand over the white head and tugged gently at the blood red ears. "Keep close to me for the next few days, till I have a collar made. Gold, I think. You're a noble-looking animal, though as a man you were a failure. I'll have my name and emblem put on the collar. Few people will steal from a wizard, especially the king's wizard.''

Ewen nosed the old man's hand, then licked the palm.

It was surprisingly easy to be a dog. Ewen had never been much of a talker. Now he didn't have to make the effort. Barks and snarls served for almost every purpose. When they failed, he bared his long sharp teeth. Even the king's dogs gave him room.

Human women had always baffled him. Now, he had no interest in them. It was female dogs that attracted him, and it was far easier to court a bitch in heat than any human woman he'd ever met. Whether high or low in rank, they always seemed to want something Ewen couldn't provide. What the bitches wanted Ewen had and gave willingly.

Arthur, laughing, said, ''All the dogs in Camelot are going to be white,'' then added, ''You wouldn't give me the dog, but I'll have his children.''

When they were alone Merlin said, ''Don't worry about fathering dogs. The king wants his bitches to bear white pups. They will, and the pups will grow up to be everything Arthur is hoping for. But they won't be your children.''

Ewen, chewing on an ox bone, had not considered the problem. After all, he'd been a younger son. His children, if any, would not have mattered much, except to his wife. Let them be dogs and hunt for the king! But he was sterile, the wizard said, at least when he mated with dogs.

''I have changed your appearance, but not your essence. You are still as human as ever you were.''

Ewen cracked the bone held between his front paws, extended his long, rough tongue and licked the marrow out.

He became famous: the big white dog with red ears and a gold collar who followed the king's wizard through Camelot, lay at Merlin's feet, ran beside his horse. He did not age in the ordinary fashion of dogs, as Arthur noticed.

''Nor do I,'' said Merlin. ''Ewen is a wizard's dog, and he

never leaves my side. Magic slows the passage of time, as you ought to have noticed.''

This was a reference to the magic in the royal lineage. The king grimaced, not wanting to think about his family or about the family he had failed to produce—unlike Ewen, whose progeny filled the kennels of Camelot, Arthur believed. The queen was childless and increasingly restless.

By this time, Merlin had fallen into the habit of talking with his dog. Ewen had retained his original intelligence, which was considerable. His problem had never been stupidity, but rather greed, rashness and brutality. These were the traits that led him to attack the maiden at the ford and the pig bones in the storage hut. He understood most of what the old man told him, though not everything, of course. He could repeat nothing. Nor could he use what he learned for his own benefit or against his master: the perfect companion for a lonely wizard.

So began a strange double life. In daylight and in public, Ewen was an animal. At night, alone with Merlin, he was an audience for the great wizard's ideas, worries, reflections, speculations. Gradually, under Merlin's influence, he learned to think, but this process—thinking—had almost nothing to do with his daylight life. There he fought for scraps, mounted bitches, confronted other males, coursed the king's prey, followed at the heels of the king's wisest counselor. Thought belonged to the evening, when Merlin drank wine and tugged Ewen's blood red ears.

In his way, he grew to love the old man. In part, it was a dog's love. In part, it was the love of a man whose own father had been stupid as well as brutish. Strange, maybe, to look at the enchanter who'd made him a domestic animal and see, not an enemy, but a loved father or master. Such things do happen. The heart hath its reasons, which reason knoweth not, as Pascal tells us.

Sometimes, when they were traveling and had stopped for the night in a place distant from other people, Merlin would turn the hound back into a man. Magic *had* slowed time. He looked no more than twenty, fair and muscular. His hair had grown just a little. It fell over his shoulders, curly and shaggy, the color of wheat at midsummer. His eyes were summer blue. His beard was like a wheat field after harvest: blond stubble shining in the light of their evening fire.

In his youth and middle age, Merlin had been a lover of men as well as women. The church forbade this kind of love, of course; but the church also forbade witchcraft and wizardry. Being a scholar, Merlin knew that the basis for these injunctions was a script that also forbade the eating of shellfish. Yet he had seen Christian kings and prelates consume oysters with the zeal of pagan Romans, pausing only to give praise to God for the excellent food. He kept his counsel and did not abandon his inclinations.

In his old age, his passions diminished. Little remained except his love for Arthur, which had always been more familial than anything else. This was the baby Merlin had carried in his arms, the boy he'd watched over, the youth he'd made king. From the beginning, Arthur's future had enveloped him like a cloak or veil of light, visible to Merlin and a few others. The babe in his hands had shone as if swaddled in moonbeams. The boy had seemed garbed in the pale, clear light of dawn. The young man had been like morning.

The veil was still present, though dimmed by age and compromise. At night, when Arthur sat in his feasting hall, surrounded by retainers, Merlin saw glory flicker around the king. Duty and a sense of history transformed the wizard's love, as iron is changed by fire and water.

Ewen was different. Merlin looked at him, on those nights when the two of them camped alone. If the weather was cold enough, the boy would wrap himself in a blanket. Otherwise, he wore nothing except the gold dog collar engraved with Merlin's name. Whatever human modesty he might once have had was gone. He'd been a dog too long.

Merlin remembered lust, and that was what he felt now, stirring in his groin. The boy had no sexual interest in men.

Merlin could force him and be a rapist. He could seduce him using magic. In either case, he'd be a brute, acting from simple need without regard for reason, consequence or the dignity of his art.

No, the old man thought. Better to end his days a celibate.

Now and then, Ewen seemed briefly uncomfortable, as if he suspected what Merlin was thinking. Usually, he was at ease, though rarely talkative. Even in human form, he preferred to listen.

When Merlin wanted to travel in disguise, he gave the boy clothing, and Ewen became a servant or a young relative. At first, Merlin insisted that he not wear the collar. It was too rich and distinctive. But Ewen missed the weight. It was difficult being a man, he told the wizard. His clothes were binding and scratchy. Women were once again exciting.

"When I see one who seems in heat, I get an erection. But what can I do with it? I know you won't let me push the woman down and mount her. As for seduction, it requires skills I don't have and more time than I'm willing to put in. It isn't time I want to put in, in these situations.

"When men brush against me or give me an insulting stare, I want to growl and bite. I know I could leave marks on them, even with human teeth. But you have told me to be mannerly.

"Let me wear the collar. It reminds me that I'll be a dog again soon. I'll keep it hidden."

Merlin gave in, though with foreboding. The inevitable happened at a little roadside lodging place. A fastening came undone. The innkeeper saw gold gleaming at the boy's throat. That night, six men came to rob the travelers.

In his old age, Merlin slept fitfully, and the robbers made the mistake of waiting. By the time they crept down the hall, the wizard had passed through the deep sleep brought on by fatigue to a state close to waking. The noise they made was enough to rouse him entirely. He roused Ewen, who pulled a sword out of their baggage.

One of the robbers had a lantern made of horn. By its dim light, they saw a man emerge from the travelers' room, naked except for a wide gold collar, bare steel in his hand. The six robbers advanced, made confident by their numbers, their knives and their cudgels. A moment later, the lantern went out, dropped or tossed aside. This proved an advantage to Ewen, who knew he had no friends in the dark hall. He charged, swinging his sword. Deep growls came from his

throat, interspersed with yelps and howls. It was the noise
that settled the battle. The robbers, stumbling into one another
in the darkness and striking out at random, became terrified.
Surely this snarling creature was a madman or a demon. They
turned and ran. Ewen followed.

Merlin picked up the horn lantern and relit it. Two men
lay in the hall. One was dead, his head crushed by a cudgel
blow. The other wept noisily, holding onto his belly. Blood
welled between the robber's fingers. Merlin lifted his hands;
the man did the same, as if in imitation. Now the wound was
visible. It was deep. Intestines spilled out. A fatal wound,
unless the wizard used his magic. Why bother? England was
already well supplied with robbers and murderers. On the
other hand, no living thing should suffer, if the suffering
could be ended. Merlin gestured a second time. The man
slept, his hands falling to his sides. The wound continued to
bleed.

The other men were in the yard: one dead and two dying.
The last robber, a lad of fifteen or so, had scrambled to the
top of the manure heap and was slinging dung at Ewen, as
the naked man climbed toward him, coated now in blood and
excrement. The moon shone down on all of this. The noise
was terrific: the dying men groaning and calling out to God,
the boy screaming curses, Ewen howling.

"Heel!" called Merlin.

Ewen paused and shook his head as if to clear it, then
climbed down to join his master.

"Who planned this?" Merlin asked the boy on the dung
heap.

"My brother. The one who keeps the inn."

They searched for the innkeeper, but he was gone.

"When he comes back," said Merlin to the boy, "tell him
that he tried to rob Merlin the wizard, and that his comrades—"

"Our brothers," said the boy. "There were seven of us,
and you have killed five."

"Tell him that his brothers were killed by my famous white
hound, which I turned into a man for the night. If I ever hear
anything about the two of you again, I'll send him back as a

dog or a man or something worse than either; and I'll tell him to spare no one.''

They cleaned up and left, going into the forest. Merlin guided them with the horn lantern, which shone more brightly than before. They stopped finally. Ewen gathered wood in the lantern's light: by this time it was a second moon, shining under the trees.

"That could lead them to us," Ewen said.

Merlin gestured. The lantern grew dim. Ewen built his fire in almost-darkness. When it was burning well, the lantern went out. The lad cared for their horses, while Merlin sat by the fire. His dark, lined faced looked weary.

At length, the young man joined him, pulling out the sword he'd used against the robbers and making sure that it was entirely clean. That done, he resheathed the weapon and unfastened the collar around his neck. "I'll miss it."

Merlin took the collar and put it away. "You did well tonight. It may be time for you to consider becoming a man."

"I was always good at doing harm," said Ewen. "In any case, it wasn't necessary. You were there. You could have turned them all into toads."

"Magic has more to do with form than substance," Merlin said after a moment. "If I had turned them into toads, they would have been extremely large toads. It's possible that their new shape and structure—the toad skeletons and muscles and organs—would not have been sufficient given their size, which would have been the size of men. They might have collapsed in on themselves and died of their own weight."

"Small loss," said Ewen.

"If this hadn't happened, you would have been dealing with mouths large enough to swallow you and long grasping tongues." The wizard paused again.

Ewen waited. He'd leaned back on his elbows and stretched his legs in front of him, comfortable in spite of the scratches and bruises he'd gotten in the fight. Tomorrow he'd feel all his injuries, as he knew. Tonight he felt tired and content.

"There is another possibility," the wizard said finally. "Magic likes to follow the rules of nature, to create things that are possible and have existed, if not now, then in the past. If I had tried to enchant the robbers in the way you have suggested, they might have turned into the ancient relatives of toads. Some of these animals were as large as men. Some were carnivores with heads like mastiffs and teeth that could put your teeth to shame.''

''My dog teeth?'' asked Ewen.

The wizard nodded. ''The Flood, or some other catastrophe, destroyed these creatures. The world does not need to see them again.''

''You are less powerful than I thought,'' Ewen said.

Merlin considered, then answered. ''For the most part, magic has to do with seeing. I saw your canine nature at the ford. I saw Arthur's future while he was *in utero*.''

Ewen knew some Latin by this time, as well as a little Arabic and Hebrew. He had no trouble understanding *in utero*.

''Doing is more difficult,'' the wizard added. ''Though it can be done.'' He glanced up, smiling. ''As you know.''

In the morning, they continued, riding through the forest shadow. The road they followed was narrow and grey. Sunlight stippled it like the spots on a trout.

As Ewen had expected, he hurt all over. Conversation might be a distraction. He said, ''I've been thinking of those animals, the ancestors of toads. How do you know about them? Are they in the Bible or Aristotle?''

His knowledge did not come from human texts, whether sacred or profane, Merlin said. Rather, he had learned it from the fairies. Humans knew those folk as students of magic, and so they were, but they studied nature with an equal zeal, and they were obsessed with the passage of time. ''They have dug out the bones that are preserved in stone, and they know these are not the bones of giants, nor are they unusual mineral formations. Rather, they are the remains of animals, unlike any animal alive today.''

Using magic, the fairy scholars had recreated these ancient animals. ''Some are solid and alive,'' Merlin told Ewen. ''The fairies keep them as pets or use them as the prey for their hunts. But most of the animals—especially the enormous ones—are illusory. A reptile the size of a feasting hall would be difficult to make, difficult to feed and possibly dangerous."

Ewen nodded his agreement.

Illusions, on the other hand, were safe, economical, and comparatively easy to make. The fairy scholars could study them, without having to cage or feed them. The fairies who were not scholars could take pleasure in their strangeness.

Ewen asked about the real animals in fairyland, the ones that could fight and had to be fed. Merlin described what he had seen on his visits to the Fair Realm: elephants covered with shaggy fur, pill bugs as big as his palm, a toothy creature with a sail on its back, a toothy creature that ran on two legs and gathered food with sharp-clawed hands.

The shaggy elephants had tusks that curved like hunting horns. The pill bugs had large eyes faceted like jewels. The sail creature was like a salamander, save that it was as big as a man and had a thick, leathery hide. The creature that ran on two legs could be compared to nothing.

The fairies had tried to train these bipeds, as they might have trained ostriches or humans; the creatures proved to be intractably wild. "Instead of being turned into a new kind of hunting dog, they became a new kind of quarry; and the fairies have bred dogs to course them and bring them down. The dogs are your size, when you are a hound, blue-grey in color with hanging jowls and long ears that are usually cropped. They are fearless, as they have to be. The bipeds have great curving claws on their feet, in addition to grasping hands and piercing teeth."

The Fair People were obsessed with all the aspects of time, Merlin told his companion. They studied the future as well as the past, though this area of study was full of challenge and obscurity. The future is always uncertain. Nonetheless, they had managed to create images of what the future might be like, and these also could be encountered in fairyland. "Though these illusions waver and shift and are rarely convincing." The wizard described groups of oddly dressed people, involved in activities that made little sense to him or the fairy scholars, and devices that seemed magical or perhaps like the devices made by ancient engineers such as Daedalus.

Cities would appear in the distance, at times as bright as adamant, at other times dark and wreathed in smoke. If one
approached the cities, they receded. They could never be
reached, nor could travelers get close enough to see them
clearly. Instead, the travelers were left with confused impres-
sions—of puissance, valor, and confidence or poverty, sadness, and pain.

Ewen had small use for illusion or for the future. Better to
concentrate on what was present and real. He glanced around.
Large ferns lined the road, so green that they seemed to glow
with their own light. Farther back, in the forest shadow, fungi
dotted the trunks of trees. Ewen recognized a number of kinds
and recited the names to himself, as a charm against unreality:
Jew's Ear, Dryad's Saddle, Witch's Butter, Poor Man's Beef.

Some of the animals in fairyland sounded interesting: the
real ones, not the illusions. Maybe some day his master would
take him there. In dog form, he'd chase the bipeds.

That evening they came to a village, and Merlin bought liniment from the local witch, a tall handsome woman of more
than fifty. She offered to put the liniment on. "I have the
healing touch. But maybe you'd prefer to do this yourself,
Merlin."

As much as possible, he did not touch the boy when he
was human. In any case, this was a situation that required
rubbing rather than magic. His own hands were stiff. He nodded his agreement to the witch's plan, and they entered her
cottage: a single room, lit by a fire that flared up as they
entered. Herbs hung from the rafters. Sealed pots stood along
the walls. A pallet lay in one corner, and there were two three-
legged stools. Merlin took one. The witch took the other. The
boy settled in front of her on the dirt floor.

It was disturbing to watch the witch's dark strong fingers
move over Ewen's back, the pale skin mottled with bruises.
The lad's evident pleasure was also disturbing, how he leaned
back against the hands, eyes closed and full lips faintly smiling. "Soon," Merlin told himself, "I am going to have an
erection, and the witch will notice." It was the kind of thing
that witches noticed. She might remember the old gossip

about the wizard. It wasn't likely she'd disapprove. It was churchmen, not witches, who called sodomy a sin. But she was likely to make a joke, and then the boy would know for certain what went on in his master's mind.

Merlin excused himself and took a walk by the river. When he got back, the two of them were on the floor, naked and entangled. The boy was incorrigible! Merlin stepped forward, intending to grab Ewen by the scruff of the neck and pull him off the woman.

"Get that look off your face," the witch said. "And take another walk. The boy is younger than I am, but old enough to know what he's doing. I used no charms. Both of us are willing."

He went back to the river. Swallows flew back and forth over the water like shuttles in a loom, though they wove nothing except the death of bugs and obedience to their own natures. Merlin waited till darkness, then returned to the cottage a second time.

They spent the night there. Twice Merlin woke to the sound of Ewen and the woman coupling. "Patience," he told himself. "You are old enough to have learned patience."

In the morning, the witch gave them food for their journey and a second jar of liniment. "You have a fine big penis," she said to Ewen. "And you're certainly willing to use it. But you lack skill. If your master ever lets you go, come to me. I'll teach you how to fuck properly."

Ewen blushed. The witch laughed.

Late in the morning, Merlin asked, "What would you have done if she'd been unwilling?"

"Have I learned restraint? Some, but probably not enough." Ewen paused to watch a woodpecker flash—black, white, and red—across the road. "It really is easier being a dog."

They traveled north. Rain fell, and the weather was unseasonably cool. Merlin's joints hurt. "We'll stay with lords this time, and I'll be the king's wizard."

Ewen, riding miserably through a misty rain, lifted his head. He'd be a dog again.

"You'll be a youth of good family, not yet a knight."

"*Why?*"

"I want you to practice being a man."

He said nothing in reply, knowing it was futile to argue with Merlin in weather like this.

"If you forget your manners and act doggishly—well, it's a long distance from the north to Camelot; and these northerners might not even notice."

The lords along the border made them welcome. These were rough men, who guarded King Arthur's realm against the incursions of bandits, infidels and Scots, as well as an occasional monster or dragon. Most were loyal in their way; all knew enough to treat the royal wizard with respect.

Ewen puzzled the lords. A promising lad, but past the age when most northern boys were knighted. He did not seem to be sickly or clerical. Everything in the south went at an odd pace, either too slowly or too quickly; and a lad in Merlin's care must be noble or even royal, though maybe not legitimate. They did not puzzle further. Instead, they loaned him armor and told their younger sons to treat him well.

By days, he practiced the arts of war or hunted on horseback, though he would sooner have run four-footed in the baying pack, as he told Merlin privately.

"Patience," said the wizard.

He killed a boar with a spear, on foot after his horse fell. The lord of that keep offered to make him a knight.

"Not yet," said Merlin. "I'm not satisfied with his manners."

"What use are manners to a soldier? D'you think dragons care about manners? Or Scots, for that matter?"

"I see things you do not," Merlin said firmly.

The lord grew quiet then.

At another keep, Ewen joined a war band going after thieves who had taken twenty head of the lord's best cattle. They got most of the cattle back, but all the thieves escaped.

When they returned, the lord held a feast, honoring the warriors who'd recovered his favorite cow, a great rough beast with wide horns. "A fountain of milk," said the lord with satisfaction. "And the daughters she's produced! She is a mother of queens!"

Ewen sat among his comrades from the war band, drinking as little as possible and trying to ignore the serving women. This had happened in other keeps. The women brushed against him. The men made sly remarks and gave him mocking names: Master Prudence, Master Silence, the Squire without Reproach.

Always before this, he'd managed to control himself. Tonight, he could feel the control slipping, though he wasn't certain why. The lord's lewd praise for his favorite cow and for the bull they'd recovered? The noisiness in the hall? Or his own weariness, after the long chase toward the Scottish border and over many weeks of self-restraint?

He knew what he wanted: to be a dog again, close to Merlin rather than separated by half the feasting hall. It had never been said aloud, but he knew this would be his reward, if he passed the test that Merlin had set him.

If he did not—Ewen shivered. Merlin might refuse to change him. He might remain as he was, awkward and uncomfortable. Worst of all, the wizard might cast him out to wander through England in human form.

The soldier next to him pushed a woman into his lap. She screamed and grabbed hold of Ewen. He wrapped one arm around her waist and with his other hand pushed up her skirt, knowing what he'd find—a wet furry hole like the witch's, though most likely wetter and furrier. The witch had been old. His penis was engorged. He would mount the woman here. Most likely, the men around him would cheer.

Merlin's hand gripped his shoulder. Merlin's voice said, "Down."

He shivered and withdrew his hand, pushed the girl away and stood. Merlin was sitting next to the lord, having never moved.

"You have a prick," said one of the other men. "We can see it. Why are you so unwilling to use it?"

"A promise," he said with difficulty. "To Merlin."

"Is he teaching you magic? Does that art require that you be celibate?"

"A hard art, if this is so," said a second man.

A third man said, "Nay, if this is so, then we must call magic a soft art, rather than a hard one, for it requires softness rather than hardness in those who practice it. Look at our squire now. His male member has diminished to nothing. If we believe him, this is the influence of magic and the wizard Merlin."

Oh God, thought Ewen, and turned and left the hall. It was raining again. He stood in the muddy yard, face lifted to the dark sky, a howl forming in his throat. He pressed his lips together. The test was too difficult. He could not endure it. On the morrow, he'd go down on his knees to Merlin and beg for an end.

"No," the wizard said. "You will continue. You did well last night." He reached out a hand, the fingers stiff with age and the weather, and touched Ewen's golden hair. "Surely it is nobler to be what you are now."

"If you hadn't intervened, I would have treated that servant the way I tried to treat the maiden at the ford. How is this noble? These men along the border are animals and do not know it. I know what I am, Merlin. Let me be content."

"Winter draws near," the wizard said finally. "Arthur waits in Camelot. Be patient. Your test is almost over."

The northern foliage began to change. So did the weather, though too late to save most of the harvest. They rode south in sunlight, through drying fields.

"Something in the north has been troubling me," said Merlin. "A sense of darkness, a feeling of oppression. For that reason I stayed as long as I did, talking to the beldams and the local magicians, trying to discover the nature of the problem. I thought a dragon might be stirring or maybe a pestilence was beginning to spread, though most plagues come to us from France."

He stretched his aching shoulders, enjoying the sun's heat. "Maybe the problem was the weather. My vision was cloudy because it was a vision of clouds."

Ewen had pulled his shirt off and rode bare to the waist, his fair skin turning ruddy. Looking at him, Merlin realized how much the lad had changed in the time he'd spent free of enchantment. His adolescent ranginess was gone. Thick muscles covered his long tall frame. His hair, which had been ragged and unruly, was short and neatly trimmed. So was the beard he'd grown. So much in only a summer, the wizard thought.

When they got close to Camelot, they stopped with a farmer, an old friend of Merlin's. That evening, the wizard got out the gold collar. "Are you certain?"

"Yes."

The wizard felt perturbed and must have looked it. "You can't take me into Camelot like this," said Ewen. "How would you explain me? Arthur knows you have no noble ward, and he certainly knows I'm not a royal bastard; and if you think I want to listen to orders from Kay or insults from the rest of Arthur's knights—the royal hounds have better manners."

The farm was built in the ruins of an ancient Roman farm. There was a tiled pool that still held water. Ewen bathed carefully—he was always cleanly—dried himself, folded his clothes and packed them, then put on the collar. "Now."

Merlin gestured. Where the man had stood was a white hound, tail wagging, tongue lolling, a look of amusement in the hazel eyes.

Ewen's horse stayed with the farmer, who knew better than to ask questions about the vanished companion or the suddenly present dog. That afternoon, they were in Camelot. Arthur greeted Merlin with a hug and gave the hound a brisk rub over the head and shoulders. "How can I do less for the sire of my kennels?" Then he took his wizard off for a conference. The white hound followed.

They talked first about the harvest in the north, the lords there, the Scottish menace, then about other problems which concerned Arthur: rebellious barons, false knights, rival kings, and a dragon on the Welsh border.

Finally, Arthur got to his chief concern. "It's Guinevere. I know she pines for children."

"Pining" was not a word that Merlin would have used for the queen. She was a large, rosy, healthy woman with enough energy for ten or twenty children. Lacking these children—there were not even any royal bastards for her to gather and raise, except for Borre, who had a perfectly good and noble mother, unwilling to give her son up—Guinevere did her best to keep busy in other ways. Camelot was full of the hangings that she and her ladies embroidered: the deeds of Sir Hercules and King Alexander in the feasting hall, the deeds of the saints and prophets in the royal chapel, blooming gardens in the royal bower and the rooms used by royal and noble guests. This was in addition to all the everyday work a queen must do: managing the king's household, training his pages, greeting his guests of high and low degree—kings, nobles, prelates, bards, and jugglers. Guinevere was especially fond of the jugglers. She was a woman in love with activity.

When Arthur made royal progresses, she accompanied him.

"She stops to visit with every good wife famous for her herbal lore and every hermit famous for his piety," the king said. "It's obvious why. I have the most famous wizard in the kingdom in my employ. I ask again, is there nothing you can do?"

"In the first place, don't presume that you know your wife's mind. Women are not easy to understand. Even I, with my vision, make mistakes about them. In the second place, my liege, I am not a village witch dealing in potions and cures, though I have met one recently who seems excellent to me. You can send for her, if you like. If she's honest, she'll tell you that the problem does not lie with Guinevere."

The king's fair skin reddened slightly. "Are you certain?"

"I've told you there's magic in your line. Most likely, one of your ancestors was a fairy. They are slow to reproduce and rarely have more than a child or two. If this were not so, they'd fill the world, since they age slowly and are difficult to kill.

"Sometimes they take our children, raise them and mate with them, hoping to produce offspring who combine fairy magic and endurance with human fecundity. In general, the fairies tell me, these experiments do not achieve the hoped-for end. Most of the half-breed children lack magical ability and die young, being barely a hundred or a hundred and fifty,

and they are only slightly more fertile than their fairy relatives.''

Merlin paused. Arthur looked uncomfortable.

''It's possible you might have better luck with a fairy wife
or with someone who, like you, has fairy blood. But I promise
nothing.''

The king shook his head. ''I love Guinevere. Tell me where
to find this witch.''

She came to Camelot on a white mare, a fine new cloak over
her shoulders. Arthur and Guinevere received her privately.
Afterward, she sought out Merlin. He was in his quarters,
reading the *Logic* of Aristotle, which a learned Jew of Cairo
had translated into Latin and sent to the wizard in return for
a book on fairy natural history. The white hound slept at his
feet.

Merlin greeted the woman and poured wine for her, which
she tasted before she spoke. ''I could have said 'no' to the
king, but not to that sweet lady. Where's your serving man?
Has he left you?''

''No.''

She laughed. ''You've hidden him, for fear that I'll seduce
him.''

Merlin stirred the white dog with a foot. Ewen, who was
dreaming of deer or possibly of bipeds, made a wuffing
sound.

''What did you tell them?'' Merlin asked the witch.

She tried the wine a second time, giving it so thorough an
assay that Merlin had to refill her cup.

''I gave the queen a potion that will calm her. In my experience, women who fret have trouble breeding, especially
if the thing they fret about is their infertility. Why this is, I
don't know, though worry can disrupt the behavior of the
body in many ways. Also, it's possible that the queen's activity—especially the traveling she does—is having an ad-
verse effect on her female functions, though I have certainly
known farm wives who worked as hard as any queen and
bred like rabbits.

''I'm not happy with the number of shrines she visits. Or

with the hermits. A pestilent lot! Full of vermin and bad advice! I told her to travel less, and if she must talk with religious folk, let them be seemly nuns and clerics who wash.''

Merlin smiled and stirred the dog again. This time Ewen was silent.

''I told the king to wear loose clothing whenever possible. Monks and priests have no trouble fathering children. I have long suspected it's their clothing that makes them fertile.''

''None of this will do any harm,'' said Merlin. ''No good either, I fear.''

''I could not say 'no' to the lady,'' the witch replied, finished her wine and rose to go. Merlin escorted her to the door of his quarters. She glanced up at him, her face flushed with wine. ''I'm going to the kitchen to brew a tisane for Sir Kay. He suffers from headaches, he has told me. After that, I'll go to my room. I would like company, if your serving man is free and willing.''

Merlin closed the door behind her, then walked back to his study. The white hound was up on all fours, ears lifted and tail wagging.

''Do you think you can behave in a seemly fashion, like a knight, instead of a cur?''

The tail-wagging grew more furious.

''Very well,'' the wizard said after a moment. ''I imagine this woman can take care of herself, but you are to act as if she were the mildest and silliest of maidens. Do you understand?''

The dog wagged harder.

Laughing, Merlin changed him into a man. He dressed quickly, pulling clothing from one of Merlin's chests, then hurried through the palace, already dark in the early evening of autumn.

In dog-form he had explored every corridor; and he had no trouble finding the witch's lodging-place. (In any case, she had described the location to Merlin.) At the moment, it was empty, unlit and as black as pitch. But the witch's aroma was everywhere. He could smell it through all the other odors: the dry herbs in the bedclothes, the dry rushes on the floor, the dust in corners and—very faintly—a mold.

He undressed and realized, when he was done, that he was still wearing the hound's gold collar. No time to take it back to Merlin. He wanted to be in the room when the witch arrived. He unfastened the collar and hid it in the middle of his clothing, then settled on the bed, among blankets that smelled of herbs and the woman.

She took longer than he had expected, in his eagerness. At last, the door opened. The witch entered, carrying a lamp. In the dim glow cast by it, she took on the appearance of a young matron, blooming the way some women do after their first few children.

Ewen raised himself on an elbow. She glanced at him, her dark eyes shining, then laughed and blew out the light.

He listened to the sound of her undressing, then felt her settle on top of him, astride his hips. In this fashion they coupled the first time: the witch on top and riding like a knight in a tournament.

The second time was side by side. They were both less eager than the first time. Their coupling was slow, gentle, and affectionate. When they finished, Ewen fell asleep.

He woke to lamplight. The witch stood in the middle of her room, dressed in a plain white shift. In one of her hands was the lamp, now relit. Her other hand held his gold collar.

"How have I deserved this?" she said.

Puzzled, he did not answer.

"I am a woman of no great birth, never beautiful, no longer young—those being the only virtues a village woman may have, as I know. My skills are nothing much, compared to Merlin's art and science. Your master might well look down on me. But to play such a trick! To make me couple with his dog!"

Now Ewen understood the expression on her face. As quickly as possible, he explained he was a man. "Though I have spent most of my time as a dog in recent years. Still, I began my life in human form, and my birth was gentle."

"Why did Merlin turn you into a dog?"

Ewen flushed with shame, sat up and told the story of his life before he met the wizard.

The witch listened, frowning. When he finished, she said,

"I'm glad that Merlin did not trick me into an act contrary to nature, which requires us to mate with our own kind. But it doesn't sound as if you're much of a man."

He flushed again and nodded.

"Though you were young and had a bad upbringing. That much is evident. Have you learned to do better?"

"I don't know."

She glanced at the collar and held it out. "Put it on."

He obeyed, then looked up. The witch wore a smile that combined affection with malice. "It certainly is a fine piece of jewelry, fit for a prince or king; and now that I know you're a man, I like how it looks on you." She set the lamp down, came over, bent and kissed him, one hand resting on his shoulder. Her fingers touched the collar. He could feel her caressing the gold links.

He pulled her down, pushing up the shift, which was made of wool, coarse and prickly. They coupled a third time, with less vigor than the first time, but more passion than the second, then slept tangled together.

At dawn, he returned to Merlin's quarters. The wizard had spent the night with Aristotle and was still up, a lamp burning next to him.

Ewen told him about the witch's discovery, then added, "I will never know enough to be a man."

"What makes you say that?" asked Merlin.

"Why was she disgusted by the collar, then enticed by it?"

"That's a question she will have to answer, though every witch and magician knows that things have many qualities that can be called accidental—or, if these qualities are not entirely accidental, then they are capable of variation, depending on context and use. The same herb may be a medicine or a poison. A knife can be used for surgery or murder. A gold collar on a man does not have the same meaning as a gold collar on a dog.

"Also—" The wizard closed his book. "Actions performed in knowledge and through choice are not the same as actions performed in ignorance, without decision. No one likes to be tricked."

Ewen frowned, not understanding much of this. Merlin told

him to go to bed. When he woke again, midway through the morning, he was a hound.

The witch left, having promised Merlin that she would keep Ewen's secret. "If you ever decide to let him remain a man, send him to me. He needs teaching, and not by men. This father of his seems to have almost ruined him, and I'm not certain about the education you have given him."

For a while after that, Guinevere took the witch's potion, and Arthur wore long robes, made by his wife and richly embroidered, so he looked (his knights said) as fine as a priest at mass.

But the potion made Guinevere languid and drowsy. She missed her energy. Kay the seneschal took Arthur aside and told him in full what the knights were saying.

"You can't keep the respect of rough fellows like these, if you dress like a priest or a lady. This isn't Constantinople or even Rome."

Arthur sighed and nodded.

"Just as well," Merlin said later to his white hound. "The queen was nodding off in the middle of banquets, and Arthur could not learn to manage his robes. He kept tripping over the hems."

Ewen listened, while chewing on his flank. Something itched in an infuriating fashion.

"Do you have fleas again?" Merlin asked, but didn't wait for an answer. "I've not told this to anyone, but the king is not fated to have a legitimate heir. I have seen this and also seen—" Merlin paused. "Harm will come to him from a child he fathers. I've been watching young Borre for years now. He seems a harmless lad. Maybe he'll turn malevolent as he ages, or maybe there is someone else I don't know about. My vision isn't as clear as it used to be. Time vanquishes everything."

Not you, thought Ewen.

The beginning of the end was ordinary: one of Arthur's fellow kings came to Camelot on a visit, bringing in his train a maiden, slim and comely with black eyes and hair. Her face was pale, except for a faint blush in the cheeks, as if wild roses—the kind that bloom along every road in spring—bloomed there. Her name was Nimue.

In the old story, it says that Merlin became "sotted," a word that means "foolish, stupid, drunk, or wasted." A sot is a dolt, a blockhead or a soaker: harsh words to use on a man so old, wise, and learned.

What happened was this: Nimue was interested in magic. While the king she followed spent time with Arthur, she sought out Arthur's ancient wizard, drawn by his wisdom and learning. Even his age was attractive, or so she explained to Merlin. Wisdom is not found in the young. Nor is true learning, which requires not only memorization, but also pondering and the testing of learned truths by experience.

Merlin, in his turn, was attracted by her interest in magic, as well as by her beauty. Ewen disliked her at once, though she fawned on him, rubbing his red ears and his snow-white neck and shoulders, praising him to his master. What a fine dog! How handsome and famous! He wanted to bite her.

How could Merlin, the wisest man in England, fail to see the calculating look in Nimue's dark eyes and fail to hear the falsity in her honey-sweet voice?

Maybe falsity is too harsh a word. Beyond any question Nimue was interested in magic and respected Merlin as a magician. But she had no interest in him as a man, as Ewen could tell by her odor and her expression, when Merlin turned away from her.

Merlin, on the other hand, was in love, as he had not been for years. That a woman so young and fair and graceful should be drawn to him! She was intelligent, as well, and knew something of magic already, enough to ask him good questions. She listened to his answers intently, her dark eyes fixed on him.

Ewen, at Merlin's feet, felt the fur on his back prickle and his upper lip lift. A growl was forming in his throat. He pushed his head down between his paws, trying to keep his hatred hidden, telling himself to be patient. The visiting king would not stay forever. When he left, he'd take the woman, and Merlin would recover.

So it went, through late spring and early summer, until the king—Nimue's host and Arthur's guest—made ready to return home. Merlin asked Nimue to stay in Camelot.

"The city is growing hot," she said in answer. "Soon it will be filled with flies and foul aromas. I will not remain in such a place. Nor should you, Lord Merlin. A man as venerable as you, a repository of so much knowledge, should guard himself against discomfort, which can lead to disease." She added that she had a villa in the country. "Which the ancient Romans built and my relatives restored to its former splendor and dignity. Come there with me."

That evening, at the end of yet another long feast and drinking bout in honor of Arthur's guest, Merlin walked back to his rooms. Ewen was beside him. The dog was uneasy, nudging his master and nipping at the old man's hand. When they were alone, Merlin changed him and said, "What is it?"

It had been months since Ewen had been a man. Something had happened. He no longer felt comfortable with nakedness. His human body seemed horribly bare. It was difficult to stand upright and face the wizard, who was frowning at him, obviously angry. Prescient as always, the old man knew he wasn't going to like what Ewen had to say. The youth thought of dropping back down on all fours, so his belly and genitals would be protected. Instead, he pulled a robe from one of Merlin's chests and put it on.

"Speak!" said the wizard.

Ewen tried, but he'd never been good at talking, and most of what he knew was canine, having to do with Nimue's scent and the tone of her voice, the way she moved, how her hands felt when she petted him or tugged his ears. The woman was selfish and dishonest. As wise as Merlin was, he was being tricked.

The wizard listened. His eyes—usually a soft faded blue, like cloth washed many times and laid out in the sun to dry—darkened, becoming the hard blue-grey color of steel. Ewen faltered and finally stopped.

"Do you think I'll listen to a dog about such matters? Or to a rapist? You have not learned much, have you, in all your years at Camelot? Not respect for women, nor courtesy, nor chivalry. My fault, I suppose. I should have kept you a man and sent you to the witch or to a monastery. What can a dog learn, except obedience and odors?''

Loyalty and love, Ewen thought. A dog can learn those as well. But he could not force his tongue to move and speak.

''I intend to go with Nimue,'' the wizard said. ''If you wish, you can stay here. Arthur will take good care of you, though he will treat you like a dog, as I never have. Or you can go to the witch in human form. That might be best.''

And leave the old man with Nimue, who stank of falsity? No. Ewen shook his head. ''Take me with you.''

Merlin pondered, saying finally, ''If I do, you will have to remain a dog. I want no more conversations like this one.''

Ewen agreed.

The three of them set out several days later, the wizard and maiden on palfreys, Ewen running beside them in dog form. The weather was pleasant, once they left the closeness of Camelot, and their journey ordinary. Because he traveled with a woman, Merlin stopped in the houses of noblemen and the hostels maintained by religious orders. In most of these places, Ewen stayed in the stables. Every morning, it seemed to him, Merlin looked happier and younger, though the wizard did not smell of satisfied lust. Nor did Nimue smell like a bitch who'd been mounted. Her odor remained the same as always: a combination of eau de rose and something Ewen could not put into words: self-containment, aloofness, an absence of sensuality so marked that it became a presence.

It was not lust that had transformed the wizard, but rather love and hope.

The villa, when they reached it, proved to be on an island in the middle of a lake and hidden by trees, so no one on the lake shore could tell the island was inhabited.

They left their horses and rowed across in a small boat. Ewen, at the prow, felt his fur go up. Something about this place was uncanny. Merlin, pulling the heavy oars, noticed nothing except his own strength—surprising in a man of his age—and a sense of happiness.

It was, in fact, a Roman villa, restored as if by magic, though a bit dusty at the moment. The floors were covered with mosaics and the walls with paintings: the deeds of Dame Venus, portrayed in the style of the ancients but with colors so fresh and bright that they could not be genuinely Roman. In one room, she rose from the ocean, as naked and lovely as a pearl. In another room, Prince Paris awarded her the golden apple. A third room showed her husband Vulcan exposing her adultery. The goddess lay with the war god Mars, the two of them imprisoned by a net, which Vulcan had made through magic and thrown over them, as they coupled. Mars grimaced, and rage was evident on Vulcan's face, but the lovely goddess remained tranquil, faintly smiling, as if none of this—her infidelity, her exposure, the trap that held her—mattered.

Nimue guided them through the villa, then out into the garden that surrounded it. If she had servants, they were careless. The garden had a half-wild look. Still, it was full of midsummer flowers, roses especially. Sweet aromas filled the air.

Some of his old acuteness returned to Merlin. "This place is a wonder. Who are your relatives?"

Nimue smiled. "I have kin in fairyland."

She settled on a marble bench, and Merlin settled next to her, Ewen at his feet, panting a little in the midday heat. There, in the overgrown and aromatic garden, the maiden told her story. She was one of the fairy experiments, not an ordinary hybrid but the product of generations of interbreeding between fairies and the human children they stole. In the end, it had been decided that the experiment was a failure. Her line would not be continued.

"The fairies had no further use for me, and I did not wish to stay in their country. There is enough of them in me so I'm not especially affected by their enchantments. Pure humans are and rarely leave, if they have the chance to stay, though you have come and gone many times, as I have heard."

Merlin said, "Yes."

She picked a rose and turned it in her hands. "They would have let me stay. They recognize their obligation to me and the other hybrids. But I didn't want to be a poor relation, and

I didn't want to grow old, while my cousins remained as fresh and blooming as this rose.''

While she spoke, she tore at the rose, apparently without noticing what she was doing. When she glanced down finally, nothing remained in her hands except the stalk. Her lap was full of bright red petals. Nimue laughed and stood, brushing the petals off, then invited Merlin into the house.

They remained there for the rest of the summer, while Merlin taught Nimue about magic. She had little interest in the other things he knew: the logic of Aristotle, the philosophy of Plato, the medicine and mathematics he had learned as a young man, traveling in India and China. Now and then, she would permit the old man to speak of such things. Ewen listened, feeling more comfortable with human knowledge than with the spells that fascinated Nimue.

The house remained empty except for the three of them. Meals appeared out of the air. So did music, pipes and stringed instruments playing through the long summer evenings. The musicians were never visible, nor were the instruments they played.

Though the house was always a little dusty and slovenly, it never became dirty. It was being cleaned somehow, by someone, though never thoroughly. This was no surprise to Ewen. Merlin had told him years before that the stories humans told about the excellent work of spirits were untrue. ''Some are quick, but also careless and slipshod. Others are so meticulous that they finish nothing. Their idea of what's important is not the same as ours. With the best will in the world—and they often lack good will—they can't do a job to our satisfaction.''

The garden remained ragged, but never turned entirely wild. Sometimes, in the morning, they would find bouquets throughout the house, filling the rooms with sweet aromas. Merlin must be doing this, thought Ewen. The old man remained sotted. Now that they were alone, away from other people, his passion grew stronger and more obvious. He began to court Nimue as a lover would, praising her beauty, speaking of his own desire, creating illusions to amuse and entice her.

Some days, the mountains of China rose outside the villa, tall and strangely shaped. Mist floated among them. The sky above was pearly grey. Now and then, Ewen saw a flash of green or blue. At first, he thought these were breaks in the clouds through which he could see the sunlit upper heavens. No, as Merlin explained to Nimue. The flashes of color were Chinese dragons. Unlike the local English dragons, who were compounded largely of earth and fire and liked living underground and causing trouble, the oriental dragons were creatures of air and water, who lived in the clouds as well as in lakes, rivers, and the Great Eastern Ocean. As a rule, they were beneficent, though powerful and very proud.

On other days, Ewen went out and found the meadows of fairyland. Animals grazed there such as he had never seen before: huge quadrupeds, their faces and necks covered with helmets made of bone and skin. Three horns—as straight and sharp as lances—protruded from each armored face.

He ran out among the animals, barking from pleasure. They, being illusions, ignored him. Still, it was pleasant to trot past gigantic leathery haunches and catch the gleam of a tiny eye, the pupil a vertical black line across an orange iris, or to sit and watch some massive cow or bull—he could not distinguish the sexes—shear grass with a great curving falcon-like beak.

Nimue was interested in the dragons, since they were magical. The quadrupeds were not, and she had seen them often before. "Make them vanish," she said to Merlin. The old man did.

She remained cool and aloof, interested in the wizard's skill, but not his body. Would any body have interested her? A handsome young knight? A fairy lord? The dog could not tell. She always smelled of distance and self-control.

Merlin's passion continued to grow, and his courtesy decreased. He began to stand close to Nimue and touch her as if by accident, his old withered hand brushing her arm or the fabric over her thigh. He spoke of his love, usually indirectly—hinting, making allusions, frowning, and heaving sighs.

She was growing angry. Ewen could see this and smell it.

But she would not send the old man away. She was too curious, too anxious to have Merlin's power and knowledge.

So the summer ended: in dry heat and a conflict of wills. Now, instead of flowers, Ewen smelled dying vegetation, the old man's frustrated lust, the woman's anger and dislike, which she hid from Merlin, but could not hide from Ewen. A bad situation! Beyond any question the woman was dangerous. He needed to speak with Merlin, to issue a warning. But how could he? The old wizard had to change him. Ewen nosed and licked Merlin's hand, whined softly, stared beseechingly.

"No," the wizard said. "I told you, no further conversation. You came here as a dog. A dog you will remain."

He had reached the limit of his endurance. He could no longer bear the sight of Merlin fawning over the woman, all his dignity and wisdom forgotten, sharing his magical knowledge with Nimue, giving her with open hands the power that made him the greatest wizard alive. In the end, Ewen knew, she would turn on his master.

Very well. If he could not speak as a man, he would act as a dog.

One morning he came upon Nimue in the garden. The day was already hot. She stood by a rose bush, as languid and drooping as the plant's last blowzy flowers, which she gathered, bending slightly, her long white neck exposed. The two of them were alone; and as far as he could tell, the woman did not realize that he was in the garden. He attacked, going straight for her throat.

The moment he began to move, she whirled, flinging her basket of flowers aside and raising an arm. His teeth closed on tender flesh, but it was not the flesh of her throat. Nimue screamed.

A moment later Merlin was with them.

The old man said nothing. Nor did he lift a hand. But Ewen felt as if he'd been struck by a giant. He let go of Nimue, falling to the ground and cowering in the dust of the garden path. The other two ignored him. The woman stood absolutely straight, holding her arm, from which blood gushed. Her lips were pressed together. No sound emerged.

The wizard touched her gently. The flow of blood stopped; the wound closed; and there was no evidence of Ewen's crime, save the bright splotches of blood on Nimue's white gown.

"Is the dog mad?"

Merlin glanced at Ewen. "He has no disease, if that's what you are asking."

"Kill him," Nimue said.

For a moment, Ewen thought the wizard would do it. Then Merlin shook his head. "I've had the brute for a long time. I won't kill him, even now. But I will tie him up."

He snapped his fingers. Ewen rose and followed him to the back of the garden. An old stone hut stood there, a storage place for garden tools and pots. Merlin led him inside. Ewen stood shaking in darkness while the wizard rummaged and found an iron collar fastened to an iron chain.

His gold collar came off; the iron collar was fastened in its place.

"When I have time, when I'm not otherwise occupied, I will decide what to do with you," Merlin said. He left the hut, closing and locking the door. Ewen began to whine. The wizard rapped on the door. Ewen found that he could make no noise.

At first, he lunged at the end of the chain, trying to break it and reach the door. At the same time, he tried to bark and howl. Neither effort produced any result, except his throat became sore, and the iron collar rubbed his neck until it was raw.

Finally, he gave up and sat. What had happened? Had he really been trying to kill Nimue? He reflected on the question, while licking his chest and paws. Some of Nimue's blood had spurted onto him. It tasted of salt and magic. Yes. Murder had been the plan, though not a deeply considered plan, but rather the impulse of a moment. Still, he had failed another test of chivalry. After years at Camelot and in Merlin's care, he'd ended as he began: a bad dog imprisoned in a hut, waiting for who knew what kind of punishment.

Ewen lay down in the dark, staring at the hut's locked door. A whimper formed in his throat like a tic that wouldn't go away. He couldn't release it, though he opened his mouth and yawned and shook his head, trying to break the noise free.

Late in the afternoon, two dishes appeared in the hut: one of water, the other of meat. Ewen ate and drank, then went to sleep.

He remained in the hut all autumn. Every day food and drink appeared, and his waste products vanished. The hut never became filthy, though it always smelled of dirt and dog. The sores on his neck became scabby and itched. Bugs came into the hut and bit him. These wounds itched as well. No one visited except the bugs and, now and then, a field mouse. The mice were timid and quick. He never managed to catch one.

In the high corners of the hut were spiders. They spun webs, catching a few of the bugs that tormented Ewen, like angels helping the damned just a little. Enough light shone in through cracks in the door so he could see his benefactors: little round bodies glowing in the sunlight, with as many legs as angels had wings.

The punishment was just, Ewen concluded. He had failed as a man and a dog.

And what was going on with Merlin? How could such a man succumb to lust and folly? The old man had, though Ewen was reluctant to admit this. Still, the dog thought, nosing at the problem, if he knew nothing else—not honor, not chivalry, not courtesy—he could recognize the urge to mount a bitch.

If Merlin had wandered from the *via media* and lost himself in wilderness, what hope was left for lesser men? Who could live wisely, if the wise could not? The problem was an itch, almost as painful as his bites and sores. He worried it whenever he was unoccupied by bugs, mice, or spiders. No answer came to him.

One day the door opened. Nimue stood before him, rimmed with sunlight. She gestured, and he felt himself change, becoming a man. The iron collar remained around his neck.

Nimue looked him over. "I wondered what lay under your enchantment. You're certainly handsome enough. Why couldn't Merlin be satisfied with you?"

He tried to speak and couldn't. She gestured a second time.

"He wasn't a man who fell in love with men," said Ewen. "What's happened to him?"

"Of course he was a lover of men. Did you know nothing about him? And of women also, of course. He would not leave me alone, though I tried every way I could to hint him off."

Ewen went up on one knee. It seemed more decent than standing, naked as he was, and less humiliating than remaining on all fours. He leaned cautiously against the chain. It held. The collar cut into his neck. "Where is he?" His voice sounded rough.

"Under a stone. A big one, which ought to serve to hold him down, though he lifted it with a gesture. There was a treasure under the stone, which he wanted to show me. He was always trying to show me wonders, as if they could win me. As a teacher, yes. I wanted nothing more than to be his student. But his leman? No.

"He went into the pit beneath the stone, the stone hanging above him, held in midair by magic; and he opened the chests and jars that held the treasure, pulling out—oh, necklaces and bracelets made of gold, silver goblets with satyrs dancing on them, bowls engraved with nymphs and goddesses, and glass that had been transmuted by time, so it shone as many-colored as an opal. All the while he smiled at me from a face made of wrinkles.

"I knew the charm he used to raise the boulder and used it to bring the boulder down."

"He's dead then," said Ewen, his heart full of sorrow.

Nimue shook her head. "It's not easy to kill a man so powerful. He is trapped beneath the stone and tangled in the spells he set to guard the place. But most likely he's still alive and will remain so."

"This was a bad action," Ewen said. "Unkind, discourteous, ungrateful, and lacking in respect. He was your teacher, an old man and very wise."

"Don't talk to me of courtesy and kindness. He made you a dog and chained you in this hut; he was after me day and night to have sex with him. Was this courteous? Or kind? Did

he respect my maidenhood or your manhood? Who knows
what he might have done next—a man of such great power,
no longer held in rein by reason?''

Ewen frowned, trying to puzzle out right and wrong. ''I'm
here as punishment, for trying to harm you and for other
crimes.''

''Is that so? I could ask what you've done. But it's not my
concern. Nor does it interest me.'' Nimue turned as if to go.

''I'll die here, if you leave me chained.''

She turned back. ''Then you have an argument with Merlin. You don't believe you deserve what's happened to you.''

''I'd prefer not to die, especially here and now. As to my
deserts, I can't answer you. I don't think Merlin would have
killed me or let me die.''

She tilted her head, considering. He waited, still on one
knee. Finally she snapped her fingers. The iron collar opened
and fell away.

Ewen leaped to his feet, lunging at Nimue. He moved less
quickly and gracefully than he had before his imprisonment.
None the less he reached her.

As soon as he laid hands on her, she turned into a dragon
of the western variety, as black as iron, rather than blue or
green. Magic is mostly illusion, Ewen told himself and held
on tightly. The dragon twisted its long serpentine neck,
opened a mouth full of teeth like daggers and spat a gout of
fire into his face.

He screamed with pain, but his grip did not loosen, though
his face felt as if a mask of red hot metal had been fastened
over it, which burned through skin and flesh to the bones of
his skull.

The pain should have killed him or at least made him let
go. It didn't. *Ergo*, it was illusion.

As soon as he decided this, the dragon became a fish as
long as he was tall. It thrashed in his arms: cold, slimy and
powerful. Better than a dragon, Ewen thought, though difficult to hold. He tightened his grip further. His face still hurt.

The fish became an eagle, which he gripped around the
lower body. The creature beat him with broad strong wings.

As the feathers brushed his face, he felt pieces of flesh fall away.

The bird lasted only briefly, turning into a spotted cat that screamed (a sound like the scream of an eagle) and bit Ewen in the neck. Blood, his own blood, ran into Ewen's lungs. He was drowning.

The cat became a troll with green skin and foul stinking breath. Ewen's arms were locked around the creature's torso. Its arms were free and beat his head and shoulders like a pair of hammers, wielded by two strong smiths. His face was almost gone by now, and blood filled his lungs, so he was no longer able to breathe. What an illusion! His old master was without equal, and Nimue had obviously been an exceptional student.

The troll became a slim young man, who stood quietly in Ewen's arms. The lad had all of Nimue's beauty, transformed so it (and he) was clearly masculine.

"Well," said the youth. "You are certainly brave, or else extremely stupid. I can't tell which. Why are you holding me?"

"I won't let you go till you promise to free Merlin," Ewen said. He looked down at the lad and thought, why should I trust him? This is still Nimue. "I won't let you go till Merlin is free."

The youth shook his head. "You're no danger to me. But if the old man were free and had the use of his powers, there's no place on Earth where I'd be safe."

"Then you are trapped, as he is trapped," said Ewen.

"Don't be ridiculous," said the youth and clicked his tongue.

Ewen's arms fell to his sides, heavy and powerless. His entire body seemed made of stone.

The youth stepped back, and Ewen could see him clearly for the first time. Dark curls fell around his shoulders. His straight young torso was garbed in fine mail; a sword with a jeweled hilt hung at his side; and his tall boots were made of a leather so thin and soft it must have come from fairyland or Constantinople. Ewen had never seen a knight or squire more comely or better dressed.

"Can you swim?" Nimue asked.

"Not well."

"I'll send the boat back for you. By the time this spell wears off, I'll be long gone. Don't bother to look for me or Merlin. You won't find either of us. If you get hungry, there are plants in the back of the garden. My kin brought them from a land in the distant west. Their fruit will give you both food and drink. Farewell." The lad turned and walked off, stepping lightly and whistling with right good cheer. Long after he'd vanished from sight, Ewen heard the whistle, still clear but growing gradually fainter, as if Nimue were departing into an unimaginably distant place. A trick of magic, Ewen thought, or a rare natural phenomenon. Still it was disturbing to hear the high clear music recede farther and farther.

Late in the afternoon, he found himself able to move. He stretched cautiously, then felt his face. It seemed as always. There was no charred flesh, no burning mask. His throat was not torn open, though it certainly felt sore.

So much to the good. He went to the villa. The rooms were empty of furniture. Carpets of dust covered the mosaic floors. The frescoes looked old and faded, as if years had passed instead of weeks. He searched every corner, though without much hope. There was only dust and cobwebs. His gold collar was gone. So were the clothes that Nimue and Merlin had brought.

In the end, he realized that he was going to find nothing; and he was filthy and hungry. He went to the shore of the island. The boat was there, waiting for him, oars shipped. He waded in next to it and washed.

After he was done, he looked at his reflection. What his hands had told him was confirmed by vision. His face was the same as always. The damage done by Nimue had been illusory. Though he'd never been vain about his human body, Ewen felt relief.

He pulled the boat farther up on shore and returned to the garden. The plants described by Nimue were there: knee-high, bushy, laden with round red fruit that was obviously too heavy for the branches. Narrow stakes had been driven into the ground, and the branches fastened to them. In spite of this support, the plants drooped, so heavy was the load they bore. He picked a fruit. Sun-warmed, almost certainly ripe, it lay comfortably in his palm. Now that he looked closely, he could see it was not perfectly round, but rather flattened at top and bottom. Grooves ran down it, dividing the flesh—soft under the thin skin—into lobes. Of what did the fruit remind him? An undersized melon? A new kind of apple?

In truth, the fruit resembled nothing he had seen before.

Was it poisonous?

Nimue could have killed him easily, or left him chained in the hut to starve. She meant him no harm, apparently, though he had tried to kill her.

Ewen took a bite. The fruit was juicy with a flavor that combined sweetness and sharpness. Both food and drink, Nimue had said. He remembered her words as liquid ran down his chin. The fruit had seeds, too many to pick out, so he ate them, then licked his palm to get the last of the sweet, acidic juice.

He was a man again, with no clothing, no weapons, no money, no master, no home. Merlin was under a stone, which stone he did not know; and he lacked the skill to free his master. Nimue had vanished. He doubted that he'd be able to find her. In addition—he counted over his problems, while his throat grew tight with grief—winter was not far off. The fairy fruit might survive cold and snow. He would not. If he stayed on the island, he'd freeze and maybe starve.

He sat a while longer in the dust, October sunlight pouring over him, the warm air full of the scent of the fairy bushes, weeping for Merlin and himself. For the most part, his weeping was silent. Now and then he groaned. It was a harsh, human sound.

At last he ate another fruit, taking pleasure in the combination of sweetness and acidity, also in the way the liquid felt running down his raw throat. A thought had come to him, and he returned to the hut where he'd been a prisoner.

The two dishes that had provided food for him were empty. That magic had ended, as he might have expected. But the spirits who had taken everything from the house had not been told to clean here, or else they had forgotten, as minor spirits often did. The iron collar and chain still lay on the dirt floor, and the corners were full of piled up pots and tools. He even found a gardening smock, folded in an ancient battered basket.

He need not go into the world entirely empty-handed. The basket would serve to carry some of the fairy fruit. The smock might hold together, though the fabric was old and badly worn. If he took the tools, the scythe especially, he'd have a way to defend himself and to earn his keep. Adam, who was the father of all humans, had kept a garden; and many hermits and pious monks still did, some of them men of noble birth. According to Merlin, there had been kings in ancient times who took pleasure in such things; and monarchs in Asia still vied with one another to build and maintain gardens. Such an activity could not dishonor him. Surely it wasn't any worse than coursing game or catching rats in Arthur's stables, as he had done now and then, mostly for his own amusement, though also to help the stable boys.

Thinking this, he carried his discoveries out of the hut.

He'd find the witch. She knew more of magic and human behavior than he did. Maybe she'd be able to explain what had happened on the island. It must have a meaning, this test that he had failed and Merlin also, apparently. Maybe she would know a way to rescue Merlin. If not—he would not think so far ahead. The important thing was to go forward, remembering what his old master had taught him.